Why Would I Love You?

By S. Shine

Copyright © 2021 Sheniqua Shine | Why Would I Love You?

Publisher: Messy Mind Publishing | sshinetheauthor.com

Prepared by: Ebony Nicole Smith Consulting, LLC | ebonynicolesmith.com

Editor: A.B. Brumfield | Omni Publishing

Cover Design: Angle Bearfield | Dynasty's Visionary Designs

ISBN: 978-0-578-70091-5

Printed in the United States of America

1st Edition – 2021

All rights reserved. No portion of this book may be reproduced in any form without permission from the publisher, except as permitted by U.S. copyright law. For permissions contact via email at sshinetheauthor@gmail.com

Dedication

This book is dedicated to the children, women and men who suffer in silence. To a world that isn't pretty and stings but always has love in it no matter when it chooses to show up in our lives. 🖤

S. Shine

PROLOGUE

Have you ever felt like your world was spinning out of control? I mean, like you can recall all the points in life that you would change just so you didn't end up where you are right at this very moment? Well, I'm at that moment no one wants to end up in. It's like my world has stopped moving and the walls are closing in on me and I'm not even sure why. All I know is that I wish I could go back and change all of the points that got me to where I am right now.

I am lying on my bathroom floor curled up in a tight and tense ball crying my heart and soul out. Why, you ask? Well, I don't know why. I'm in pain, I think. I know that I'm not happy, I haven't been happy in a very long time. I've gone through so much misery that I'm all cried out. Honestly, I've been looking for the answer to that same question. *Why* am *I crying?* Maybe, just maybe if I tell you my story, you can help me understand why. Then maybe the tears will stop. Maybe. . .

ONE

I was born O'Zella Bella Grife to Tonya Lail, a drug addict, and Leon Grife, a monster, two people that were a match made in hell. How or why they ever got together will forever be a mystery to me. One thing I can say for sure was that those two, should never have met in any lifetime.

As a young child, before I had the chance to get to know what Leon was really like, he'd disappeared from our lives. It was always just me and Mama. In fact, there was no other family to speak of, no aunts, no uncles, no cousins, no grandparents. It was literally just the two of us. I was so young, I didn't think much about it. As a matter of fact, up until I was about eight years old, I'd thought I had a normal childhood, if there is such a thing. It was a childhood that consisted of a roof over my head and love from my mother. I would like to tell you that there were good and bad times like any other childhood, but honestly, it's such a blur now that I can't even remember.

One of the few things I do remember is that my mother had a sickness that kept her from doing a lot of things with me. It wasn't the kind of sickness that kept her in and out of the hospital, it was the kind where she wanted to be left alone a lot, the kind where she stayed locked in her room and when she did come out, she didn't seem like herself. As a result, I learned very early on how to care for myself. But when Mama wasn't sick, she was fun and cheerful and she always made sure I had at least the basics. That is until I had to start taking care of her like I had been taking care of myself because she was barely able to provide those basics anymore.

It was my first week of fourth grade and I couldn't have been happier. I was really excited that I finally lived far enough away from school that I could ride the big yellow bus. It had always made me sad to see the bus drive past my house. I would see the kids laughing and having so much fun. For years I wished I could be like them and ride the bus too.

The excitement I felt as I waited outside for the bus was overwhelming. I was finally going to be one of those kids that got to laugh and have fun on the way to school. When the bus pulled up and I got on, the first thing I found was that no one wanted me to sit next to them, so it was hard to find somewhere to sit. When I finally did get a seat, it was next to this kid that pushed as far away from me as possible. She was acting as if I was dirty or something and that hurt my feelings. To top it all off, the kids that I used to think were having tons of fun were really just wild, rowdy, and noisy. It only took me sixty seconds to learn that riding the school bus was overrated.

To take my mind off of my huge disappointment, I simply ignored what was happening on the bus and looked out of the window at the scenery we were riding past. I read each and every sign we drove by, that kept my mind off of the foolishness that was to be my morning commute to school. School itself was nothing spectacular either. I was the new girl that some kids talked to and most ignored. The schoolwork was pretty much the same as it had been at my other school, and the teachers, with very few exceptions, were just as normal and as boring as my old teachers were. Lunch was okay, if you like bland food with almost no taste. Since I'd had to learn to cook for myself, I knew how to throw a meal together with seasoning, apparently the school did not.

Why Would I Love You?

On the bus ride home from school that day, I again focused on the windows and what was going on outside of them. I was enjoying the different streets and stores which made my ride go by much faster. I was so lost in the view that it caught me off guard when my bus got to my house and I saw that there were police cars with bright flashing lights everywhere. My heart started to pound when I noticed the ambulance and the yellow caution tape that blocked off my house from the street. Without thinking, as soon as the bus came to a stop I jumped up and ran to the door. Just as I got to the stairs, the driver stopped me from getting off until he figured out what happened and figured out if it was safe to release me from his care.

"Stay here little girl," he said with a look of concern. He turned the bus off, took the keys out of the ignition, and stepped outside the doors. I watched as he spoke with the cop that came over to tell him to keep it moving.

While they were talking, I looked over and saw the EMT's leaving my house and pushing a gurney covered with a black bag. It was at that moment that I knew my mother was dead. I stood there in shock, staring out of those damn bus windows, unable to truly process what was happening. My body went completely numb, my emotions did the same. I didn't scream, I didn't move or cry. I just watched, remembering her face and knowing that my mother was never coming back.

Two

I was nine years old when I finally felt the sting of being alone in the world. I'd known my mother was an addict and that she was killing herself with the stuff she was putting into her body, but even with her doing that, she'd still made me feel loved. The first night without her in my world was a hard night, but not as hard as everything that was in store for me. I didn't know any of that yet though, all I knew then was that my life had been completely shattered and there was no one left that would love me or take care of me. For the first time in my short life I was scared and completely alone.

It wasn't long before the driver got back on the bus with a pitiful look on his face. I kept asking him to let me off and he just said, "I gotta take you back to school first."

I wasn't dumb, I knew that meant I wasn't ever going back home. Still, I did exactly what he said. When I got back to the school, I stepped off the bus and was met by a short, black, curly haired lady with thick glasses that said she was from the child protection agency. She told me that her name was Janet as she looked at me with sad eyes and told me that my mommy had an accident and that she was never coming back. Somehow, I'd already known, but hearing her say it was still hard. She tried to comfort me by telling me that she would find a safe family for me to stay with, but there was no comfort in her words. I had lost my mother, I didn't think I'd ever feel comfort again.

Why Would I Love You?

"I know you'd like to get some of your things out of your house," she spoke to me in a voice that was meant to soothe. "However, because the police are still at your house, I'm not able to let you in there yet." She cleared her throat when I gave her no response, then she continued. "As soon as we're allowed inside, I'll bring you to get some of your things, okay?" I didn't even bother to respond, I just looked away from her and remained quiet.

I was still numb as Janet drove me to another house. I hadn't figured out how to process what happened. My entire world had changed and I wasn't sure how I was feeling about it. All I knew was that I no longer had a mother and that I was now alone in the world. I was at the mercy of strangers, strangers I just wanted to leave me alone.

Once we arrived at a house, I saw that it resembled a library on the outside. We were greeted at the door by a couple. They said their names were Teresa and Bill, I really didn't care. I did notice that they were an odd-looking couple. Bill was a tall, thin, and pasty white man with glasses that looked thicker than coke bottle bottoms. Teresa was a short, olive colored woman with a round face and a body to match. They both smiled a smile that said it was late and that they were ready for bed but they didn't want to be rude while being forced to take me into their home well past their bedtime.

"Hello, Zella," Bill said, leaning down to make proper eye contact with me.

"My name is *O'Zella!*" I enunciated the O as from somewhere deep inside of me anger flared up and I snapped at him. He was no one to me, he had no right to even say my name let alone say it wrong. Immediately, everything in me disliked him and I just wanted to go home, home to where my mother knew my name.

Bill stood up straight and looked at me like someone had just killed his favorite pet, but he kept that weird fake smile on his face. It was all in his eyes that he wanted to deal with me for correcting him. Even though I saw that I'd angered him, my feelings were still too muted to care. Teresa looked like she wanted to put me in my place too, but neither would dare while Janet was there.

"Well, she's a spirited one, isn't she?" Teresa chimed in with a laugh that was nowhere near friendly.

I just looked at them, thinking of how much I wanted my mommy. The adults, Janet included, then engaged in a conversation about me as if I wasn't standing right there in the doorway with them. No one asked me any questions. No one tried to find out if I even wanted to be there. No one asked me how I was feeling even though I wouldn't have been able to tell them anyway. They just kept discussing me as if I were a thing and not a person. "Bill, Teresa, this is as always temporary until we can find her next of kin or permanent placement," Janet informed them.

"No problem, Janet. You know we're always willing to be there for these poor souls," Bill said as Teresa remained quiet. I knew his words were fake and wondered if Janet could tell as well.

As if she could hear my thoughts, Janet bent down to talk to me in what I quickly learned was her friendly, kid voice. "O'Zella, this is a safe place for you until we either find a family member or a nice forever home for you, okay?" And with that, she gently pushed me through the doorway, wished me luck, and closed the door behind me.

She didn't tell me when I could see my mother's body, didn't tell me how long it would take to find family that I knew she would never find, didn't even tell me what a forever home was. She was a stranger that only did her job to the bare minimum and abandoned me with more strangers.

When the door closed, it was like all of the niceties that Bill and Teresa had pretended to possess were left on the other side of the door with Janet. Suddenly they became like the monsters they truly were.

Why Would I Love You?

"Little girl," Bill spoke in a voice that let me know he wasn't nearly as nice as he had just faked being with Janet, "throw your shit in that closet and follow Teresa to your bed." I went from angry to scared. These people made me feel like they would hurt me if they could get away with it. I knew there was nothing I could do about it, I was nine years old and all by myself in the world. They could rip me to shreds and I was too little to even defend myself. I was quickly realizing that my once friendly world could turn ugly and dangerous in a heartbeat.

On my way to the bedroom, I saw that there was only one dim light at the end of the hallway and lots of doors. We walked past at least five other rooms before Teresa pushed the sixth door open and whipped around to angrily face me. "Here! And you better not be loud or get yo ass up out this room til' someone tell you to. If you have to use the bathroom, follow the light then bring yo ass back here," she finished her sentence with a snarl. I guess I took too long to answer, because she yelled so hard that she made me jump, "Got it?"

"Yeah," I blurted out in sheer terror, unable to think of a single other word to say.

"Yes, Ma'am!" Teresa snarled with anger in her eyes.

"Yes, Ma'am." I whispered with a shaky voice

"And fix yo motha fuckin' face!" Teresa said as she walked away, leaving me in a room so small that it was only big enough to fit a twin bed and a small dresser.

Her statement made me feel confused on top of everything else. What did she mean by telling me to fix my face? My mom had just died and I was terrified and wanted to get the hell away from there. I knew then that Teresa wasn't going to be anything like the loving mother I'd had and I decided then and there to stay as far away from her as I could until I could get out of there.

Looking around at my new environment, I went from terrified to really sad. The room was small with very little standing room and not much else. I stared at the bed for the longest time, wishing it was my bed at my house, but it wasn't. I would never share a home anywhere with my mother again, and I had to learn to adjust to whatever my new life was going to be. So, without a single word, I lay down and didn't even try to turn on the light. I just used the moonlight to find my spot in the bed where I curled up and quietly cried myself to sleep.

Three

The next morning wasn't any better than the night before. I was up and sitting on my bed for what seemed like hours. I was sad and just staring into space, trying to adjust to my new existence, when someone finally showed up to get me out of the little room. It was Bill that opened the door and threw clothes at me while yelling, "Get changed and let's go!"

I was startled out of my daze by his abrupt tone, but still started to move and do as I was told, at least until I noticed Bill standing in the doorway with a creepy grin plastered on his face. The look on his face and the fact that he was just standing there made me feel uncomfortable. It was like something was wrong, but I was far too young to know what the wrong thing was. His presence made me feel so uneasy that I began to squirm a little.

Why was he just watching me? How was I supposed to get dressed if he was going to just stand there? I didn't move, I just kept standing next to my bed as he watched me. When he finally realized that I'd stopped moving because I was watching him watch me, he turned a bright shade of red, coughed a little, and then walked away, closing the door behind him. I wasn't yet mature enough to understand the dark significance of what was happening then, but I did understand that no one was supposed to watch me while I was dressing, not even the people that were supposed to be taking care of me. Mommy hadn't done it, no one else was supposed to do it either.

When I finally made it out of my room and into what was called the common area, I saw that there were tons of kids running around. However, they were all weirdly quiet, playing and laughing but not making a sound while they did it. Everything about this seemed different to me and only made the depression that was coming over me feel even heavier. I missed my mom, I wanted to go home, I wanted to be where things were normal again. Those thoughts had unshed tears coming to my eyes as I stood at the end of the hallway looking for any sign of what I was to do next.

Suddenly, someone my size grabbed me by the hand and pulled me to a table. It was a girl that looked really familiar to me. I thought I knew her from school, but my mind was so messed up that I honestly couldn't remember. Before I could understand what was going on, she was already whispering to me.

"Only whisper in the morning because Teresa is still sleep and we don't want to wake her. She's mean when you wake her before she's ready to be up," she said as she looked at me with a serious expression on her face. Then, "You look sad," she told me as her eyes bore into mine. I said nothing, only hunched my shoulders. Realizing that I didn't want to talk, she continued her previous conversation. "I'm Jazz, by the way. I've been here for a year. It's not that bad," she assured me. I guess the look on my face told her that I was not at all comfortable with my new surroundings because she smiled warmly and said, "It's not that bad. All you have to do is make sure you stay out of the way, do what you're told, don't talk back, and you'll be fine."

"Okay," I whispered as I silently processed what she was saying, then I shyly introduced myself. "I... I'm O'Zella," I stuttered as I reached out my hand to give a proper introduction because that's what I had been taught to do. She just looked at my hand for a minute and then shocked me by grabbing my wrist. I was confused as to why she grabbed my wrist instead of my hand, but I didn't say anything, she didn't give me time to.

Why Would I Love You?

"My real name isn't really Jazz, it's Lauren. But everybody calls me Jazz," she rushed her words out as she tightened that grip on my wrist and dragged me to the kitchen where she began to make me breakfast. Then we sat and ate while Jazz asked me tons of questions until we were done and it was time for school.

My school day was frustrating to say the least. I was pulled out of class no less than three times and brought into my counselor's office to speak to different people about how I was feeling. The truth was that other than sadness, I wasn't sure how I was feeling and I didn't want to talk about it either. My world had literally been turned upside down less than twenty-four hours ago, and they were all in my ear trying to get emotions out of me that I wasn't even sure were there. I was only nine, but I fully understood what happened, I just didn't think I was ready to believe it yet.

I told every person that questioned me, everyone that looked at me like they pitied me, "I'm sad and I just want to go home." I gave each of them the same answer and they always gave me the puppy dog eyes in return. I hated that look, but what could I do to stop them?

At the end of my school day, Janet showed up again. I had already decided to dislike seeing her because I associated her with bad stuff. After all, she was the one that showed up after my mom had died and she was the one that took me to that home I didn't like.

"I'm cleared to enter your home, so I can take you there to gather some of your things. And since we've found no living relatives to take you in, you are now considered a ward of the state." I just looked at her and wished I could make her disappear because there she was again with the bad news. I thought that my mean glare would have made her stop talking, but she continued being the bearer of news I didn't want to hear. "And since there is no one to claim you or your mother's body, there will be no funeral. I'm afraid that the last time you saw your mother, Zella, was the last time you got to see her. But I will let you know where she is buried as soon as I find out where the state will place her, okay?"

I wanted to scream. I wanted to cry. I wanted to run away and hide from the world that had become so cruel to me, but I did none of that. I simply said, "My name is *O'Zella*!" My voice was firm and quiet.

She stared at me, and for a moment it looked as if she felt pity for me. However, even though Janet seemed smart enough to not express that pity, she still wasn't smart enough to stop bringing the unwelcomed news. "Well, okay, O'Zella," she said respectfully before she continued wrecking my world. "Also, because you were renters and not homeowners, anything you leave in the house, after a certain amount of time, the landlord will either keep, sell, or toss. So, you'll have to get everything you want and lose the rest. I'm so sorry," her apology was sincere.

Lose the rest! Lose the rest? That was the only thought playing through my mind as she led me to her car and drove in the direction of what used to be my home. The sadness that had been covering me like a wet, heavy blanket all day had become heavier. Not only was there no one to claim me, no one to love me, but there was also no way I could see and say goodbye to my mother, the only person in the world that had ever loved me. And to make matters worse, in addition to losing my mother, I was also going to lose everything I owned, everything that was familiar to me. I had no one and I had nothing. The little I could take with me had to be chosen carefully because there was only so much I could carry into my new life.

It was becoming really hard to understand what I should do, because who knew at nine years old what to grab, or what to hang on to that would keep the memory of someone who cared for you in your head and in your heart? I had no clue, and that added stress to whatever it was that I was feeling. I remained quiet as we rode towards what used to be my home. In fact, I said nothing until we reached the house.

Once inside, Janet allowed me to roam around on my own. That was when the sadness kicked in. Without knowing what I should do, I just started grabbing teddy bears and dolls, things that were the most familiar to me, things that had once brought me a sense of comfort and happiness. Then I noticed the picture in my room, the one on my dresser. It was a picture of me and Momma, one that had been taken on the day that I was born. Momma was so beautiful, so I grabbed the picture and sat on the floor in the corner of my room. That had been my safe place, the place I would always sit in whenever I had been sad about anything.

For the longest time I sat there staring at the picture, tracing my finger over my momma's face. I really wanted to cry, the tears hiding behind my eyelids burned so bad. But for some reason I didn't cry or maybe I just couldn't. So, I sat there, cradling the picture, moving my hand over the picture as if just my touch could bring Momma back to life. As crazy as everything was around me, this moment in my room, in my safe corner, brought me a small sense of peace, the first peace I'd had since I watched her being rolled out the front door in a black bag. I let out a deep breath and began to relax a little, and then the moment was ruined.

I hadn't been sitting there long before I heard Bad News Janet clomping up the stairs and calling my name. "O'Zella, honey? Are you almost ready?" She walked in with an empty duffle bag in her hand and was shocked when she saw me sitting in the corner hugging the picture. Her face said *'aww'*, but her movements said she didn't have time for the bull. So, she stood in the doorway for a few seconds longer before saying, "Hey, O'Zella, you ok?"

That was a stupid question. My mother was gone, I was now living with strangers, and my world would never be the same, No, I was not okay. But I answered her anyway. "Yes," I gave her a lie that was just as stupid as her question.

"You sure?" she asked with genuine concern in her voice. I just stared at her, there were no words worth saying at that moment. Then, "What are you doing in the corner over here?" she asked as she began to walk toward me.

"Nothing," I quickly lied again. I didn't want her in my safe space and I didn't want her to see my picture. It wasn't that I thought she would have taken it away from me, I just didn't want her to fake like she cared about what happened to my mom. I knew she didn't. I wasn't mad about that either, I understood that she had a job to do and that was it. With the way I was feeling, all I wanted her to do was her job and then to leave me alone like she'd been doing.

Slowly, I stood just as she held the duffle bag out to me. "Here, I thought you would need this for your clothes."

Honestly, I had forgotten all about clothes. So, I took the bag from her and immediately started stuffing it with any piece of clothing I could see. I didn't care if the clothes were clean or dirty, if they were old or new, I just grabbed whatever. After I finished filling the bag, I put the picture of me and my mom on top of everything and zipped up the bag.

On the way out, I stopped at the door to my mom's bedroom and looked in one final time. Memories flooded my mind and the tears that I had fought so hard to keep at bay finally rolled in silence down my face. The last time I saw that room my mother had been in it, now she would never be in it again. Closing my eyes to rid myself of the pain, I turned toward Janet and followed her out. It was the last time I would ever see the place I once called home, and that hurt almost as much as losing my mom.

Janet and I made it back to the library house before dark. Teresa was by herself when she greeted us this time and she wasn't looking as mean or as miserable as she had the night before. That made me feel a

Why Would I Love You?

little bit comfortable, but not much. Janet didn't help my situation at all because she dropped me off at the door without even coming in, and before the door could close good enough, she was gone.

Without so much as a word, I took my bag to my room, I just wanted to shut them all out. I had closed the door to my room and was prepared to climb into the center of my bed, lie there in a ball, and cry like I had done the night before when suddenly, I heard a knock on my door that made me jump. Then the door creaked open and I saw that it was Jazz looking just as happy as she wanted to.

"Hey, Zella!" she chirped.

"Hi, Jazz," I spoke somberly. For some reason she was the only person I didn't mind calling me Zella.

"I just came to tell you that it's time for dinner."

I sighed as I gave up my desire to lie in bed, then began to get up to participate in the dinner even though I was nowhere near hungry. I didn't care about food, as a matter of fact I didn't care about anything. I just hoped this living situation wasn't going to be long term. All I knew was that until Janet came back with news that I was being moved somewhere else, I would do what I needed to do.

I was never going to make that place my home, but for the time being I could at least make it comfortable for me. So, before I left my room for dinner, I went to my duffle bag, pulled out Momma's picture, and set it on the dresser. I knew she was gone, but I also knew that she hadn't left me. As far as I was concerned, Momma would be watching over me for the rest of my life.

Four

    Being in a group home was exactly the way people made it out to be. A nightmare. The only saving grace for that place was that Jazz and I became really close, so close that we were more like sisters than like the best friends we called ourselves. She was the only person that I talked to, the only person my age that I could relate to. Other than that, I hated that place. And even though I didn't stay at the library house long, it was just long enough to get the ball rolling on a series of traumatic events that would follow me for the rest of my life. And those traumas all started with Mr. Bill.

    It happened on a weekend when most of the older kids and some of the younger ones were away on overnights with their families. I had gone to bed early because there was nowhere for me to go and nothing for me to do. The only friend I'd had in that place was Jazz and she was one of the kids that was lucky enough to go home on a weekend visit. I remember it was dark out and that Teresa had also left to spend some hang time with her friends. There were very few of us left in the house.

    I was lying in bed, wishing that sleep would come and take me to the place where I didn't have to face the bleakness of my reality when I heard my door make a sound. It creaked as it always did when it was opening slowly. Looking over at it, I saw it open and saw that the light in the hall was on. Since it shined directly into my room, all I could really make out was an outline standing in my doorway. I didn't even know that it was Mr. Bill standing there until after he'd opened the door about halfway and came in. He closed the door behind him just as slowly as he had opened it.

I was trying to figure out why he was in my room that time of evening, when the smell of the beer and cigarettes on his breath hit me immediately. The room wasn't that big to begin with, so when he whispered my name, the funk permeated the air and made my skin crawl. In fact, Mr. Bill always made me uneasy. I didn't know if it was his voice or the way he peered at me with his beady eyes, but either way, I was always uncomfortable whenever that man came around.

To keep from having to deal with him and whatever he had in mind, I lay in my bed, not moving, trying to pretend as if I was asleep. I prayed that he would go away if I didn't answer, but I should be so lucky! Instead of Bill retreating when he realized that I wasn't answering, he tiptoed the six steps to my bedside and was quietly standing over me.

With that beer and cigarette smell burning my nose, he shook my shoulder and slurred my name on a whisper again. "O'Zella," he called out, but I didn't move. I just stayed still with my eyes slightly open as I watched him. I was scared out of my mind. He realized that I wasn't moving from him calling my name so he reached out and pinched me on my leg. "O'Zzzellaaa," he spoke in a louder voice with an even harder slur, "you awake, girl?" After his hard pinch I made a noise of pain. I could no longer pretend I was asleep anymore.

Slowly, I sat up, fake rubbing my eyes. "Yes, Mr. Bill?" I hoped my pretending to be asleep would stop him and he would go away.

"I been watching you, girl!" he said as he sat next to me on the bed and started stroking my hair with his gross hands. "You know yousa beautiful lil' girl, right? Just so pretty."

"Thank you, Mr. Bill." I replied quietly as I shifted my body to get away from his touch.

"And because you're so pretty, I want to share a special secret with you," he looked at me with red eyes that said he'd had too much to drink. "Do you know what a secret is?"

I was confused as to why he would ask me that question, but I replied, "Yes," anyway.

"Ok, ok, good," his beady red eyes lit up. "I have a secret. Can you keep my secret?" There was just something about him that was wrong, something about the way that he kept looking at me that was wrong.

I didn't answer, I just sat there frozen, feeling like this secret was bad. Then without even waiting for me to say something, Mr. Bill stood up in front of me and started unzipping his pants. My eyes bugged out of my head and my jaw dropped. My heart started racing and doing flips. I wasn't sure what was about to happen, but everything in me knew that it was wrong. I had never seen mommy undress in front of me and definitely never saw a boy do it. And Mr. Bill wasn't a boy, he was a grown man, so that made it even worse. I was suddenly terrified. I wanted my mommy, but the sad truth was that mommy would never come. Nobody would ever come.

In a very aggressive whisper Mr. Bill continued with whatever plan he had going on in his head. "If you weren't always teasing me with your pretty face, I wouldn't want to share my secret with you. So, you better appreciate it, and you better keep my secret or I'm gonna make sure you end up like ya momma. You hear me?" He threatened me as he stared at me hard and mean.

Shakily, I moved my head up and down and answered, "Yes, Mr. Bill."

After hearing the answer he was looking for, his tone and his ugly face softened and a creepy smile spread over his mouth. "When we havin' secret time, you can call me Daddy," he whispered as his voice started to sound funny and he started breathing like he was really happy about something.

I didn't understand how he could be so happy when I was so scared. But I was determined to do what he said with the hopes that after he took off his clothes, he would simply go away. "Ok, Mr—" I caught myself, cutting myself off as I shook my head up and down, "I mean Daddy."

"Good, good," he said as his voice changed once again and the expression on his face changed too. "Now, come closer to me and stick your tongue out, baby." My eyes became as big as saucers and it was my very first instinct to back away from him. Seeing that I was on the verge of freaking out, Mr. Bill quickly said, "It's okay, I promise it won't hurt." When I still didn't move, he said, "But I can make it hurt real bad and make you end up like your momma if you don't do what I say." His voice was strange now, with just a hint of anger in it. "Now come on back over here and stick that tongue out!"

I was scared to death. Tears stung my eyes and my entire body began to shake. Slowly, I eased closer to the edge of the bed, closer to him and that thing he was holding in his hand. And as the tears of fear and sadness rolled down my face, I did what Mr. Bill told me to do. All because I was scared and because I didn't want to end up like Momma.

At the time, I wasn't sure of what was happening that night, but thinking back on it, I eventually came to realize that at nine years old, I had been forced to suck my first dick. And although that had been the first time, it wouldn't be the last time Mr. Bill, a.k.a Daddy, showed me his secret. There were plenty of other times that followed.

Every chance Mr. Bill got for almost three months, he would sneak into my room. He seemed really excited each time, I was really scared each time, but nothing I did or said would make him leave me alone and stop sneaking into my room. Even though I wanted it to stop, I never said anything to anyone who might have been able to make it stop. I didn't even tell Jazz because I didn't want him to keep his promise and make me end up like my momma. My life wasn't the best, but it wasn't enough to make me want to be dead, at least not yet. Back then, I think I was more scared of the death he had promised me than I was of the secret he'd told me to keep. So, I kept his secret and kept my mouth shut for as long as I could.

That first night, after Mr. Bill was done, he cleaned up all of the evidence and quickly left my room just as quietly as he had entered it. I felt so alone and so unprotected in the world. The adults around me were showing me how hurtful and dangerous they could be. Sadly, I was too little to protect myself from them. Not only that, but there was no one to protect me from them either and I wasn't sure that there ever would be. At that point I trusted no one and I didn't want anyone to get close to me, not physically and definitely not emotionally.

At nine years old, I had already learned that when you let people get close to you emotionally, they died like my momma and that hurt a lot. And when you let them close to you physically, they did bad things like Mr. Bill and that hurt a lot. So, I despised closeness of any kind and vowed to keep my distance in every way possible. And when I was sure that Mr. Bill was gone and wasn't coming back into my room, I cried and cried and cried so hard that I almost made myself sick. When I was done, when I had no more tears to shed, I swore to myself that those tears would be the last tears that ever fell from my eyes. It was actually that night and that moment when I began conditioning myself to become a distant and cold hearted bitch.

Every encounter with "Daddy" from then on broke me down piece by piece. I had become withdrawn and quiet. I shut down in school, shied away from making any friends. The counselors at school would try and talk to me, but after a while I think they just attributed my quietness to being my way of coping with the loss of my mom. The truth was that not only was I not coping well with the loss of my mom, I also wasn't coping well with the loss of my innocence. Life had turned cold and so had I.

Finally, the day came that Janet showed up at the home just as she said she eventually would. This time she wasn't bringing bad news with her, or at least I thought the news wasn't bad at first. She told me

Why Would I Love You?

that she had found a place for me to stay for a while. It was supposed to be a nice place with a nice lady named Linda and her three nice kids. Although I was happy at the thought of leaving Mr. Bill behind, I was scared of what the new adults in my world were going to do me.

As I was up in my room packing my things, Mr. Bill eased in and closed the door behind him. Immediately, I was terrified because I thought he was going to make me give him secret Daddy time once more before I left, but that wasn't what he wanted. He wanted something else.

"You better keep that mouth of yours shut, little girl," he warned me as his face took on a mean and scary look. "Because if you tell anybody what happened, I'm going to send you to your momma. You understand me?" he asked as he stepped close enough for some spit to land on my cheek.

"Yes, Sir," I said as I vigorously shook my head up and down.

If it was his plan to terrify me, it worked. I had no intention of telling anybody anything. I just wanted to gather my things and get out of that house. Besides, there was nothing and no one I would miss from that place except Jazz who wasn't there when Janet arrived to take me away. So, I simply filed Jazz away in my mind as another person I didn't get to say goodbye to.

On the ride to my new house, I was quiet, reflecting on what Mr. Bill had said to me and on how Teresa had acted so sad to see me go but had never once cared about me when I was in the house. Janet, on the other hand, would not stop talking. "...Jillian is nineteen, but she's away at college so you probably won't see her much. Tyler is her thirteen year old son and he's in honor classes. And then there is Gabe, he's her eight year old and from what she's told me, he's her little troublemaker."

The word troublemaker snapped me out of my thoughts and had me now listening intently. I didn't want to go to a place where there was going to be trouble. Seemingly oblivious to my worry, Janet just kept on talking about 'her', but I had been so caught up in my thoughts that I had no clue who the 'her' was that Janet was referring to. Instead of saying a word, I remained quiet and listened. I figured that eventually she would say 'her' name again.

When we finally pulled up to the house, I was amazed. It was in a part of town I had never been in before. On the way over, I read a sign that said, Welcome To Suburbia. I didn't know what Suburbia was, but it looked quiet and very pretty. The house itself was like a mansion and my eyes were huge as I tried to take all of it in. It was three stories high and the outside was clean, and the yard was cut. It even had a long driveway that led to a two car garage. From what Janet told me, I was going to be living there.

I had never lived in a house that big before. My old house was a small one, but that was because it had been just me and Momma. The library house had been a decent size, but that's because there were a lot of kids living there. But this one was amazing, it was like a fairytale house that somebody on Tv would live in. What I saw so far, the house was too big for just me and 'Her' and Tyler, and Gabe and Jillian who wouldn't be there that much anyway. I was curious and scared at the same time, but I refused to show either emotion to anybody.

Janet and I walked up to the door where we were immediately met by the friendliest adult face I had seen in months. "Please come in?" She practically sang to us while wearing a pretty smile. When I took too long to move, Janet grabbed my hand and gently led me into my new placement. Once we were inside and she closed the door, the lady kneeled down so we were eye to eye. Before Janet had the chance to say a word, she held her hand out toward me and said, "Hello, you must be O'Zella. My name is Linda, and welcome to my home. As long as you're here, this will be your home too." Shyly, I reached out and shook her extended hand.

Why Would I Love You?

This was nothing like the library house, so I used the manners my mother had taught me. "Hello, Ms. Linda. It's a pleasure to meet you."

She squealed excitedly and unexpectedly grabbed me for a hug which caught me completely off guard. I was scared at first so my whole body stiffened. But when I realized that this was like a real momma hug, I relaxed and enjoyed it before it was taken away like momma had been.

"The kids are at their dad's house," Ms. Linda continued chattering happily, "but they will be home later tonight. I figured you and I could use this time alone. We can get to know a little about each other, set your things up in your room, and have a late lunch together. Are you hungry?" her smile was big and genuine.

I hadn't really had an appetite, but once she mentioned food my stomach began to talk. "Yes, Ma'am."

At that moment Janet said she was going to step outside to make a phone call and then she would be back in to check on me before she left. The minute Janet disappeared, Linda grabbed my hand and took me on a tour of the first floor on our way to the kitchen. She was being so nice to me that I felt comfortable with her and before I even realized it, my fear had completely disappeared.

If I thought the outside of the house was nice, the inside of the house was even more impressive. There were beautiful marble tile floors and a big sparkly chandelier that could be seen from the entry way all the way to the dining room where it hung. The house was so big that we walked through at least four rooms before we got to the kitchen, and Ms. Linda kept her sweet voice on while she told me about each of the rooms we passed in the house.

"Ok, now, this is the family room," she kept talking, trying to get me familiar with my new environment. "The kids don't really hang out here, it's more for when we are hosting parties or when we have company. This room on the other hand," she said when we made it to what looked like a living room, "is the living room. We sit in here all the time. I don't like anyone to have food in here, but sometimes if we're watching a show or a movie, we have dinner or snacks in here."

After she spoke her peace, we continued moving through the house as she gave me a tour. "This is our formal dining room and this," she said as she kept moving through the huge house, "is our kitchen-dining area," Linda led me, still holding my hand, to a seat at the kitchen table. Then she stopped talking and looked at me for a second, concern was written all over her face. "You're very quiet, you haven't said a word. Is there something in particular that you like to eat?"

"I like peanut butter and jelly," was the only reply I could think of.

"Then that is what I will make you, my famous P, B, and J."

For the first time since my mom died, I'd found someone that I actually liked. Linda seemed really nice and a little goofy, and she was the first adult that had paid me any real attention since I'd become an orphan. I found myself looking at her and smiling a lot in the short time I'd been there, something I hadn't done even once at the library house.

Five

As I sat and watched her, Linda focused on making my sandwich. She smiled and hummed and danced a little as if she actually enjoyed what she was doing. That made me feel even better. When she cut my sandwich into cute little triangles before she put it on the table in front of me along with a glass of milk, that reminded me of the good times with momma and I couldn't help the smile that spread across my face.

"Thank you," I beamed just before I began to devour my food.

Linda sat with me and watched me eat while she told me little things about herself and her kids, things that she hoped we may have had in common. While eating, I looked up at her occasionally, just my way of letting her know that I was listening. But then she said the one thing that stopped my happy mood in its tracks. "You are a very beautiful little girl."

Instantly, I eased my sandwich onto the plate and dropped my head. That sentence immediately tossed me back into that little room with Mr. Bill standing over me, smelling like beer and cigarettes. My heart started to race, my palms started to sweat, my vision started to blur. I didn't want to be in that room, I didn't want to experience what I knew Mr. Bill was going to make happen. Shaking my head slightly, I shook that vision away from me and breathed in and out deeply. I needed to clear my head and calm my body.

After a few seconds, I was back in the kitchen with Ms. Linda, and when I looked up at her, I saw how she was looking down at me. There was extreme sadness and bitter recognition on her face.

Linda had seen the drastic change in my demeanor, the sorrow I saw reflected in her eyes made me feel ashamed. "I'm *so* sorry, Zella," she spoke in the saddest voice I had ever heard. But I didn't want her sorrow and I didn't want her pity. "Did I say something wrong?"

I refused to say a word. Emotionally and mentally, I began the process of shutting down. I didn't move, didn't look up at her, or answer her. I just tried to separate myself from that situation until she was able to realize that I didn't want to talk about it. Because Linda had already known that I was a child of trauma due to the circumstances of my mother's death, she didn't walk away and leave me there to deal with things alone. She also didn't try to touch me, she respected my physical space which I appreciated. But when she made a move to scoot closer to me, just to be near in case I needed her, I jumped hard and she froze in her tracks.

I didn't know it at that first awkward moment between us, but Linda was a grief counselor for adults. She knew the signs of abuse. Still looking at me, she chose her next moves and words very carefully because she wanted to gain my trust. Scooting back to her original spot, she spoke softly. "O'Zella? I don't know what happened, but you are in a safe place here." Her voice was calm and kind and soothing. I liked it, but I was still uncomfortable and still shutting down. "I'm not here to hurt you, and when you're ready, I'll be here to support you in any way you need me to be," she assured me.

For some reason, the way she spoke to me made me believe her and the fact that she wasn't trying to force me to give her answers made me feel just a little bit safer. Slowly, I looked up at her as she continued talking, using that soft voice that made me not so scared anymore. "I want to start over, is that okay with you?" she asked as she waited patiently for me to respond in some way.

Why Would I Love You?

I liked the fact that she was including me in the decision making process, that she was making me feel as if I had a say in what took place in my life. It made me feel safe knowing that instead of just throwing things on me and leaving me to sink or swim while I dealt with them, Linda was going to move at the pace I felt was most comfortable. Remaining quiet, I shook my head up and down which prompted her to continue.

"If there is ever, ever," she spoke softly but sincerely, "a time that you don't like something I've said or done, you can tell me. And by telling me you are letting me know that you would prefer it if I didn't do that again. Is it okay with you if we handle things like that from now on?" Slowly, I shook my head up and down again just before I picked up my PB & J and started eating it again.

Just then there was a knock on the front door Janet came back in. "Hello?" Janet called out.

"Yes, Janet," Linda replied, "we're back here in the kitchen."

"How is everything going?" the social worker asked once she made it through the house.

"Seems as if it's going pretty well to me, but how about we ask O'Zella," Linda said as both she and Janet turned in my direction. "O'Zella, are you ok with staying here in this home with me?" When I remained quiet for a second, still not ready to talk yet, Linda went on. "You have every right to say no, and that will be okay. The decision of whether you stay here or not is totally up to you."

Those words made me feel safer than I had in a long time. That security made me feel as though I was ready to speak. And when I did, I looked up from my plate to say a very simple, "Yes."

"Ok," Janet spoke with a little excitement in her voice. That was the first time since I'd met her that she expressed any real emotion. Her behavior made me suspicious of her. "I'll be back this time next week to check in on you. Ok, dear?"

I didn't bother to respond to her, Janet seemed a little too happy at my willingness to stay with Ms. Linda. Her excitement made me feel as if I had been a burden to her and that she was grateful to finally be unloading me. So, I merely looked back down at my plate and gave her a dismissive nod that didn't include any eye contact at all. Taking that as her que, Janet said her final goodbyes and as quickly as she came, she left.

After I was done with my food, Ms. Linda wasted no time showing me to my new room. Because of what happened earlier, she didn't try to hold my hand like she'd done on our tour to the kitchen. However, she did keep her jovial tone as she talked my ear off while leading me up to the second story of her big house. The room she took me to was nice and big, bigger than any bedroom I'd ever seen. There was a full sized bed with a pretty purple and pink butterfly blanket. The dresser was long and short with a huge mirror mounted to the back of it. On the opposite side of the room was a little comfy corner. It had a recliner that was fit for a child my size and it was piled high with dolls and teddy bears. On the side of the chair was a chalkboard wall with different color chalks in a little cup.

"This is for me?" I finally spoke, looking at her in astonishment. I had never seen anything like it. I was so impressed by it, that I'd forgotten about hiding my emotions and allowed my excitement to show.

"Yes," she said as she smiled, clearly happy that I was happy. "This is your room. And everything in it is yours."

"Thank you, Ms. Linda," I said softly and sincerely. This was the best room I had ever seen and the best room I had ever lived in.

"You don't have to thank me, sweetheart," she spoke with a gentle smile on her face. "This is your home now, I'll be doing things like this for you all of the time." I shook my head to acknowledge what she was saying, but I was still in awe of the fairytale room that was mine. "Is it ok if I help you put your clothes away?" she asked cautiously, still letting me know that I had a say in what happened in my life.

I nodded as I began to roam around the beautiful room. She set my bag down and started to close the door. It was her intention to unpack my bag in private and start putting my things in the drawers. That caught my attention and I gasped as I reached out my hand in a panic. "Ms. Linda!" I almost shouted.

Immediately, she jumped and quickly gave me her undivided attention. "Yes, O'Zella? What's the matter, sweetheart?" The look on her face was one of shocked concern.

"Please don't close the door?" I said as my voice shook.

"No problem," her voice was filled with worry as she opened the door she had started to close. I could see in her eyes that she definitely knew someone had abused me. But she didn't say anything about it, she didn't try to push me to say anything about it, not that she could. I hadn't opened my mouth since Mr. Bill had threatened me that first night, I wasn't about to open my mouth to anyone now. After opening the door to my room, she walked over to the dresser with the bag and began putting my things away. She kept a concerned eye on me the entire time. I was so grateful to her that I wanted to say thank you again, but caught myself. She told me that I didn't have to thank her, so I would just show her how thankful I was when given the chance.

Later that day, after Ms. Linda made sure I'd gotten to know as much about her and her family as she possibly could, her boys finally came home. They were nice to me as well, just as nice as their mother. They were also really helpful, but they had their own things going on and didn't really bother me much. I was ok with that. I didn't want to be a bother to them, and I didn't want them to bother me. So far, things at my new house were comfortable and I was settling into a routine that I liked, one that was safe to me.

The days went by and turned into weeks and then into months. Janet had finally stopped coming by after the first six weeks, which was right after Christmas. I was still comfortable and feeling safe. I was actually happy for the first time since being tossed into the system. I spent time with my new family, but I spent most of my time in my room sitting in the recliner playing with dolls and reading.

Even though I was in fifth grade, the school said that I was reading at an eighth grade level. Ms. Linda was so proud of me that she would make it a point to come into my room and read with me every night before bed. I loved the one-on-one time she spent with me because she wasn't like the other adults. She treated me as if I mattered and she never once tried to force me to do anything just like she promised she wouldn't. I didn't have to explain my pain, she just respected me and my ways and accommodated me as much as I needed her to.

One night after we finished a book and she was tucking me in, Ms. Linda kneeled by the bed to talk to me. "O'Zella?" she began in that voice that always made me feel safe and protected. "You know your birthday is in three weeks, right?"

"Yes, Ms. Linda," I spoke up. I didn't even bother telling her that I didn't pay attention to my birthday because I had never celebrated it.

"Would it be ok if we celebrated your birthday?" she asked quietly.

"Celebrate?" I asked as surprise crossed my face. "Like how?" I was curious because I had no clue what a birthday celebration was even about.

"What would you like to do?" She decided to see what I wanted.

"I don't know. Kids don't really like me, so I don't want a party," I told her the truth. I knew I should have been sad about my lack of friends, but to be honest, I wanted to stay as far away from people as I could, I didn't trust them. So, keeping away from them was perfectly fine with me. "That's ok," I spoke happily I don't want anything. Thank you, though."

Why Would I Love You?

"Ok," her voice sounded sad. Then she looked at me and asked another question. "Well, would it be ok if you, me, and Jillian had a special girl's day?"

I thought about it for a second. I liked Ms. Linda and Jillian. I knew that spending a girl's day with them wouldn't be a bad idea, so I said, "Ok, I would like that."

"Good," Ms. Linda's mood seemed to have brightened at my answer. "We're going to have so much fun. Jillian will be visiting in two weeks, so we'll make your birthday weekend all about us girls."

Ms. Linda did a lot for me. If letting her show me a good time for my birthday would make her happy, I was willing to let her do that. Besides, she wasn't forcing anything on me, she had asked, and I had agreed. I liked that she was still including me in my own life's decisions, that made me feel really good at that moment, just as it had done the first time she'd included me.

"Okay," I said with a shy smile as she stood and headed for the bedroom door. Once she flipped the light switch and the room was immersed in a comfortable darkness, I said, "Goodnight, Ms. Linda."

"Goodnight, my dear," was her kind reply.

Six

The day had finally come and Ms. Linda was making a really big deal about our girls' day. She did her best to keep from referring to it as my birthday, but she was doing a poor job of it. I'd caught her almost calling me the birthday girl a few times when she was asking my opinion about things she chose to do. Even though I was uncomfortable with all of the attention, I went along with the program because it felt really nice to be spoiled and because I enjoyed doing something nice for her as much as she enjoyed doing nice things for me.

When it was finally time, we went to pick up Jillian from the airport. I hadn't seen her since Christmas and was excited about seeing her again. She was just as nice as her mother and seemed genuinely happy to see me when she spotted me in that airport with her mother.

"O'Zellaaaa!" Jillian sang happily as she hugged me, and unlike Ms. Linda, she wished me a happy birthday.

I was a little uncomfortable with that, but I replied with a shy, "Thank you." I saw the look of happiness that crossed Ms. Linda's face when she heard my response and that made me smile as well. I was really beginning to feel like I was a part of the family.

After hugs and too much conversation was exchanged in that airport, we were finally off on our girl's day adventures. Our first stop was at a boutique downtown. It was time for Ms. Linda to shop for some clothes. When we walked in, a lady greeted us but I was barely aware because of my shock at how pretty all of the clothes were. As I

Why Would I Love You?

looked around at everything, Linda let the saleswoman know that this was a special weekend for us girls and that we were looking for special outfits for the following day. Everything was so beautiful in that boutique. There were sparkly dresses, silky shirts, and fuzzy pants, things that were really nice and super expensive.

I wandered around for a good while taking everything in, reflecting on how Momma was never able to take me shopping at places like that. Even with that being the case, if I could've had my momma back, I would have walked away from Ms. Linda and Jillian and gone back to living a less privileged life with Momma. After checking out everything, we found one dress that we all really liked and we each decided that dressing alike was what we wanted to do. The dresses were pink and white, pin striped, sweater dresses that went past our knees. The lady that was helping us commented on how the colors of the dress went so well with my beautiful skin and my sandy brown hair. "You're so gorgeous and that dress will be especially pretty on you," was what she said. Immediately, I was uncomfortable. My mind flashed back to when Mr. Bill had told me that I was pretty and instantly I froze. I didn't like to be looked at like that, didn't like anyone paying that much attention to my physical appearance. So far, my life has taught me that when people thought that I was pretty, they wanted to do some ugly things to me. Her innocent words had messed me up and she had no clue.

Linda heard those words as well, and knowing that comments on my beauty were triggers, she quickly ran to my side just as I tensed up. Kneeling down so that she and I were on eye level, she put up a hand as a way of asking the lady to give her a moment. She knew not to touch me, knowing that I didn't like hands on me in any way when I was in that state and she respected my need for that space.

She then looked at me and spoke softly. "O'Zella, you think your dress looks nice, right?" she asked as a way of addressing the situation without addressing the situation.

With my head hung low, and my eyes now closed tightly to shut Mr. Bill out of my mind, I answered with a very soft voice, "Yes, Ma'am."

"Well," she spoke in that gentle voice that was working hard to make me feel safe again, "we all think the dress looks great on you. And," she added a big smile to that calming voice, "we are going to be three divas in our fabulous dresses."

Her words were always the perfect ones to put me at ease. In no time at all I had pushed my discomfort to the corners of my mind. Even though it took some serious effort, I was heading back toward enjoying my girl's day.

At that moment, Jillian came out of the dressing room, unaware of what just happened. She took one look at me and screamed, "Zellyyyy, we look like twins!"

That broke me almost all the way out of my trance and put a huge smile on my face. Once Linda saw that the scare was over and that the mood had lightened, she reached over and hugged me, whispering in my ear, "Everything is ok, dear."

The rest of the day was really nice. We got our hair and nails done, we bought matching shoes and accessories for our dresses, and Ms. Linda even bought us the same perfume so that we could smell good too. Then we went out for dinner, stayed the night at a hotel playing games, went in the pool, and then at the end of what Jillian called our staycation, I got to see a real live play at the local downtown theatre. I was really enamored by the costumes, the stage changes, and all the people moving around under the bright lights. I got lost in the fact that they could pretend to be someone else, that they could be anyone other than who they actually were.

Why Would I Love You?

Getting back to the house was like returning home from a long drive. Ms. Linda, Jillian, and myself were so tired that we all passed out and didn't wake until late that next Sunday morning which was my actual birthday. I woke to what smelled like a big breakfast cooking. I stayed in bed because I didn't want a big fuss and all kinds of attention focused on me, but that feeling didn't last too long. After only a few short minutes, my stomach started to grumble so hard that it took all the power away from me. When that happened, I didn't care about Ms. Linda making a big fuss anymore, I needed to eat.

After putting on the robe that Ms. Linda had gotten for me to wear in the hotel, I headed downstairs. When I entered the kitchen and looked around, I was surprised to see that there was no Ms. Linda or Jillian anywhere. Instead, it was just the boys there. As soon as they saw me, they smiled and told me that they knew today was special and that they asked their dad to drop them off early so they could make us breakfast.

My relationship with the boys was mainly like ships passing in the night and that was ok with me. I wasn't much of a fan of the male species since I grew up around none, and especially since Mr. Bill. So, I actually preferred the whole passing ship's relationship with them. We had small talk occasionally, and we would eat meals or hang out in the family room together with everyone, but that was as close as I had gotten to the boys up to that point and I saw no reason for that to change.

I said, "Hi, and thank you," as I made my way to the kitchen table and took a seat. Then I sat quietly and watched as Tyler finished making scramble eggs while Gabe bounced around and handed his brother the things he asked for from the kitchen.

"So, how was your girl's day?" Tyler asked me.

"It was nice," I spoke in that shy voice that had somehow become my signature sound.

"What did you do?"

As I ran down all the great things I had experienced from Friday and Saturday, Gabe set the table while Tyler put the food on dishes and brought them to where I was sitting so we could have a family style brunch.

"Go get Mom and Jill, Gabe!" Tyler ordered his younger brother and Gabe obediently ran off to wake them.

Tyler was putting the pitcher of OJ on the table when he suddenly began to stare at me. I didn't like that, and I disliked it even more when his stare lasted as long as it did

I said nothing and he said nothing, so the awkward silence made it even more uncomfortable. For a second I felt like I was caught under the gaze of Mr. Bill again and I began to look away.

Finally, Tyler broke the silence by saying, "Nice hair, O'Zella."

As I responded with, "Thanks," Gabe came zipping back into the room followed closely by Ms. Linda and Jillian. I was no longer comfortable, but I didn't want to make another scene like the one at the boutique, so I put on a smile and enjoyed breakfast with the family. Even though he hadn't called me beautiful, he was giving off a vibe that made me want to shut down, all the way down.

After that day, it seemed that Tyler began making more of an effort to hang out with me. It all appeared to be harmless at first. He would do little things like invite me on walks or on bike rides with him and Gabe, or make it a point to be in the family room whenever I ventured out of my room and went there. He didn't look at me again like he did on my birthday, but every once in a while I would catch him sneaking stares at me which still brought me discomfort.

It had been six months since my birthday and the weather was cold and snowy. I was in my room reading as I always did when there was a soft knock at the door. It was Ms. Linda.

"Hey, you!" That was the friendly greeting she would always use with me.

"Hi," was always my shy and quiet reply.

Why Would I Love You?

"I think Gabe got food poisoning. I'm going to take him to urgent care, but I don't know how long we're going to be gone. Since it's close to your bedtime, and since you have school in the morning, I'd like to leave you and Tyler here and I'll just call to check in on you two if we're gone too long. Is that okay with you?"

There she was including me in decisions, making me feel safe with her. "Yes' Ma'am," I replied.

"Thank you, O'Zella," she said, seemingly happy with my response. Then she started toward the door, but stopped to say, "Make sure you brush your teeth before bed, and I will see you in the morning, ok?"

"Ok, Ms. Linda," I smiled at her. "I'll just brush my teeth and go to bed now. And I hope Gabe will be okay."

"You are such a good girl," she said in a voice that sounded grateful.

"Thank you," I replied in response.

I liked the way Ms. Linda talked to me, she was so positive and loving. She knew how to treat me and she did her best to make me feel safe and included. I appreciated her so much that I didn't ever want to be any trouble to her, so I did my nightly routine immediately.

I'd been taught to brush my teeth, wash my face, and put on my bonnet before bed. I had a head full of sandy brown hair and because Ms. Linda didn't know how to take care of my type of hair, she took me to get it braided in all different kinds of styles every two weeks. After putting my bonnet on and heading toward my bed, I climbed onto it and stared at the streak of light that was shining underneath my door. Occasionally a shadow would pass, but I knew that was just Tyler going to the bathroom.

I don't remember going to sleep, but I do remember being suddenly shaken awake. I was disoriented at first because I'd been in a deep sleep. I sat up, rubbed my eyes, and as they began to focus I realized that I was looking at Tyler standing over me.

"What's wrong Tyler?" I asked, thinking that Ms. Linda had called to say that something bad was going on with Gabe.

"Were you sleep?" he asked, and I frowned.

Of course I'd been asleep, that was why he had to shake me to wake me. "Yes," I replied to his weird question anyway. "Why? Is it time to get up?" When he didn't say anything about Gabe, I figured that I must have been late for school.

"No, I just wanted to talk." With that sentence, he sat on the edge of my bed. The light from the door was giving me just enough light to make out his face and what I saw shook me down to the bone. He was giving me the same look Mr. Bill had given me the night he started to sneak into my room. Immediately my nerves were shattered.

Just as I was about to back away from him on my bed, Tyler reached toward my face and softly touched my cheek. The tension that shot through my body was instant and my muscles quickly tightened as I swatted his hand away from me.

"What are you doing?" I asked as I stared at him, praying that he wasn't going to make me do what Mr. Bill had made me do.

"I am just admiring your beautiful skin." Alarm bells sounded loud and hard in my head.

"Thanks," I said as I managed to scoot back just a little.

"O'Zella, you know that you're beautiful, right?" I hated those words so much. They were usually followed by bad things and it seemed like Tyler had some of those bad things in mind for me. I inched back just a tiny bit more.

"Ok," was all I dared to say.

Not seeming to care that I was pulling away from him, Tyler started to move one of his hands down my shoulder while using his other hand to push the blanket to the side off of my legs. My initial reaction was to cross my ankles and stiffen up.

"It's ok, Zell," he said as he looked at me with that look of lust in his eyes. "Don't be scared," he leaned over and whispered in my ear.

Why Would I Love You?

I was shaking so hard as I watched him with squinted eyes. I had been conditioned for shit like this, so I knew what was coming. Very carefully, I watched as his eyes roamed over my body, all the way down to my ankle where his hand had begun its journey toward the top of my legs. With the lightest of touches, he moved his hand from my ankle and slowly to my knee. He then started to push his hand past the hem of my nightgown, I was just about to scream when the alarm on the front door beeped and the automated voice rang out, "Front door open."

As quickly as he could, Tyler jumped up and tiptoed to my bedroom door. When he saw that the coast was clear, he looked back at me and whispered, "Good night, O'Zella. See you in the morning." With that, he stepped out and pulled the door closed behind him.

It was only a few seconds later when I heard Ms. Linda come up the stairs with Gabe and then it was quiet again. I lay there in my bed, feeling Tyler's hands on my body. I wanted to cry, I wanted to be scared, I even wanted to say something, but I did none of that. I just curled up in a ball and tried to think of something happy.

In the months since my mom had been gone, things had finally begun to seem normal. Life was looking better for me and I wasn't so afraid of the world anymore. So, for a male to sneak into my room in the middle of the night to do the same things Mr. Bill had done to me had me feeling jaded and wondering why this place that had seemed so perfect would actually be any different from the last place. That night I learned that there were just not very many good things in the world, at least not many that would come to me.

When morning finally came, I was so devastated by what Tyler had done that I didn't want to get out of bed. But when Ms. Linda came in the room with her big smile and her bubbly personality, my fear of leaving the room disappeared. I knew that as long as I was with her, she wouldn't let anything bad happen to me.

"Come on, sleepy head. Time to get ready for school," she said as I lay with my back to her, not responding.

"O'Zella," she called out to me, her voice a little concerned, "did you hear me, dear? It's time to get up." Since I had never gone to sleep, I had to fake waking up. Once she saw me roll over and saw my eyes open, she headed for the door. "Ok, little Ms., let's get a move on. I'm making pancakes and you know those don't last very long in this house." She then headed for the door and exited my room.

I closed my eyes for just another moment, hoping that Tyler was not going to make today awkward. I had no intention of saying anything and I hoped he would do the same. As much as I hated his behavior from the night before, I just wanted it all to be a bad memory that went away. *And as long as he didn't do it again everything would be fine*, I tried to convince myself, but something deep inside of me knew that would never be the case.

Reluctantly rolling out of bed, I grabbed my clothes and headed for the bathroom. I wanted to groom myself and get dressed as fast as I could so that Linda would not have to come back up and get me like she so often had to do with the boys. I was determined to be as little of a nuisance to her as possible. Grabbing the things I would need, I hurried from the room, closing my door behind me. As soon as I stepped outside of my room, there was Tyler leaning on his bedroom door frame.

"Good morning, O'Zella," he said with a slick grin. The way he greeted me made me feel uncomfortable again, so I looked to the ground as I rushed past his room and into the bathroom.

I had never in my life checked a lock on a door as much as I did when I got inside of that bathroom. Satisfied that it would keep the bathroom secure as long as I was in it, I leaned on the door as worry began to set in. From what it looked like, Tyler was going to be taunting me. The peace I had found inside of Ms. Linda's home seemed to quickly be disappearing.

Why Would I Love You?

To keep the sanity that was trying to escape me because of Tyler, as I was getting dressed for school I decided to come up with a game plan. I knew that Tyler wasn't going to stop just like Mr. Bill never stopped, so it became my goal to make sure that we were never alone again. Nighttime was going to be the hardest, but I was going to do what I could to keep him out of my room and away from me.

Seven

It had been weeks since Tyler woke me that night, and I was ok with that. The first week or so I would wait for a little while and then go to Ms. Linda's room and tell her that there was something that scared me. She would let me bring my blanket and cover into her room and I would sleep in her bed. Any time she said she was going to the store or for a walk, I would be stuck to her like glue, offering to go with her. She would always smile and say that I reminded her of Jillian. She had no clue that I was really running from the things I knew her son wanted to do to me.

One day Ms. Linda was going out for a walk and as usual I asked if I could walk with her. She was happy to have me along for the walk. She then helped me tie my sneakers and off we went, leaving the boys at home. On each of our walks, she always went the same way, down two blocks, over three blocks, back up two and straight until we were back home. This particular day she decided to take a different route.

I was holding her hand and couldn't help but to ask, "Ms. Linda, where are we going?"

"O'Zella," she spoke happily as she normally did, "I'm sure you're tired of the same old houses over and over, so we are going to walk a different way today. Is that ok?"

"Uhhuh," was my innocent reply.

We walked four blocks in the opposite direction of the one we usually traveled. Then as we took a right, my eyes immediately gravitated to the big park with lots of kids that were playing and to their parents that were keeping a watchful eye on them. While I was still holding her hand, Ms. Linda walked us to a bench where I didn't take my eyes off of the empty swing until we stopped.

"I'm going to be right here keeping an eye on you. Do you want to go and play?" she asked me, already knowing what I wanted to do.

Quickly, I shook my head yes, and she let my hand go. I took off like a bullet running to the only empty swing that I had my eye on. The park was really nice, nicer than any of the parks I was used to playing in. This one had three slides, a monkey bar, two rope bridges, and lots of ladders and tunnels. I was seriously enjoying my time at the park, and things became especially fun when kids my age invited me to a game of tag. That surprised me a lot because kids my age, especially at my school, never seemed interested in playing with me.

So, I said, "Yes," and for the first time since my mom died, I was playing with children my own age. That made me really happy the entire time we played. I was good at playing the game, in fact I was a beast at it because I was never it. I smiled and laughed and played so much that by the time Ms. Linda called out to me, I was almost exhausted.

On the way back to the house, I noticed that Ms. Linda was unusually quiet. I was wondering what I had done that would make her not want to talk to me on the way home like she usually did, when all of a sudden she stopped, kneeled in front of me and started to talk. "O'Zella, it has been a pleasure having you in our home these past months, a real pleasure," she said with the most sincere eyes. "But I've noticed that over the last few weeks you've been more attached to me than usual. Is everything ok? Are you as pleased with us as we are with you?"

This was the moment I was supposed to tell her about Mr. Bill and how he crept into my room like a thief in the night and took my innocence away. I was supposed to tell her how Tyler was now trying to become my new Mr. Bill and that he was the reason I was stuck at her hip. I was supposed to tell her that her son almost had his way with me when she was at the hospital with Gabe and that I feared him. This was my moment, this was my time to free myself from the mental and emotional prison I was trapped in.

"No, nothing's wrong," I lied, choosing to remain imprisoned. "I just really like spending time with you," was what I decided to say.

"Are sure there is nothing else" she asked me as she searched my eyes for the truth she wanted me to tell her. "You can talk to me, you know that, right?"

But I refused to give her that truth, I was too scared to. "Yes, I know," I said with honesty. "Is it ok that I go places with you?" I asked her instead of telling her the truth.

"Of course it is, dear," she assured me. "I just want to make sure you are ok. I always want to make sure that you're okay."

"I'm ok, Ms. Linda," I insisted. There was no way I could bring myself to tell her the truth. I was too afraid of the consequences of me doing that.

"Ok, good," she said with a smile as she let out a deep breath. "Now let's go make some lunch."

She then grabbed my hand and gave it a quick squeeze before she started leading me in the direction of the house I wanted to think of as home.

"We're back, boys!" she yelled as we walked in the door. Gabe came tumbling down the stairs, yelling from around the corner and up the stairs. "Mom, mom, mom!"

"Whoa, Gabe where's the fire?" she asked as motherly concern entered her voice and plastered itself all over her face.

"I'm hungry! I'm really hungry," he spoke excitedly. "Are you still making lunch?"

Why Would I Love You?

"Nice to meet you, Mr. Hungry." Ms. Linda giggled because whenever she said that Gabe would frown his face up into a really funny expression. "And yes, I'm still making lunch. In fact, O'Zella and I are going to wash up and then whip up some sandwiches," she said as she tousled his hair. "Would you please go get Tyler and wash your hands before you come back down?"

"Ok!" Gabe happily replied, and with that he went running off as fast as he'd come running in.

A short while later, Ms. Linda was helping me to put a plate of sandwiches together. When we were done, I set the table with paper plates, several bags of chips, and asked for help with the drink because it was too heavy. As she bent down to get the pitcher out of the fridge, Tyler came around the corner with no shirt on. I looked over in the direction where I saw movement and caught his eyes scanning me up and down. Before Ms. Linda and Gabe could notice, Tyler blew me a kiss and winked at me. A chill flew down my spine and deep down I knew that was not the end of his efforts to do to me what I didn't want done.

Unaware of what her son had just done, Ms. Linda walked over to the table with the pitcher in hand, and finally noticed him. Immediately she began scolding Tyler for coming downstairs without a shirt on. I didn't hear everything she said to him because my nerves had taken over and I was in the process of blocking the noise out as I stared at the table top in front of me.

"...now you get yourself upstairs and put on a shirt this instant!" she said as she plopped the pitcher down and started to turn away to get the plate. Suddenly, I grabbed her sleeve. "O'Zella," her voice took on that note of concern, "is everything ok?"

"Ms. Linda," I said as I swallowed the lump that had lodged itself in my throat, "I have to tell you something."

"What is it dear?" At that point she had bent down so that we were face to face.

I looked her into her eyes and fidgeted with my hands. This was it, I was finally going to speak up for myself and tell the woman who was caring for me as if I was her own child, that her son had touched me. *Tell her, tell her,* my mind screamed for me to open my mouth, shouting that it would do the rest of the work if only I spoke. However, at the exact moment that I finally parted my lips, Gabe came rushing down the stairs.

"I'm not hungry anymore because my stomach hurts," I took the coward's way out. "Can I go lay on the couch?"

I had quickly learned to adapt to my situation. Any other day, I would have gone to my room and cuddled up with a book to avoid the triggering events that were going on in my world. This particular time, though, I knew that my room wasn't safe, and I wanted to be where I knew safety was. I needed to make sure that if Ms. Linda was leaving, I was for damn sure going with her. So, instead of running away to be alone in my room, I stayed in the thick of things and used the woman that cared for me as my safety shield.

Later that night, I was in the family room with Ms. Linda, lying there curled up in a fuzzy blanket watching cartoons until I dozed off. I was in a really good sleep when I was suddenly awakened by a touch on my shoulder. I jumped out of my sleep in a crazed frenzy, swinging and screaming, "Leave me alone!"

"O'Zella?" I heard my name being called in a firm and concerned voice.

The moment I realized that it was Ms. Linda, I stopped fighting and just broke down crying. I was so tired and so exhausted from being on alert all of the time that I just couldn't take it anymore. I sobbed so hard that my body shook, and my throat began to burn. Ms. Linda reached out and hugged me. She didn't ask any questions and I didn't try to tell her what I had been through. She just held me, and I let her. That was the night that I began to feel as if she'd started to look at me different, almost like she felt bad for me.

Over the next couple of weeks, she tried to talk with me about what was going on with me, but I kept shutting down, shutting her out, or changing the subject altogether. No matter what I did, however, Ms. Linda kept me close to her and I was just fine with that. From that day on I felt safe because I felt that she was keeping a close eye on me. As much as I clung to her, she kept her eyes on me even harder. I was finally beginning to relax again.

On one of the weekends when the boys had gone to their dad's house, Ms. Linda woke me up early and said that she wanted to take me to see someone. I trusted her, so I didn't bother to ask her any questions at all. I knew something was strange because the ride to our destination was a quiet one. Other than her telling me that she was taking me to a doctor's appointment, there was no real conversation that took place.

As we rode along, I began to take note of what was going on outside of the car window. From what I was seeing, it looked like we were going from one side of the city to the other. Then we began to travel down a long road with tall trees on either side to get to the expressway. On the highway, I enjoyed looking at the different cars, trucks and busses that we passed or that passed us by. It seemed like none of the vehicles were the same and counting them and seeing what was different about them became like my own little personal game. It helped me to shut my thoughts out even if just for the moment of a drive to an unknown place.

When the car finally slowed and turned into a parking lot, I saw that we had pulled up to a medical complex, one that we hadn't been to before. I looked over to Ms. Linda and she looked back at me while giving me a weak smile. When we got out of the car, I held her hand tightly as she walked me up to a door. There was a weird feeling that came over me, a feeling that let me know that this wasn't just a regular appointment.

The etching on the glass door read, Dr. H. Shabazz M.D. *Nope, I haven't been here before*, I thought as we entered a waiting room. Ms. Linda was still trying to act like everything was ok as she checked me in and we headed for a seat. Ms. Linda had never been that quiet, and I was worried that I had done something wrong.

The moment we were seated, she quickly turned to me and spoke as if the words in her mouth were hot coals that burned her tongue. "O'Zella," she began, "I'm not sure what is going on with you and I'm very concerned. Since you won't say anything to me, I brought you here to talk with someone about what has been bothering you and about why you have been so clingy and jumpy lately."

All in one breath she let those words flow, but I didn't know how to respond. I had no clue how to answer her. Over the last few months I'd had so many perfect chances to tell her what had happened to me with Mr. Bill, and even to tell her what her son had been attempting to do, but I could never bring myself to say the words. So, I took in what she said to me in that waiting room, turned my body forward, and waited for Dr. H. Shabazz.

"O'Zella Grife?" I heard my name being called a short while later.

Here goes nothing, I silently told myself. Together Ms. Linda and I got up and followed a petite lady with short blond hair and pretty unicorn scrubs. Briskly, she led us through a set of double doors that led to an office. When we first walked in, I took in everything. There were two upholstered, Victorian chairs, a long-slanted back chaise lounge, and a small matching coffee table with tissue and magazines in the center of it. On the other side of the office was a cluttered, medium sized desk, and all along the floor and up the walls were children's toys, books, and games. Seeing those toys, things I could relate to, had me relaxing and thinking that maybe this appointment wasn't going to be so bad. Boy was I wrong.

Why Would I Love You?

Suddenly, at the entrance of the office doorway was a tall, slender, black woman with a big afro. She was wearing wooden earrings and bright red lipstick. Her smile was big and inviting.

"Hello," she spoke in a calming and smoky voice, "you must be O'Zella." She walked until she was standing directly in front of me, her long jean skirt flowing on the floor around her. Reaching out, she shook my hand. It was kind of weird to me that this lady was so happy to see me, but I shrugged her demeanor off and took her hand. "My name is Dr. Shabazz, and it is so nice to meet you!"

"Nice to meet you, too," I courteously replied. If there was one thing that no one could say about me, it was that I was rude and that I didn't speak well. My mother had taught me at least that much. Seemingly impressed with my manners, Dr. Shabazz then turned and greeted Ms. Linda with the same friendly smile.

"O'Zella," she kept speaking in that calm and friendly voice, "over there is what I call my wonderland." She directed her hand to the wall of toys. "You are welcome to play with whatever toy you like, and if you find a game you want to try, let me know and maybe we can play together."

I looked over to that corner and saw so many things to choose from that I just stood there for a moment, frozen as I surveyed the scene.

When I was finally able to process everything, I walked toward the wonderland and noticed that Ms. Linda and Dr. Shabazz were having a seat on the other side of the room. They were talking in a low tone and watching me. I didn't even bother paying them any mind because I was seeing some toys and games that I wanted to play with. As I went digging in the basket, I saw two barbie dolls. Immediately I pulled them out and began playing with them. After a while, Ms. Linda said that she was going to step out so that I could talk with Dr. Shabazz alone.

"O'Zella?" Ms. Linda called out to me. I turned in her direction and looked at her. I'll be right outside the door if you need me. Are you ok with me stepping out?" she asked as she looked at me to let me know that if I said no or if she saw one ounce of discomfort in me, she would stay in that room with me and Dr. Shabazz.

Because I trusted her, my immediate response was, "Yes, Ms. Linda." If she could trust Dr. Shabazz, I believed that I could too.

The door closed behind Ms. Linda and it was just me and the good ole doc. She looked like she was sizing me up but with a smile before opening her mouth and saying, "Hello O'Zella," as if she hadn't already greeted me.

"Hello," I replied in turn.

"How old are you?"

"Ten," I answered as I kept playing with the dolls.

"What grade are you in?"

"I'm in the fifth grade now."

"Do you like your school?"

"It's ok."

"Just ok?"

"Yes."

"What's your favorite subject?"

"Math."

"What do you like about math?"

"I am really good with numbers, so I get good grades in that subject."

Dr. Shabazz and I spent a good half hour doing the back and forth with the questions and answers before Ms. Linda stuck her head back in the room to see if I was ok. At least that's what she said. However, the moment Dr. Shabazz saw her, the session was over.

"O'Zella," the doctor called out to me again.

"Yes?" my response was immediate.

"It was really nice to meet you and I hope we can sit and talk again soon."

"Thank you," my response was as kind as hers was, "me too."

Why Would I Love You?

On the ride home, things were still quiet between me and Ms. Linda, but this time I could tell that Ms. Linda wanted to say something to me or that she wanted to ask about what me and Dr. Shabazz had discussed while she was gone. The questions never came. She just filled the quiet with the radio. And when we got back to the house, she didn't even ask me then. Instead, it was the normal routine, dinner and then off to bed I went.

Eight

I had been seeing Dr. Shabazz once a week for almost three months and the sessions were always the same. She would ask me the usual, how my week was, how school was, how was life with friends, with home, things of that nature. After a few visits with her, I found myself becoming comfortable and I began telling her more things, the good things, but I was always careful to leave out the bad. Although I was comfortable with her, I still wasn't *that* comfortable.

After one particular session with Doctor Shabazz, at first things were like any other day. Ms. Linda drove home, once inside, I started on my homework, and she started on dinner. The boys did after school sports, so I always got home before them. Gabe was the next one to get home and as usual he came bursting in the door, happily telling us about his day. In the middle of him talking, Tyler came in and it was immediately noticed that he wasn't as happy at all.

Stomping into the kitchen, he threw his bag down which got everyone's attention. Ms. Linda held up a finger to Gabe to gently silence him and then addressed Tyler.

"Tyler, what's wrong?" she asked in that concerned mother's voice.

"Just leave me alone," he snapped at her.

"Excuse me, young man" she said, anger coming into her voice for the first time since I'd known her. "Exactly who do you think you're speaking to like that?"

Why Would I Love You?

"I'm sorry," he began to control his anger and calm down. "I got into it with a boy on the bus and I'm just upset."

"What do you mean got into it?" She wanted details and a better understanding.

"I mean he called me a baby and I didn't like it, so I punched him, and we started fighting."

"Oh, my goodness! Why would you do that?" she asked as frustration replaced her anger. "You should have used your words."

"I did use my words, and he called me a baby. So, I used my fists."

"Tyler!" Ms. Linda was back to anger again, "go into your room and take a moment. I'll be up to talk to you in a minute."

Tyler did as he was told and walked away grumbling after snatching his backpack up off of the floor. You could hear him stomping the whole way upstairs, every step ending with a big boom. Ms. Linda was really flustered, but she was also trying really hard to hide it. She started mumbling under her breath about how Tyler was getting out of control and how she didn't know what she was gonna do with that boy. I thought about how much more flustered she would be if she only knew what kind of a boy he was really turning into. I wondered if she would have still just mumbled under her breath then.

Without saying much more, Ms. Linda finished cooking dinner, excused herself, and then headed upstairs. Unlike Tyler's loud departure, her steps were slow, deliberate, and barely audible. Gabe and I gave each other a cautious look, we both were curious about what they were talking about and about what was going to happen. In the year that I had been there, Ms. Linda had never put her hands on her children, so I knew he wasn't gonna get the whooping he deserved. However, I was extremely hopeful that his punishment would be severe enough.

Gabe and I sat in the kitchen, silently finishing our homework. When we were done, we took it upon ourselves to begin setting the table when out of the blue there was a loud bam. Those same loud and heavy steps came down the stairs quickly just before Tyler yelled up the stairs "...and I'm never coming back!" Without even looking at me or Gabe, he stormed out the front door and slammed it hard behind him.

The tension in the house was so thick that evening that a chainsaw was needed to cut through it. I knew Ms. Linda was going to come down and act like everything was okay, but everything wasn't okay and that gave me the feeling that something bad was going to happen next.

Just like I thought, Ms. Linda came down with a forced smile on her face while Gabe continuously asked her, "What happened with Tyler? Where did he go?"

Her youngest son was badgering her with questions she couldn't answer until eventually her cool became a little warm and she snapped at him. "He'll be back! Now, stop asking me questions!" Gabe took that as a sign to leave the issue alone.

In unusual silence, we finished out the night with our routine the same as always. We ate dinner, read a book together in the living room, and then brushed our teeth. We all took our showers and went to bed. I know I was young, but I could tell that Ms. Linda was really stressed. So after tossing and turning for about an hour after bedtime, I got up and went to her room, softly knocking on her door as I did so.

"Ms. Linda? Can I come in?"

"Sure, Zell," her normally happy voice sounded very different, "come in."

I don't know when it had started, but my name had gone from O'Zella to just Zell, and amazingly enough, coming from her, I liked it. As I slowly opened the door thinking about how much I liked her and the life I was living with her, I noticed her wiping her face, trying to hide the tears that I know the argument with Tyler brought on.

"Are you okay?" I questioned her with concern in my voice.

"Yes, Zell, I'm fine," she lied. "Why aren't you in bed? You know you have school in the morning."

Why Would I Love You?

"I couldn't sleep, and I wanted to make sure you were okay like you always do with me," I told her the truth. That brought on a warm smile from her. Then I asked, "Is Tyler back yet?"

"No," she sighed deeply, worriedly," he's not back yet, but I promise you that everything is okay, sweetheart. Now, you go on to bed and get some sleep because we have to get up early for school tomorrow. Okay?"

"Okay," I said, wanting to give her a comforting hug like she always did when I wasn't okay, but I decided against it. "Goodnight Ms. Linda."

The walk back to my room felt so strange, I didn't know why but it did. And to make matters worse, for some reason I still couldn't sleep. I was tossing and turning for so long that eventually I just lay on my back and stared at the ceiling. That's when I heard the door downstairs open and close. The sound was faint, but I'd still heard it nevertheless. I knew it was Tyler trying to sneak in and I quickly glanced at the alarm clock that Ms. Linda had given me to help me keep track of time. It read three A.M.

I tried really hard to listen, to see if I could identify which direction Tyler was traveling in the house. Every once in a while I would hear a slight movement, but it was difficult because he was very light on his feet. To hear even better, I decided to close my eyes and close out all distractions. As I listened intently, it shocked me to hear my bedroom door creak. My eyes immediately shot open and I struggled to adjust to the darkness that was surrounding me. In less than three seconds I could clearly make out Tyler's shadowy form and I saw him silently slide into my room, close the door behind him, and tiptoe to my bed.

My body began to shake, and I began to tell myself that this was it. The closer he got to my bed, the more my mind raced with panicked thoughts. *Should I yell or should I just shut up and say nothing like I did when Mr. Bill came into my room?* Fearful and not sure of what move to make, I held my breath and waited. Then I closed my eyes again and just

56

listened, but it was so hard to hear past the banging and racing of my heart.

Finally hearing him, I realized that even though every step he took was intentionally soft, they each sounded like a jackhammer going off in my head. Then I felt his body move my bed as he took his last step. Before my mind could react to whatever decision I'd made, Tyler's hand swiftly covered my mouth. That's when he leaned in and roughly whispered in my ear, "If you yell, I'll kill you before anyone makes it to the room."

I was instantly nauseated. His breath smelled just like Mr. Bills had, like he had been drinking, and in that moment my decision had been made for me. I didn't want to die, so I was going to go numb and act like it was just another nightmare. I never even put up a fight when Tyler pulled the cover back and moved his hand up my leg. When he kissed my neck, the only move I made was to cringe.

He seemed so desperate to get at me that it didn't take him long to get to my panties. In a heartbeat, he started tugging at my waistband while keeping his hand on my mouth. His face was still by my ear, he growled, "Lift your body so I can take it off."

I wasted no time in doing as he said because I was scared even though I was trying to be numb. I was only ten years old and he was fourteen at this point. He was big and I was still very little. There was no way I could fight him, and after he'd said that he punched that boy in the face I just knew that he would beat me until he killed me just like he said he would do if I made one sound.

He removed my panties and tossed them to the floor, Tyler used that same hand to spread my legs apart and roughly shoved two fingers into me. My eyes shot wide open and I squealed from the unbearable pain. My squeal was muffled by the hand that he was pressing on my face even harder. "Shut up!" he growled at me. My heart was racing so fast and I was breathing hard as I tried with everything in me not to make a sound.

Why Would I Love You?

"I know you've been trying to stay away from me." His words were slurred, but still had evil dripping off of every syllable. "But I knew I was gonna get you one day."

Without another word, and while still keeping his hand over my mouth, Tyler climbed on top of me. With his free hand, he fumbled with his pants, pulling them down to his thighs, and then he forced himself inside of me. He was rough, and flopped on top of me like a fish out of water. I kept my eyes closed as tears of anguish streamed from my eyes, something I'd promised myself I would never do again. But these tears were different, they were soul deep tears, that came from a place of sheer and utter hell. This was a different type of pain altogether, not just physical, but mental as well and my tears reflected that.

The only saving grace for me that night was the fact that just as fast as he began, Tyler was finished. Quickly, he climbed off of me and pulled up his pants. When he let me go, I said nothing and did nothing other than curl up into a ball that faced away from him. Then I bit my bottom lip so that I wouldn't dare make a sound, especially not with him still in the room.

Before he left, he reached over and stroked my arm while whispering, "You better not tell anyone about this! This is our secret!"

Those were the words that rang in my ear repeatedly. Over and over. A secret that Mr. Bill told me to keep, now a secret that Tyler was telling me to keep. I hated secrets from that moment on, because secrets hurt. The only person that was hurting from those secrets was me. Falling back into that same depression that had filled me in the library house, I didn't move as I heard Tyler stumble to the door and walk out, leaving it cracked behind him. I heard him go to the bathroom instead of to his room, then I heard the water running before he exited it and made his way to his room. He might have been drunk, but he knew how to move and close doors very quietly.

The next morning came and I hadn't gotten a wink of sleep, I'd simply lay curled up in the fetal position until dawn. In my head I could still hear Tyler mumbling, "This is our secret, this is our secret." I tried to drown the sound of his voice and the memory of his horrible actions out, but that was useless. Those sounds and those images refused to depart from my mind. I was devastated and was smart enough to know that I would live with those words for the rest of my life.

Since I couldn't empty my mind enough to free myself from that torture, I spent the night talking to God, asking him why He had to take my mother, asking him why He kept sending me to places where people would hurt me. I wanted to know why I wasn't standing up for myself, why wasn't I screaming and why I didn't tell someone the first time it happened to me? I thought about asking God to never let it happen again, but somehow I just didn't believe He would hear me.

Knock, knock, knock, is the sound that interrupted my thoughts.

"Good morning, Zell!" I heard Ms. Linda's happy voice while I felt anything but happy. "Time to get up and get ready for school," she said as she made her first rounds to get everybody started on their day.

Before she'd gotten to my room, I heard her go to Tyler's room to see if he was back. When she'd found him there, the two of them had a heated discussion, but then I heard her tell him that she loved him and that she just wanted him to be safe. By the time she got to my room, if I'd had any plans to tell her anything, all of that went right out of the window at her confession of love for her son. I was the odd man out in that family and I truly believed that she wouldn't believe me if I told her what her monster of a son had done. So I figured that there was no point in uttering a single syllable about it.

Agonizingly slow, I dragged myself out of bed and started to get ready while trying to act like nothing had happened. My body was sore, and my mind was hallowed out. I felt more like a zombie that morning than I felt like a human being. I was simply going through the motions. To make matters even worse, while on my way back from the bathroom, I looked up only to see Tyler standing in his doorway watching me. Instantly, my body froze, I literally could not move.

All I could do was stand there as he put a finger to his mouth and said, "Shhh." And with a smug and satisfied look on his face, Ms. Linda's son headed down the stairs.

I didn't notice at first, but Gabe was looking through the crack of his door and he had seen everything. As I was finally able to move and began walking into my room, Gabe popped up behind me, scaring me so bad that I jumped and turned around to look at him while grabbing at my chest. I was back to being terrified of everything.

"I'm sorry I scared you, O'Zella," he began quietly, unlike his usual self, "but I wanna know the secret too?"

"What secret?" I played dumb. "What are you talking about?"

"I saw Tyler tell you to shush like you were keeping a secret, now I wanna know too!"

"Gabe, there is no secret," I lied.

"Yes, there is, and it's not fair because I wanna know too."

Gabe was younger than me by a year, but still close enough that maybe if I told him, someone would believe him if he told them. Or maybe he would join his brother in torturing me. I wanted to tell someone, but I was so lost, so hurt, so confused. I still had to come up with a lie because I knew Gabe wasn't the type of kid that would give up easily. He would keep pressing and pushing until someone told him something.

"Okay," I said while thinking quickly on my feet, "he doesn't want me to tell Ms. Linda that I saw him when he came home really late last night."

"Oh, that's not a really good secret," he spoke as if deflated. "But okay. Besides, I think my mom knows he got home late anyway."

"Yeah, I guess she does, doesn't she?"

Another moment to tell the truth had come and gone. I actually could have told someone that I was being hurt, and yet again I didn't say anything. Fear had me choosing not to say a single word.

Nine

A week had gone by and it was time for my visit with Doctor Shabazz. I tried so hard not to change my attitude because I didn't want anyone to suspect anything and start asking me questions. I did stop spending so much time with Ms. Linda and spent more time in my room reading, or at least that's what I said I was doing. However, I'd lied because instead of reading, I was curled up on my bed as the words, "This is our secret," haunted me mercilessly.

Ms. Linda and I pulled up to the office building, went inside and checked in as usual. This had become such a normal thing for us that Ms. Linda had started to sit in the waiting room while I would go in for my appointment. No longer did she feel the need to wait right outside of the door and I no longer felt the need for her to be right outside of that door. We both felt comfortable enough that such drastic measures no longer had to be taken.

"Hello, Ms. Lady, how are you today?" Dr. Shabazz began our session,

"Hello," came my usual reply. "I'm okay."

"Just okay?" She spoke in a different voice now, a curious one.

"Yes," I replied cautiously. I thought I was behaving normally, but apparently, I wasn't. I was speaking slowly so that I wouldn't tell her anything I didn't want her to know.

"Why are you just okay?"

"I don't know. I just am."

"How is school going?"

"Okay"

"Hmmmm," there was that curious voice again. "So everything is just okay?"

"Yes."

"What would you like to talk about today?"

"I don't know."

"O'Zella?"

"Yes"

"Usually, you have more to say than this." She looked at me with serious eyes. "Today your conversation is different. Is something bothering you?"

"Yes..." I let slip out even though I wasn't sure if I could bring myself to say anything. "I-I-I," frustration and confusion had me stuttering hard. "I don't know!" I finally just blurted out.

Dr. Shabazz raised a curious brow at me before saying, "Do you remember what we talked about when we first started meeting?"

"Yes," I replied as I put the toys down and stared at the floor where I had been sitting to play with the toys. "You are my friend and I can share my feelings with you."

"Right," she confirmed, "so is there something you need to share with me that you don't feel like you can talk with anyone else about?" She paused for the longest time, giving me a moment to process and accept her words as truth. "I'm here to listen."

"I know," I spoke shyly, barely above a whisper, "I kinda just don't feel like talking today."

"Alright," she was quick to stand in agreement with me. "Then what would you like to do today?"

I knew I should've been telling the doctor about everything that was going on with me, about how I was afraid of Mr. Bill and the fact that he had touched me, and about how Tyler had climbed on top of me and did bad things to me. At that moment, though, I was afraid all over again. I felt the fear crawling over me like red ants on my skin.

So instead of talking, I walked over, grabbed the coloring book and some crayons. "I think today I would just like for us to color."

"I would like that as well. Will you pick out a picture for us to color?"

"I chose from the coloring book of emotions and found a picture of a girl who looked afraid. "This one."

"Hmmmmm," that curious voice emerged again. "Can I ask why you chose this picture?"

"I don't know."

"Okay," she refused to push. "Well, what color do you want to start with?"

Instead of talking, I shared my pain through the picture as I drew tears rolling down the girl's face and began to color that first. Dr. Shabazz didn't pester me about talking or ask me any more questions about how I was feeling. Instead, she made small conversation as we colored a couple of pictures until our time was up.

When Linda and I got back to the house, I went straight up to my room. The boys were gone to their dad's house, so I felt comfortable and safe enough to take a nap. I'm not sure how long I had been asleep, but when I woke up I noticed that it was dark outside. Deciding that it was safe enough to venture outside of my room, I went downstairs to find Ms. Linda in the family room reading a book. She looked up the moment I stepped in the doorway.

"Well, hello, sleeping beauty," she spoke to me with that pretty smile of hers. "You must have been really tired. I made you something to eat, it's in the microwave. Are you hungry?" I liked the fact that she was always taking care of me, it made me feel warm and fuzzy inside.

I didn't say anything though, I just nodded my head and made my way to the kitchen. Ms. Linda came into the kitchen with me and grabbed a drink out of the fridge while I warmed up the food. We sat at the table together even though I was the only one eating. For the longest time, she didn't say anything while I grubbed on my dinner. When I was almost done eating, that was when Ms. Linda decided to break the silence that had been building between us.

"Zell, I was thinking that since the boys are gone, and we have the house to ourselves we can have a movie night. What do you think?"

"That sounds good," I shook my head up and down as I spoke, liking the sound of spending time with her.

After I finished eating, we went to the living room and curled up on the couch together, looking for a good movie on the Firestick. I found myself enjoying that peaceful time with her while she hugged me as we watched movies.

I couldn't help but to think that I hadn't felt safe like this in a while. It gave me an odd sense of satisfaction to know that even in a world full of bad people, there was someone that actually cared about me and that wasn't trying to harm me in any way. Occasionally, Ms. Linda would give me a light squeeze almost as if to assure me that I was safe with her, then she would ask me if I was ok. I would nod my head slightly and keep watching the movie until we fell asleep curled up on the couch together. That was one of the memories from my childhood that whenever I thought of it, it always made me smile. Deep down inside, I wanted to believe that this particular moment of happiness was the beginning of a better life for me, but I would have been lying to myself because things only got worse after that.

After Tyler's first assault, he kept his distance from me, but that only lasted about a week. I think he was waiting to see if I would tell, but because I said nothing to anyone, nobody said anything to him. After that first week was over, Tyler snuck into my room at least twice a week for the next two months. It was like a reoccurring nightmare, one that refused to stop plaguing me. But to make it through the torment, I just lay there, letting my mind take me somewhere else while knowing it would be over quickly.

Why Would I Love You?

A short while later, I went to school and received a very unwelcome surprise. During lunch time, I was called to the office. As I sat in the waiting area, I was seriously confused about what I had done wrong because despite everything going on in my life, I was a great student.

"O'Zella?"

It confused me even more to look up and see that it was Janet with her fat body, curly hair, and thick glasses that was calling my name. I knew nothing good was happening whenever I saw her, so I immediately began a silent panic. My principal stepped to her side and told me to come into his office. When I did so, Janet was the first to speak.

"O'Zella, how are you, dear?" she was using her squeaky pity voice.

"Fine," I refused to tell the bearer of bad news anything.

"Do you feel safe at your foster home?" She got straight to the point.

"I guess," I said as I wondered where that question came from.

"Has anything happened that has made you feel uncomfortable or has anyone hurt you?" she pressed as my nerves suddenly became shot.

My palms began to clam up. I fidgeted in my seat and fumbled with my hands as Janet and the principal watched for my answer. I didn't want to talk to them anymore and I looked down and stared at a chipped piece of tile on the floor.

"I don't know," I mumbled, I needed time to think, time to figure out the right answer. I could hear Janet's frustration coming through in the big sigh she took before she began to speak again. I knew in my heart that she wanted nothing but to help me, unfortunately, I was not making it very easy for her to do.

"O'Zella," she spoke my name more firmly this time, "has anyone touched you in a way that you didn't like or without your permission?"

Again, with my eyes still trying to focus on the chipped tile, I said, "I don't know."

In one swift, frustrated movement, Janet gently grabbed my chin, lifted it, and forced me to look her into the eyes, "You talk to me, ya hear. I know you don't like me, but I am here to protect you and I can't do that if you don't tell me that something is going on." I knew she meant business by the way she spoke, but her delivery also made it so that I didn't feel comfortable telling her anything. "Did anyone touch you?" she asked once more.

While Janet's hand was still on my chin and not a word was coming from the principal sitting behind her, I burst into tears. Janet didn't try to get any more words from me, she just pulled me into her bosom, rocked me and whispered, "It's ok, dear."

The rest of that day was a complete blur. The next thing I remember after leaving that office was waking up in a strange room. Sitting in a chair at the foot of my bed was Janet. I had cried myself to sleep and because I hadn't really been sleeping for the last two months, I finally let it catch up with me.

Quietly, she moved to the side of the bed. "O'Zella, because of you potentially being harmed, I've taken you from Ms. Linda's home and brought you to an all girls foster home instead. The mother of the house is a dear friend of mine, so I know she will take great care of you, ok?"

"But what about Ms. Linda?" I asked as a great sadness covered and gripped me.

"I sent someone over to her home to pick up the rest of your belongings."

"But what happened? Why did you come and take me away?"

"This morning, Linda's youngest son told the school staff that he saw his brother touching your private parts. Is that true?" For the first time, I finally told the truth. I lowered my eyes and slightly shook my head up and down to let her know that it was the truth.

"Oh God!" she whispered.

Why Would I Love You?

    Janet didn't ask me for details or try to torture me by making me talk at all. She just sat with me for a little while, whispering the whole time. I think she was praying over me without trying to be obvious about it. The entire time she prayed, I thought about Ms. Linda and how much I was going to miss everything about her and Gabe and Jillian even though she was gone most of the time. That made me really sad. I had finally felt like I belonged to a family and Ms. Linda had made me feel as though I was really cared about. I was going to miss them so much. While Janet prayed, I prayed that God would help me to get past losing them.

    Then I was worried about what was happening to Ms. Linda and to Tyler now that Gabe had told everything. I wondered if Tyler would go to jail or if Ms. Linda would be punished because of what her son had done to me. I felt so bad and so scared for her. I truly believed that if I had said something, maybe Ms. Linda wouldn't be suffering the way I knew she was at that moment. And as much as I wanted to ask questions and find out about the people that had been my family for the past year, I pushed all of those questions and feelings into the back of my mind like I did with everything else, and I focused on the here and now.

    I refused to allow myself to break down or to shed another tear. It was time to toughen up, accept the fact that the world was a hard and cruel place to me and that it would always be. I had to deal with it and just move on. As I came to those harsh conclusions and decided to accept my reality, Janet finally stopped praying and asked me if I was ready to meet the rest of the people in the house I was going to be living in. I hadn't really said much since I woke up, so I just nodded my head again and followed her out of the room. Whether I was ready to meet them or not, I was about to be thrust into yet another living situation. There was no need to complain or to tell Janet that I wasn't ready. I just kept my mouth shut and went with whatever flow came my way.

This new house wasn't loud at all, but it was well lit and the decor was very homely. At first, I didn't think anyone was even home, but when we walked around the corner there was a large table with about eight girls of varying ages eating dinner. Janet cleared her throat and when she did so, the whole room turned and stared at us, well, they were actually staring at me. Instantly, my eyes hit the floor. I couldn't stand to be looked at, especially not by a room full of people that I didn't know. It felt like forever that I'd been standing there, but only a few seconds had gone by before I heard a high pitched squeal come from across the room.

"O'ZELLA!" My eyes shot up because I knew that voice, squeal and all. Before I could brace myself, Jazz came running across the room and jumped on me. She was screaming and hugging me really tight as she jumped up and down with me in her arms. "I didn't think I was ever going to see you again!" she said when she finally stopped hugging me. Then she grabbed my arm and turned me to face the room full of girls that still had their eyes glued in my direction. "Everybody, this is Zella, my best friend in the world!" She spoke those words so sincerely that it touched my heart.

The girls all mumbled back in unison "Hi, Zella."

Clap, clap!

At the head of the table farthest from me there was a woman that I hadn't even noticed was there. She stood to her feet and addressed the table. "Ok, girls, now that you have been introduced, let's get back to dinner so that we can get ready for bed. We all have school in the morning, including me."

Jazz let my hand go and made her way back to the table, but not before giving me one more tight hug. That hug was the thing that really felt like home to me because Jazz was actually my friend and she showed it.

Why Would I Love You?

Focusing my attention back on the woman, I noticed that she favored Janet in many ways. Her hair was curly like Janet's and she had the same round body type. The only difference was that she didn't wear glasses and she was much taller. Smiling, she walked toward me. I wasn't sure if it was that her complexion was so dark or that her teeth were extra white, but either way, her smile was bright and blinding.

"Hello O'Zella." she said, with an outstretched hand, "I'm Ms. Bailey, but everyone calls me Aunt Bee."

I reached out my hand for her to shake and then I spoke. "Nice to meet you, Aunt Bee."

After that, she invited us to dinner and Janet and I joined them. The meal was delicious, it almost tasted like something my momma would make when she wasn't on a bender. I decided to take the empty seat next to Jazz and the whole time she kept trying to whisper to me about what had been happening with her in the year that we hadn't seen each other.

After a few attempts of trying to talk to me, Aunt Bee nipped that conversation in the bud with a, "Ms. Jazz," and a look. I knew that after dinner we would have time to talk, so I gave her a wink and she stopped talking, knowing that we'd eventually catch up on everything.

From that day on, Jazz and I were inseparable. Aunt Bee saw how close we were and ended up agreeing to let us share one of the double rooms. I don't know how it happened, but we also had almost all the same classes in school. We would stay up all night talking about everything and nothing. I don't know how we managed to never run out of stuff to talk about, but Jazz was my best friend, so it didn't take much for us to find a good conversation or to be acting silly and cracking up.

I remember us being up late one night and all of a sudden we heard some banging and some incoherent mumbling outside of our room. It sounded like a regular *I stubbed my toe and it hurt* kind of sound, but the way Jazz's body tensed up made me wonder. This was my best and only friend, so if I couldn't ask her any questions, who could I ask?

Before speaking, I studied her frightened silence for a second.

"What's wrong with you, Jazz?"

"Oh, huh…" she began as if extremely distracted. Then, "nothin'" she clearly lied.

"Why you jump like that then?" The whole time I was talking to her she was stiff as a board and watching our bedroom door. No matter how much I tried getting her attention, she never loosened up or paid me any mind until she heard another bedroom door close.

Then, "Zella?" She looked up to find me staring in her face. "You have only been here a couple weeks so you need to know that even though Aunt Bee seems nice, she has a really mean side to her."

"Whatchu mean by that?" I asked as my brows furrowed in confusion.

"I mean that witch don't know how to keep her hands to herself at times," she spoke in a whisper so noone passing by would hear her. "She gets drunk, and when she does or when she has an argument with one of the men she thinks she's sneaking in and out of here, she likes to make her way through the house and mess with some of us. We call her the Tornado when that happens." She looked toward the door again, waited a few seconds before she continued.

"Most of the time it's after we're asleep. She'll wander through the rooms until she finally picks somebody to slap around. Then she'll make them clean something that was already clean to begin with. She can't say it was because of no man, but we all know that's the reason she does it." Jazz paused for a moment to giggle as if the situation she was describing was funny, then she went on. "It don't happen that often, and it's a hell of a lot better than Mr—" she cut herself off as if she had said way too much.

"Mr. who, Jazz?" her words didn't trail off like that was the man's name, she just stopped abruptly and then looked away.

Why Would I Love You?

"Nobody," she spoke quickly. "Forget I even said anything."

I had been through enough abuse to recognize when someone else had been abused. So, I decided to share my experience to see if she would share hers. "Jazz, can I tell you something that I ain't neva eva told anyone before?"

"Yeah, I'm ya best friend, dummy," she said as she looked at me like I was slow.

"When we were at the library house, Mr. Bill used to come in my room and touch me. I didn't say anything to anybody because he said he would kill me." I felt sad as I remembered, but I was not going to cry not over Mr. Bill or over Tyler's punk ass. However, I didn't dare look up because I was afraid of what was coming next. The last thing I wanted to see in my best friend's eyes was sadness and pity.

"Zella?" she said my name as if she could feel my pain. "He used to come into my room too. It's ok!" she told me as she came over and touched my shoulder.

When I looked up at her, I saw that her face was covered with tears that I absolutely refused to shed.

Wasting no time at all, I grabbed her and hugged her tight. It was real messed up what had happened to us, and I sincerely hoped that one day someone would deal with Mr. Bill for what it seemed he'd been doing to a lot of innocent girls.

"Do you want to talk about it?' I asked her.

She shook her head no and just held on to me as if for dear life. Because I knew what it felt like to not want to talk, I just held on to my friend for as long as she needed me to. To be honest, I needed her to hold on to me as well. I don't know how long we sat there giving each other silent support, but when we finally did let one another go, I knew that from that moment on, Jazz was going to be my best friend forever and that I would have to kill somebody over her.

Ten

Over the course of the next two years, Jazz and I had become inseparable. If you saw me you knew she was there too. We were known around town as the gruesome twosome. We didn't go looking for trouble, but it sure seemed to always find us. Whenever we would get into trouble, whether it be in school or just arguing and fighting with the neighborhood girls, Aunt Bee would always hear about it and beat us both. Sometimes it was to teach us a lesson, other times it was just because she was mean as hell. She could just be cruel with her beatings, but as long as Jazz and I were together, everything else was bearable. She was my best friend, my sister, the only person I had grown to love outside of my mother.

By the time we turned thirteen, Aunt Bee stopped beating us because we'd gotten too big for her to whoop on. Whenever she came at us like she wanted to harm us, we would look her in the eye to show her that we weren't afraid of her. She never showed us any fear, but I think she just stopped giving a damn about us. She was tired of us and would often tell us that we were lost causes and that the system would forever be our home. We didn't care about that, though, we had each other and that was all that mattered.

Jazz and I were so unruly that we would skip school and go to ditch parties. At the time, I thought that was the life, and I was in a good place, a place where I could get attention from boys our age and actually like it. I didn't cringe at the thought of being touched like I did

Why Would I Love You?

after Mr. Bill and Tyler, and as I got older, I realized that the attention was really nice. I couldn't say I was a virgin per se, but because I hadn't given permission to be touched by them, whenever anyone asked me about my virginity, I would say that I was still untouched. When the boys would find that out, it stopped being about liking me and all of a sudden I became everyone's conquest. They would try and buy me shit to like them or try to sweet talk me out of my pants. I was not having it, though. Just because I wasn't a virgin didn't mean I was going to give it up easily.

Jazz on the other hand was open like a 7-Eleven. I never judged her though, Jazz was my sister and even blood couldn't make us any closer. Even after so many years of constantly being around each other, we still never ran out of things to stay up all night talking about. Once she started having sex, there was even more things for us to talk about, juicy new things. Our conversations had now become exciting with her telling me details about her guy of the week. I would just sit and take it all in. No question I asked her was ever too dumb or off limits. That was one of the many reasons I loved her so much, I never had to fake it with her and she always kept it real with me.

One night she tells me that she is in love and has finally found the one. I looked at her funny because I had heard that from her before, however, that didn't stop me from asking about this new guy in her life. Because it was late, we had a flashlight pointed at the ceiling as we both lay in my bed, side by side, on our backs, looking at the light.

"Zella, girl, he is so cute and nice. He don't even act like he wanna fuck me," she spoke as if impressed. "He gives me money and tells me that I am the most beautiful girl he has ever seen," the sigh she let out revealed her feelings for him. "He also told me he wants to marry me. He's older, a senior in high school, so he's probably ready for marriage now."

"What?" I asked in shock. "He's in high school? Where did you meet him?"

"At the corner store over there by the park. I gave him my number but didn't think nothing of it because it took him like a week before he called."

"Well, where was I? Because I don't remember you going to no store without me."

"I know we're with each other most of the time, but I do have *some* time that I am not with you, thank you very much," She laughed like she'd told the joke of the century. I, on the other hand, was not happy. I knew what happened when someone's interest was taken over by a man, and all that meant was that I was about to disappear from her life.

Like I said, we knew each other well, so when she saw my face, she knew something was wrong. "Zella, why you lookin' like that?"

"What you mean?"

"I know you better than you know yourself sometimes. Sooo," she sang happily and nudged my shoulder, trying to cheer me up, "what's wrong?"

"Nothing." I felt myself pouting but couldn't seem to help it.

"Zella?" she spoke more seriously this time. I think she was hurt because she knew that I was keeping the truth from her. To be honest, I wanted to say nothing again, to keep my feelings to myself again, but I had to tell her because that was the nature of our relationship. We were real with each other, the rest of the world may have deceived those around them, but Jazz and I promised that there would always be honesty with us.

"Ok," I let out a deep breath and went for it, "so, whenever my mom would get a boyfriend, she used to fall so deep in love that she forgot about me. I think you're going to do that."

"Zella, stop it!" she chastised, her voice now revealing that she was kind of hurt about the way I thought she would handle me. "You will never be forgotten by me, I swear," she looked at me and stuck her pinky out at me.

Why Would I Love You?

Whenever we wanted to say that we were serious about what we were saying, like most people, we pinky promised. And since I never knew Jazz to go back on a pinky promise, it made me feel secure in her promise that she wasn't going to forget me.

Some time had gone by and as expected, Jazz had gotten close to the high school guy. Even though she didn't go back on her word to me, and she made sure that I was included with everything even when the boy was around, I still felt like a third wheel. And to make matters worse, I'd noticed some things I didn't like when it came to dealing with him. After about a month, I couldn't take it anymore and I had the urge to say something.

It was a week away from my 14th birthday and I asked Jazz to go with me to pick a birthday outfit. As usual, she and I hopped on the bus and headed to the mall. On the ride there, Jazz leaned over to show me a funny video and her coat sleeve rode up her arm just high enough for me to see a bruise in the shape of fingers. Immediately, I asked her what happened to her arm, and before I knew it, she had snatched her sleeve down and said it was nothing. I had the same connection with her that she had with me, so I knew it was not nothing. For the time being I let it go, though.

Once we finally made it to the mall, we had put the incident to the side and I was having a blast. It felt like I had my friend back and I was able to be selfish with her attention. I took full advantage of that. Because I didn't have much money, Jazz and I went cruising through the clearance rack of all the department stores. Then I found the perfect one piece romper in Old Navy with some matching flip flops. I decided to try on a couple of them to get the right size because I knew their clothes sometimes ran small.

I was in the dressing room getting a look at how the romper fit me when I heard Jazz's cell phone ring. "I'll be right back," she called out to me, and then she answered the phone as I heard her stepping out of the dressing area.

After a few minutes of me trying on the rompers to get the right fit, I had finally found the size that was perfect and went to show Jazz. I walked to the entrance of the fitting room in search of her and that was where I peeped her off to the side talking on her phone. From her body language and from the jerkiness of her gestures, it looked like she was having a heated discussion. Instead of yelling over to her to get her attention, I just took the few extra steps to where she was to tap her on the shoulder so she could see.

"Nah, P," she was saying, "that shit wasn't cool. You keep telling me you sorry, but you bruised my arm this time. What about next time?" she spoke angrily, then paused as if listening before she spoke again. "I don't want to hear that, there will always be a next time if I take you back." I knew I shouldn't have been listening in on her conversation, but it seemed like that was going to be the only way I was going to know anything about my friend who had begun keeping secrets. "Whatever," she went on, "I'm out with Zella. You know, the friend I have been ignoring for your sorry ass," she spoke heatedly. And without even giving him a chance to say anything, she said a loud, "Bye!" and ended the call.

Before I could move away from her, Jazz spun around to see me standing there staring at her. There were tears streaming down her face as I was trying to think up a good lie or a good excuse about how I'd just so happen to hear her conversation. All of that was cut short when she came over to me, wrapped her arms around me and cried. She was sobbing so hard into the shoulder of my hoodie that I was struggling to understand the words she was crying out. I tried filling in the blanks, adding my own words to the ones I couldn't quite comprehend.

I believed she'd said something along the lines of, "I'm sorry I've been a shitty best friend. I am done with P's stupid, possessive ass."

Why Would I Love You?

I wanted to tell her that it was okay, but I didn't because it wasn't okay and she knew that. However, instead of making her feel worse, I hugged her back and told her that I loved her. For the longest time, we stood there with our arms wrapped around one another until she was finally able to pull herself together. After that, we let each other go and she finally got a look at the romper. She said she liked it and since I liked it as well, I bought the outfit and then we headed to the food court.

Inside the food court, we bought smoothies and then found a corner where we could sit and talk. From what I had witnessed, I now knew for sure that their relationship wasn't all kisses and hugs. She was in a place where she had no choice but to either tell me the truth about what had been going on or lie to me which we didn't normally do with one another. I wanted her to choose the truth because the secrets she had been keeping were starting to take a toll on us.

For a little while Jazz and I just sat there, neither of us saying a word. Even though there was so much going on around us, so much noise and life happening, the silence between the two us was deafening. It didn't take long before I grew tired of just staring at her and not saying anything. I figured I'd have to be the one to break the silence because it didn't seem like she wanted to.

"So, what is going on with you?" I asked gently, trying to keep any emotion from my voice so wouldn't upset her any more than she had already been.

"Nothing is going on," she lied. "What you mean?" she asked, trying to play dumb.

"Stop playing with me, Jazz. We know each other, so I know when you're not telling the truth just like you know when I'm not telling the truth. And right now, I know you're not being honest." I tried to hide my irritation with a gentle sound to my voice, but her little secrets were getting old. "I didn't want to say anything, but I heard you talking on the phone."

"So, if you heard me talking, why you asking me what's going on?" She on the other hand wasn't trying to hide the irritation at all. "You clearly heard. That nigga P put his fucking hands on me and now I'm not dealing with him no more."

"What the fuck!" I was beyond pissed now. I'd heard her say that he'd bruised her, but I didn't know it had been intentional. "Why would he do that?"

"Because I told him I was going to be chilling with you today and he didn't like that shit. I can't deal with no nigga that act like he my fucking daddy, tryna tell me where to go and shit. And that putting his hands on me shit is for the fuckin birds. Ya feel me?" She was practically yelling at this point.

"Damn, Jazz, you ok?" I spoke sincerely, I was really worried about her now. "I didn't know all that shit was going down. I hope me asking to spend time with you alone wasn't what caused this to happen. Either way, you know how I get about you." She looked at me and I looked at her and she could clearly see the meaning in my eyes. "So you know that I want to put my hands on him now, right?"

"Chill, Zella," she spoke more calmly as she shook her head no, "he ain't no fuckin' body to waste your time on. Besides, he's gonna be somebody else's problem now because he damn sure won't get another chance to put his hands on me."

"I heard that," was my very satisfied reply.

Jazz wasn't lying about him not being in her life anymore. He tried so hard to get her back, sent her flowers and notes and shit. He called her phone all hours of the day and night. When she blocked him, he would call from a private number. When she blocked private calls, he started calling from random numbers. The whole situation was crazy, but she was cool as a cucumber about it. Even though she was dealing with all that, I was selfishly happy to have my right hand back again. Things hadn't really been the same without her and I was happy to have him gone so that I could have Jazz back. Immediately, we went back to doing everything together.

    My birthday came and Jazz and I planned on changing shit up. We were only fourteen, but we wanted to start making money. Because we were known around, it wasn't hard for us to get odd jobs doing some cleaning in stores and in barber shops in the neighborhood. We were always so much better together, and because of the great job we did together the store owners and barbershop owners started to refer us to their friends who had other businesses. Within three months Jazz and I had three stores, two barbershops, and a salon that we cleaned each day after school. We only cleaned each place once a week, so we were able to do our job and still make it back to the house with enough time to do our homework and chores.

    After about a month, the shit with P finally died down and my best friend and I were stacking our paper and minding our business. Four months into our job, business was really booming, the money was flowing, and the two of us were getting straight A's. Life couldn't get any better. We had an amazing routine that kept everyone happy and that also gave us time to be kids, running the streets with all the other kids in the neighborhood. Don't get it twisted though, we kept our noses clean and stayed out of trouble because business was too good to be getting into some petty bullshit that would make us lose our money.

Eleven

What happened next is something that I still remember like it was yesterday. The store around the corner from the house is where we started and where we made the most money because the old man who ran the store would always have extra projects for us to do. One Thursday, the day that we usually worked at this particular location, old man James had a big project for us. Of course we accepted because we never said no to him. It wasn't just the money that endeared us to him, it was the fact that he was really sweet to everyone, especially to the kids that would come in the store. So, we made it a point to ensure he was straight.

Anyway, because of how big the project was, Jazz and I ended up staying really late that night. The sun had just set and the streetlights had just come on, so he told us we could come and finish doing his inventory over the weekend. I was exhausted, so I didn't argue with him at all and neither did Jazz. We just grabbed our bags and headed out the door. As soon as we stepped outside, there was P, leaning on his car, waiting outside the store with a sad ass look on his face and an even sadder excuse for a bouquet hanging from his hands.

I was the first to see him, so pure instinct had me grabbing Jazz's arm.

"Ouch, bitch, what's that for?" she said as she looked at me like I was crazy.

"Look!" I spoke in a voice that let her know to get her guard up.

Why Would I Love You?

Instantly, Jazz looked up and saw his face. Once they locked eyes, he wasted no time pushing off of his car and heading our way. Jazz sucked her teeth and murmured, "Fuck!" She took steps toward him and I quickly reached out and grabbed her arm again. She whipped her head in my direction and with a dry tone she looked at me and said, "It's ok. I'll be home in a minute, let me just talk to him and get it over with."

I wanted so badly to ask her if she was sure, but I already knew what her answer was going to be, so I reluctantly began walking away. I made sure I told her my phone would be on and that she had better call. She told me she would as I headed in the direction of home. When I hit the corner, I looked back one more time just to make sure she was good. All I saw was them standing close to each other and talking like old lovers. Disgusted, I rolled my eyes and took my ass home.

I remember thinking that night that she wasn't going to learn if she took his ass back. I was so annoyed that I stayed up waiting by the phone. Finally, a few minutes after midnight her number came flashing across my phone screen. I jumped and answered, "Bitch, you know what time it is?" I was about to go in on Jazz about how she knew Aunt Bee was pissed and we were going to both be in trouble, but a sound coming through the phone penetrated my ears and gripped my voice box so tight it almost shut it completely. It was Jazz, and she wasn't talking normally. She sounded like she was crying and gurgling while calling my name. I didn't know what to do, the whole situation was like a horrible nightmare.

My body would only let me stand in the middle of the room with the phone to my ear while I screamed, "JAZZ! JAAZZ! JAAAZZ!" I kept screaming her name until the line went dead and disconnected. It felt like I was on the phone for a long ass time, but it literally was only a minute.

Not long after the disconnect, Aunt Bee burst in my door. She was geared up to curse me the fuck out and slap me around until she saw the terror on my face. "What the hell is going on?" She looked at me and spoke angrily. When I said nothing because I couldn't, she shouted at me, "Where is Jazz?" Still, I couldn't form a single word, so she grabbed me by my shoulders and started to shake me.

I had blacked out, passing out in Aunt Bee's arms. I honestly don't remember anything about the rest of that night, all I can remember is that Jazz never made it home. When my mom died, I was too young to understand what was going on, but this, this was way too familiar and I understood every single thing that was happening.

The next morning the house was crawling with cops. I stayed locked up in my room, balled up in my bed. They didn't need to tell me shit, everything in me knew what happened and it made me feel weak, like I had just lost a limb. A few times some detectives came into my room to ask me questions because other than P, I was the last person to see Jazz alive. I couldn't formulate real sentences to even answer them. All I could do was rock and repeat, "He killed her. I know it was him. He did it."

Early that morning they found Jazz's body downtown behind a dumpster on the side of a Volunteers of America soup kitchen. People were lining up to get free food when a bum who'd been looking for cans stumbled upon her body. She'd been beaten until she was bloody, her clothes had been torn almost to shreds, and she was holding onto her phone. It had died and so had she.

I want to say that losing Jazz was the defining moment in my life, the moment that made me swear to make something of myself, to get out of the hood and to be a better person. Yeah ok, that shit only happens in movies because Jazz's death didn't make me better, it made me bitter. After losing her, my attitude changed, my grades dropped, I started skipping school. I stopped caring about everything. Mr. James would see me coming down the street and try to be friendly, but that was the old me. I wouldn't disrespect him, but I wasn't stopping to have conversations with him either. I made it a point to shut people out

Why Would I Love You?

because in my fourteen years of living, the people that got close to me either touched me inappropriately, couldn't protect me, or died on me, and none of that was good for me.

    To make matters worse, if things weren't already bad enough, time wound down and Jazz's family didn't come forward to claim her body. They said they didn't have the money to bury her, so they left her as a ward of the state which meant that the state had her cremated. No funeral. Not even a memorial service. Another life that I loved was lost to me and yet again, I didn't get the chance to say goodbye. With all that I had endured in my life, I honestly felt like that was the first of the major events that was responsible for my undoing.

    Almost two months had gone by and the cops didn't seem like they cared enough to solve Jazz's murder. It was almost like she didn't matter at all, not to her family, not to the system, not to the justice system, not to the state. I just kept going deeper and deeper down a hole of depression. I stopped speaking altogether and no matter how many beatings Aunt Bee promised, I just did whatever I wanted because I didn't give a rats ass about anything or anyone. I had become so despondent that I was only attending school once a week, but because I was actually smart, I was able to do everything for the week in that one day. I wasn't passing with straight A's like before, but I was passing and that was enough for me.

    I had come home early one Friday, hoping my on time arrival would keep me from hearing Aunt Bee's mouth. Instead, I was met by another headache, her homegirl Janet. It had been well over two years since I'd last seen the bearer of bad news, and she hadn't changed a bit. She was still short, still round, and still wearing that same tired ass wig. She and Aunt Bee were sitting in the living room when I got in. They were both looking so weird that I wasn't sure if they were happy or sad, but I walked toward them anyway. I smiled politely as Janet smiled back at me and patted the spot on the couch next to her, an indication for me to join them.

"Hello, Ms. Grife," she spoke in that same old tired but kind voice. "Come on in and have a seat, will you? I have some news I'd like to share with you."

Here we go again, I thought. "Hello Ms. Janet. What's the news?" is what I said.

"We've found your father. Isn't that exciting?" She looked at me expectantly.

I didn't give anyone what they were expecting. I just sat there with Janet's words bouncing around in my head. *Is this a good thing? I mean, he is the man who walked out on me and my mother when I was an infant.* As my thoughts processed, I didn't say anything. I just sat on that couch wondering why this man was showing up in my life after almost fifteen years of being missing in action. As much as I tried to find the good in that situation, everything in me was telling me that the return of my father was not the good and exciting news Janet thought it should be.

Before I could go any further down the rabbit hole of distrust, Janet reached out and touched my shoulder, breaking me out of my trance. "O'Zella, are you ok?" she asked as concern rang loud and clear in her voice.

No, I wasn't okay. I was not going to hear the word father and instantly think my life was going to be better. I didn't know him, didn't know anything about this man except the fact that he hadn't been there for my mother or for me. I had questions that I had no intention of biting my tongue to suppress, but I wanted to hear the answers to those questions straight from the horse's mouth. So, I plastered a fake smile on my face and began to put on a show.

"Oh, yes, Ms. Janet, that's great news," I lied. "When do I get to see him?" Janet looked pleased with my response, but Aunt Bee was sitting there with a sour expression on her face.

Why Would I Love You?

I knew why she looked like a sour patch kid. Aunt Bee didn't really care about us as much as she cared about the checks she got for us. Every time one of us would piss her off, she would say, "You lucky I don't want to mess up my check or I would send you off to another home."

Now that I could possibly be going to another home, she was sitting there with that mean ass mug trying to act bootleg happy. I would've bet good money that she was thinking about how she'd already lost Jazz's money and how she was about to lose my money as well. She was probably plotting and planning on ways to get some new girls to replace us so that she could keep her pocket as fat as she was. I wanted to laugh in her face, but I wasn't even sure that my dad coming back around was any better. So, I kept my laughter to myself as I focused on the fact that I would soon find out all I needed to know about the man who claimed to be my father, good or bad.

All weekend long, I went on about my regular business. If I had learned anything in my short life, I damn sure learned never to look forward to anything. So, I didn't. Monday morning came and as promised Janet was there bright and early to take me to reunite with my "father." The car ride was pretty awkward just like they had always been because seeing Janet was like seeing the grim reaper. She usually brought nothing but bad news. To top the awkwardness off, I was annoyed. She kept randomly asking me if I was ok or if I was nervous and I didn't want to share my emotions or anything that I was feeling with anybody. I'd done enough of that and didn't like the outcomes.

To break the random checks, I asked her if I could play the radio and she agreed. When I turned on the radio, gospel music came blaring out through the speakers. It wasn't the music I would've preferred, but it stopped her from questioning me the rest of the ride. After a good while of driving, we finally pulled up to a huge broken down building. It was the welfare building. There was a long line of many different types of people overflowing out one of the doors that lead to a metal detector.

It saddened me a little that all of those people were there so they could plead their case for assistance. Janet and I walked past the crowds and through another set of doors that led straight to the security desk on the opposite side of the waiting area. We didn't have to go through the metal detectors which got us some funny looks from those that were waiting. However, Janet didn't even notice the looks, she just signed us in, swiped her badge and got us access to a separate set of elevators.

Once we got on, she pushed the button to take us to the third floor. On the ride up, I began to realize how close I was to finally meeting the man who'd abandoned me. My heart began to race, I could feel it beating hard through my chest as the elevator dinged. Janet wasted no time stepping off and I was close on her heels. To keep my nerves from getting too far out of control, I took my mind off of the meeting and began to focus on my surroundings.

The waiting area was full of women and children. I could tell as I looked around that most of the people with children were social workers or family members waiting to bring the little ones to visit with a parent that had been separated from their kid. For a split moment, my observation of the room made me forget that I was just like all of those children, a kid with no parents to live or be with. Janet, my own social worker, broke me out of my trance when she called my name and told me to take a seat while she checked in. I did as she asked me and watched her as she interacted with the lady behind the desk. They giggled with one another and spoke briefly before she turned around and waved me over to them.

"O'Zella, your dad is already in a room in back. I know I keep asking you, but it is my job to make sure you are absolutely comfortable with any situation. Are you ok?"

Why Would I Love You?

    Before I answered I thought of the irony. There she was taking me to be with a man that had helped create me and therefore shouldn't have been as concerned, but she was constantly checking and rechecking my comfort level. I found it even more ironic that she'd been my social worker from the very beginning and this was the first time she seemed to care that much. Where was that concern from Janet when she dropped me off to Mr.Bill at the library house in the middle of the night? Where was that concern when she left me with Ms. Linda and stopped coming back to check on me? Where was her concern when I went through the trauma of listening to my best and only friend die over the phone? She didn't check on me, hell I don't think she even called to see how I was doing.

    I felt a dark cloud of bitterness build up in me and my patience was beginning to grow very thin with her. "Ms. Janet, you've done your job, I'm fine. Now, let's get this over with!" I responded through gritted teeth. She was a little shocked at my tone as I stood there watching her, waiting for her to make a move so that I could follow her.

    Without saying anything, she then led me down several hallways toward my final destination. And as we walked in silence, she seemed more nervous than I was. Every turn she made would cause her to pause in hesitation. After a couple times, that shit started to get on my nerves. When she finally made it to a door and paused again, that was the straw that broke the camel's back.

    In frustration, I pushed past her, said, "Excuse me," and burst through the door not knowing what to expect.

    When I stepped in the room, however, I immediately knew that I was in the right place. There, sitting on the other side of a table in the middle of the room, was a man that looked like the male version of me.

    Quickly, his head jerked up and he hopped to his feet. For an instant we stared at one another, locking eyes. For me it was like I was looking in a mirror. Although his face was covered by a five o'clock shadow, I could still see the high cheekbones and the deep dimples that I obviously inherited from him. I couldn't decipher if the emotion I was feeling was happy or sad, so while I sifted through my feelings I just sat down. A smile spread across his face as he watched me take steps toward the table and then have a seat. At that point, he joined me while never taking his eyes off of me until Janet cleared her throat.

Slowly, she waddled to the table and forced a smile as she addressed him. "Hello, Mr. Leon," she began in a voice that gave away how nervous she was. "I'm Janet, O'Zella's case worker since she lost her mother."

"Hello, Janet," he looked at her for a fleeting moment. "And hello, O'Zella," he spoke in a buttery smooth voice as he directed his attention back to me, his smile never leaving his face. Then he took a deep breath before he continued. "O'Zella, I know you may think the worst of me, I'm sure you think that I abandoned you, and I want so badly to explain what was happening in my life when I left. I feel like they would all sound like stupid excuses though, so I'll save that conversation for another time." He paused, never removing his eyes from mine. When I said nothing, he let out another deep breath and started talking again. "I do want to say that I just found out about your mom passing away and for about a month now I've been searching for you."

The entire time he was speaking I stared at him, my face void of all emotion. As the words flowed from his mouth and I gave him no words in return and no facial expression to read, I watched his smile slowly fade to a frown. He was trying to figure out what was going on in my head and all I could think was, *Oh, hell naw! You owe me a real explanation!*

"Leon?" I said when I finally found the words I wanted to say, "Try me! Try giving me one of your excuses, because saving that conversation for later is not good enough. As a matter of fact, how about you start by telling me what made you leave us in the first place?"

Why Would I Love You?

I could see shock register on his face before he quickly suppressed it. Then cautiously he began to speak. "Okay," he said, still watching me, "I was young and not ready. It's as simple as that." Then he hunched his shoulders as if unsure of any other answer to give. "I know that sounds like bullshit," he continued, "but to be honest, that's the truth. That, and the fact that I felt as if I had nothing to contribute to you guys. So, since my band was heading out on tour, I left with them. I just ran like hell. I kept telling myself that I left to become somebody for you, but the truth is that I was just a scared boy that thought he was a grown man." He paused again, contemplated and spoke once more. "By the time I had gotten myself together some years later, I was just too ashamed to come back and face you two."

"That's bullshit!" I blurted out.

"O'Zella!" Janet interjected.

"Excuse me," I told her, then I directed my words back to him. "That is a load of crap and you know it! You've been gone all of this time, I'm literally about to be fifteen years old, what makes you think I need you now?"

"Honestly," his voice was still calm and still as smooth as butter, "I don't think you need me now. I just finally built up the courage to face you guys only to find out that your mother had passed. All I'm looking to do now is get to know you." He spread his hands in mock surrender before continuing. "O'Zella, I never stopped thinking about you, I swear," he pleaded as he let tears fall from his face.

I didn't really know what to say. The last few years of my life had succeeded in turning my heart to stone, so instead of telling this stranger who looked like me that I didn't give a fuck about his tears because my own burned so much hotter, I simply stood and told Janet I was ready to leave. Without so much as a second thoughy she stood up, shook his hand, and we left.

Twelve

Contrary to what I wanted, it didn't take long for the system to proudly reunite me with my 'Long Lost Father'. They'd sent me to his house for a couple of visits and after doing a thorough check that let them know he could provide me with a stable home, I was moving in.

Leaving Aunt Bee's house was not a tearful event for me. I walked out of her door hoping that the next stop on my journey through life was going to be much better than the places I'd already been. With Jazz no longer there, there wasn't a single soul that I really cared to even say goodbye to at that house. So I packed my bags and waited on the porch for Janet to show up and take me to meet Leon.

On the entire drive over to his place, I went back and forth in my mind about what I should call him. I finally settled on calling him by his name. Leon. He wasn't my father, he was a stranger that donated his DNA and left. The only difference was that Leon had knowingly donated his DNA to my mother and not anonymously to a sperm bank.

Showing up to his house wasn't a big shocker as it had been when I was brought to Ms. Linda's house. I had already had my room established from the few visits I'd had in the previous weeks, so there was going to be no getting me settled in and no tours around the place. Been there, done that, knew what it was going to be before I moved in.

When we arrived, Leon opened the door with the biggest smile, just as he always did, but this time was different. He was bouncing all over

Why Would I Love You?

the house, checking and rechecking things like pillows that didn't even look out of place. He seemed as nervous as Janet had the first time he and I met, and he kept asking me and Janet if we wanted something to drink or if we were comfortable. I had to admit that at the time it actually made me feel a little joy. Finally, there was someone excited to see me out of genuine care and not because there was a check telling them they had to be. It didn't take long for him to relax a little and the three of us began to talk. After only about an hour or so Janet left, but not before telling us that she would be visiting frequently over the next three months to make sure that the situation was adequate for us both.

Living with Leon wasn't that bad. He didn't push the issue with me about not calling him dad. He said, "I know it's going to take some time for you to feel like I'm your dad, but I'm willing to earn it."

Things between us were weird at first and we were both walking on eggshells. I wasn't trying to get in his way and he wasn't trying to be pushy. Once a week we had a fun day together as a way for us to bond. We would go to the movies, the public market, the arcade and stuff like that. One day, we were enjoying a game of miniature golf when he began to tell me stories about when he and my mom met. That was the first time I'd had him and my mother in the same thought.

Him telling me about their first date was so surreal to me. As he talked, in my mind I saw my mom smiling. I envisioned her in that burgundy dress with her long, sandy brown curls pinned up into a bun. I saw them spinning in each other's arms to some music at a local juke joint. I looked and listened with a growing smile, living in the moment of the story. I hadn't been around people who knew my mom and could share their memories of her, so to hear a story that made me think of my mom in a light that didn't involve her being a crackhead was refreshing. That was the first time I'd actually felt like being with Leon was a good thing.

Two months had gone by and I was finally doing better in school. I had almost given up caring about an education after Jazz died but living with an actual parent that seemed to care about me so far, had me in a better head space than I'd been in a while. Leon had started working a new job at a factory, but he made it a point to get home and make dinner to eat with me every night. One of the things I liked about him was that he was a creature of habit with the same routine every morning and every evening. That routine gave me a sense of security that I liked, especially since I'd experienced enough unwanted change to last me a lifetime.

I think I noticed a change in Leon the day I got home from school and for the first time saw that he was visibly upset. I asked him what was wrong, and instead of responding to me the way he normally did, he snapped at me, cursing and all. I already knew those signs from Aunt Bee, so I took my ass in my room and stayed real quiet. The last thing I needed was to get smacked around for something I didn't do. An hour later, Leon came to my room and sat on the end of my bed. He was calm and quiet, but he smelled like an entire bottle of liquor. My experience was that substances made some people do mean shit, so I scooted back in the corner, just waiting for the first hit that I was sure would come.

Instead of hitting me, Leon looked at me, saw my fear, and took a deep breath just before he began talking. "Listen, O'Zella," he said after clearing his throat, "I'm sorry I yelled at you when you got home. I just lost my job today and I was frustrated, but that's no reason for me to take it out on you."

I sat there for the longest time not knowing what to say or do. So, I remained quiet until he turned around to see if I accepted his apology. Our eye contact didn't last very long because after getting a good enough look at him, I shot my gaze to my covers and focused on one of the purple flowers. Then I mumbled, "It's cool, Leon." That was

Why Would I Love You?

the first time I'd seen what could happen when Leon drank, but it damn sure wasn't the last.

After he was let go from the factory, all he did was sit around collecting his unemployment and getting drunk. He didn't try to get another job, didn't try to do anything with himself, he just let himself fall into a depression and looked as if all the life had been sucked out of him. He knew better than to allow anyone to see him in that condition, especially not Janet. And since it was the end of her three month visitations, we only had one more monthly visit from her at the end of the month. Leon was smart enough to pull his shit together just long enough to make it through the short visit.

The month had passed, and the visit had come. Janet clearly liked what she had seen and once the visit was over and he'd walked her to the door and locked it behind her, he began jumping around like a mad man. He had the biggest smile on his face as he spun in circles and started howling. He grabbed me by the hands and started twirling me in a circle. At first, I thought he had lost his marbles, but after a while, seeing him let loose started to tickle me. The next thing I knew I was laughing and spinning with him until he finally let go and fell on the couch.

"Girl, I done spun myself dizzy," he spoke happily. I was laughing and smiling, but still looking at him like he was crazy. "Why you standing there looking at me like that?" he asked once he noticed me staring.

"I don't know," I began as I continued beaming at him. "Why did you start yelling and jumpin' around?"

Leon sat forward quickly and looked at me, "Come here!" I slowly walked over to him and he stood up to look me in the eye. "I was jumpin' and yelling because I am happy to have you back in my life."

I didn't say anything, I just kept smiling, especially since he seemed so sincere. That night, he made a big dinner that consisted of all my favorites and told me that he had invited a special guest.

I watched him busy himself in the kitchen for over an hour, and no matter how much I asked, he wouldn't tell me who the special guest was. However, I knew they had to be really special because for the first time since he had been laid off, I saw the light come back into his eyes. I was happy for him, happy to see that he was coming out of that funk and getting back to what was normal.

When Leon was almost done with dinner, he sent me to wash up. While I was in the bathroom, I heard the doorbell ring and began to hurry. I was very interested in knowing who had Leon so happy, so I rushed out of the bathroom and quickly made my way around the corner. When I finally laid my eyes on the person, I was surprised to see a woman who seemed a little too old to be a love interest for Leon especially since they looked too much like each other. They both quickly looked my way when they heard my foot fall forward while I was peeking around the corner.

Her smile was as big as Texas and she was the first one to speak. "Hello, little lady." Her voice was smooth and calming. I stepped out from the corner I'd been standing in and straightened my shirt out before giving her a small wave.

"Come over here, Zell," Leon said. "I want you to meet my sister, ya auntie."

I walked over slowly and put my hand out to shake hers but she laughed, a soft, feminine giggle. And as she reached out to me, she said, "We hug in this family." Then she embraced me. I stiffened up at first, but there was something about her hug that reminded me of when I used to sit on the couch curled up with my mom when she was sober.

"Nice to meet you, Ms…" I trailed off as I had no clue what to call her.

"Call me Aunt Lori, baby," her smile was even bigger.

"Ok, Aunt Lori," I tried the words out on my tongue.

Then she looked me up and down for just an instant before saying, "Wow, you are such a beautiful girl! You look just like my mother, your grandmother." When she said that I was beautiful, my skin started to crawl, but when she added that I looked like my grandma it was like the weird feeling went away and all I could do was blush and smile. Aunt Lori was the first person since before Mr. Bill that I was cool with calling me beautiful or pretty.

That evening provided me with one of the nicest nights and meals I'd had in a while. Meeting my aunt and watching Leon smile made me feel good, and the way he talked with his sister was different, I got to see a side of him that I hadn't seen yet. They laughed and talked, and I just watched them and listened. They reminisced about when they were growing up and how they used to run around, they even talked about the times Leon used to perform with his band. It was great to hear them talk about my family members that I had never heard about from my mother, my own flesh and blood family members.

Then my aunt started asking me questions about things I liked, about school, and other stuff like that. I was taken by surprise at first because other than my therapist and Jazz, nobody had really asked me about who I was. Even Leon hadn't asked. Although he wanted to know, he was always walking on eggshells and never wanted to push because he was still on my shit list for abandoning me and my mom when we needed him most. But Aunt Lori? I liked her, like I really liked her, so it was cool that she wanted to know. There was something about how open and loving she was that made me trust her and it was the first time that I didn't need a guard. Aunt Lori had broken through my wall instantly and I knew after that night that she was one of my favorite people.

Through our conversations, I found out that she was visiting from down south and that she was making plans to move closer so that she could get to know her only niece. It was confirmed that Leon had in fact been looking for me for quite some time when he'd found out that my mom had passed. Knowing that he'd been honest about that didn't change how I felt about him. Truthfully, at that time I wasn't sure how

I felt about anything, so processing the release of the pain that was alive in me because of his absence was hard to do.

Unfortunately, the night ended, but not before Aunt Lori promised that she would make sure she called regularly and send packages frequently. In her words, "I have some catching up to do with spoiling my niece."

Over time, I had come to see that living with Leon wasn't that bad. He'd found another job working as a stocker at the Walmart in the city, but he didn't like it the way he liked the job before. As a result of his dissatisfaction with his employment situation, there were moments where I felt he would flip out yelling for nothing. However, he still wasn't as bad as Aunt Bee.

It had been about five months since I'd moved in and everything was going good. Leon and I talked more and more, and he shared great stories of him and my mom, times like when they met or most things that had occurred with them before there was me. To make things even better, Aunt Lori called me every night and I found myself looking forward to those conversations with her. Whenever she and I talked, it was like a ray of sunshine no matter what time of day and no matter what the weather was outside.

My fifteenth birthday was around the corner and as a result, Leon decided to pick up some extra hours at work. I tried to talk him out of doing anything because I never liked anyone making a big deal for my birthday. And to make this birthday worse, the one year anniversary of Jazz's death was coming up and I was feeling kind of depressed. I missed my friend and really wanted to share the details of my new life with her. It still angered me that P's bastard ass had taken her away from me and there wasn't a damn thing I could do about it.

Despite my protests, Leon was determined to celebrate my birthday. He said that this was the first birthday he got to share with his daughter and he wanted to take me somewhere special. Then he added that fifteen was the year of becoming a woman. I wasn't sure

Why Would I Love You?

what that meant, but he was adamant that this was a special day in a young girl's life and that we were going to memorialize it together. Aunt Lori even joined in. She sent me a beautiful dress and money for my hair and nails. Then she told me to just relax and allow myself to enjoy my daddy-daughter birthday.

Finally, the day had arrived. I'd gotten my hair styled in some really pretty curls and my nails were painted in a French manicure. My dress was an off white ball gown that flowed down my body and flared out at my knees. My body seemed to have gotten the memo of me transitioning into womanhood way before my mind did because the top part of the dress hugged and showed off all of my curves. I wasn't into heels, so I put on a pair of rhinestone covered, off white flats. I hated to admit it, but not only did I like the way I looked, I was really excited and I felt very special.

Tap, tap.

Leon knocked on my door. "Are you ready, birthday girl?"

"Yes, Leon," I replied hastily. "Let me just grab my purse and I'll be out."

"Ok," was his quiet response.

I checked myself in the mirror and admired the woman I was becoming. Then I grabbed my little sparkly clutch, threw my lip gloss in it, and headed for the door. Nervously, I walked down the short hallway, and when I hit the corner and turned, Leon was standing at the front door with a corsage in his hand and tears rolling down his face. I had to give it to him, he cleaned up well.

"Oh, wow," his voice was really choked up. "You look so much like your mother," he said as if in awe.

"Thanks," I replied shyly. I wasn't usually comfortable with people complimenting me, but for some reason this time didn't bother me at all.

"Are you ready for a night on the town, young lady?" He beamed at me as he wiped his tears away.

"Yes," I smiled right back at him.

Wasting no more time, I took his outstretched hand and followed him out to a waiting Uber. I just couldn't stop smiling. Leon was such a gentleman as he opened the door for me. "After you, Ma'am," he said and I giggled a little before hopping in. The ride to the restaurant was very quiet. Even though I was happy, I looked out of the window and had a flashback. For a split moment, I felt like I was back on that bus going home to find out there was no more home. The next thing I knew, in my mind, we were pulling up to the scene where I found out my mom was gone. Apparently, I had spent the entire ride in a kind of flashback trance because before I knew it, Leon's was tapping on my shoulder and bringing me back to reality. "Zell, we're here."

Then I turned to him and said, "Okay."

"You ready to do this, Princess?" he asked as he looked at me and smiled.

I smiled back as I shook my head yes, then he opened the door, got out, walked around to my side, and helped me out of the car.

Thirteen

I was really impressed when we walked into an Italian restaurant. It was fancy and all the other people that were in there eating were dressed up nice as well. I felt like the place was too upscale for me, but I kept a smile plastered on my face as we followed a waitress to our table and took our seats.

"Hello, I'm Tiff," she began in a voice that was professional and polite. "I will be your server tonight. Can I start you two off with drinks?"

"Hey, Tiff," Leon began in that smooth as butter voice. "It's my baby girls' birthday and she is going to order whatever she wants."

"Happy birthday!" Tiff said with a genuine smile.

"Thank you," I gave back a shy smile.

"What would you like to drink?"

"Ginger ale, please."

"And for you sir?"

"A Jameson neat."

"Ok, got it. You two look over the menus while I go and put your drinks in!"

"Thank you," we both said in unison.

As soon as Tiff disappeared around the corner, I gave my full attention to the menu. It was a rare thing for me to be taken anywhere, but especially to a restaurant that didn't have a dollar menu, so I was in my glory. I must have been seriously focusing on the selection of great food because I was startled by a tap on my arm.

"Earth to Zell," I heard Leon say. Then I looked up to find our server standing back at our table waiting on me to tell her what I wanted.

"Did you decide what you were going to eat?" she asked.

"Can I have the seafood lasagna and the garlic knots?"

"Sure thing, and for you sir?" she looked toward Leon.

"I'd like the sixteen ounce T-bone steak, a twice baked potato, and another Jameson neat," he gave her that smile of his. "And make it a double."

"Sure thing," she returned his smile with one of her own.

In the server's absence, Leon and I engaged in our normal conversation, him reminiscing about my mother and me loving to hear about her life before I was born. The way he talked about her gave me the impression that he really cared for her a lot and that he missed her too. As much as I could appreciate his feelings for her, I was still pissed that he hadn't cared enough to stay with her, with us. So, I listened without judgment and imagined what she must have looked like and been like back then.

By the time our food showed up, Leon was about four double neat Jameson's in. The food was delicious, and I was genuinely enjoying myself even though Leon kept getting louder with each drink he took. Despite how much he was drinking, he and I ate like royalty. When we were done, we looked like stuffed pigs as the both of us sat back making room in our bellies.

When Tiff made her rounds, we informed her that we were ready for our check. She said, "Okay," and let us know that she would be back with the check shortly.

Instantly, I knew something was up because as soon as Tiff walked away, Leon started acting strange. It didn't take long for me to realize why. I saw Tiff coming around the corner carrying a slice of cake with a candle in it, and she was followed by a lot of friends. Before I could process the spotlight that was all of a sudden on me, Tiff and the Gang were all gathering around our table as they broke out into the Stevie Wonder rendition of Happy Birthday. They got closer and closer and by the time they had completely circled me, I was already in full blown freak out mode. My palms began to sweat, my body was shaking, and I couldn't breathe. I had to get out of there and quickly, so before they could close the circle any tighter around the table, I hopped up and without a word ran for the exit as if I was running for my life.

    I was standing outside hyperventilating when not far behind me, Leon came stumbling out. "Baby, what happened?" his speech was seriously slurred.

    "I- I- I don't know!" I tried to breathe as I spoke but was still having trouble.

    "So, you don't know why you up and ran out when they were singing happy birthday to you?"

    I couldn't think, couldn't process a single thought. All I could do was feel raw panic envelop me like a fiery, hot blanket. "Leon, I just want to go home," I managed to say.

    "Sure, thing baby," he said as he rubbed my shoulders to help me relax. When he saw that I had calmed down a little, he spoke again. "I'm just gonna go back in, pay the bill, and call an uber, okay?" I shook my head up and down in agreement and he kissed me on the cheek before he stumbled back into the restaurant.

    The Uber showed up in record time because Leon hadn't even come out of the restaurant yet. When I walked to the doorway to let him know that our ride was there, I wasn't at all surprised to spot him at the bar throwing back another shot of liquor before heading toward the sound of my voice. I shook my head and turned to exit the restaurant again.

    The ride to our house was a quiet one. I wasn't mad or anything like that, I was just overwhelmed, done with the day, and ready to begin a new one in the morning. The silence in the car was broken when Leon put his hand on my knee and asked me if I was ok. For a second I thought he called me by my mother's name, but he was talking so low that I couldn't really be sure so I didn't pay it any mind. He kept talking, though, kept asking me questions, and I kept giving him short answers the whole way home. I just didn't feel like talking, all I wanted at that moment was to go home and go to my bed.

When we got to the door of our house, Leon unlocked it and stepped aside, allowing me to walk in first. Before I could run off to my room like I had planned, he grabbed my arm, "Wait a minute now, Tonya."

"Leon, I'm not Tonya!" I said as I tried to yank away from him.

"Oh, you wanna play," he asked as he pulled me into his chest. "Well, then who are you tonight?" he asked as he planted a forceful kiss on my lips.

"Leon, stop!" was all I said as I wiggled and pushed under the pressure of his tight hold.

"Oh, so you wanna play hard to get, huh?" he growled with a smirk as he pushed me down onto the couch. As soon as I hit that sofa, I tried to scurry away from him, but he grabbed me by my ankle and harshly yanked me back, quickly sliding his heavy frame on top of me so that I couldn't get away from him anymore. He then leaned his liquor soaked mouth near my ear as he put a decent amount of his body weight on me, "So you want me to take it? Huh, T?"

At this point I couldn't say anything. Between me fighting back, the tears that were blinding me, and my small one hundred and twenty pound frame being crushed beneath him, I was completely helpless. With one swift movement, Leon shifted his weight slightly, and reaching down, he ripped my panties and rammed his dick into me as fast as he could. Then he started to move while he grunted and panted.

As sad as it is to say, I wasn't new to scenarios like this. And even though this man was supposed be my father, he was still a stranger to me, just like Mr.Bill, and Tyler, and all of the other boys who tried to get me to fuck or suck them in school. So, I didn't panic, I didn't even try to fight him anymore. I tried using the coping mechanism I'd developed, I tried to detach myself from him and that entire situation. Except this time was different because as I tried to stare at a spot on the ceiling and pretend I was anywhere else, this mothafucka kept me firmly present in that nightmare by repeatedly moaning, "Damn, Tonya, I missed you so much! Oh, Tonya, baby. Fuck yes, Tonya, this pussy always gonna be mine!"

At one point, he leaned up and effortlessly flipped my body over. I tried to make a break for it, grabbing at the arm of the couch to pull myself away from him. Just as my stomach was over the arm, he caught me and pulled me back. "Where you going, baby?" he growled as he slammed his dick in me from behind.

Leon let out a wild, primal grunt as I let tears fall from my eyes and stared at the door to my room, wishing with everything in me that I could get away. And knowing that I couldn't, I lay there wondering if he really thought he was fucking my dead mother instead of violating the daughter he'd made with her. I wanted so badly to believe so many other things in that moment of being defiled, but this was not like the other strangers that had taken advantage of me. This was my father, the man that was as responsible as my mother was for me being in the world. My mind was struggling to wrap around the vileness of what was happening.

After a long time, I finally stopped trying to escape. Then I lay there accepting what was happening as I started focusing on killing him and on the many ways I could make killing him look like an accident.

"Uuggggh, baby," he groaned as his voice hitched up a notch. "I'm cumming! TOOOOONYA! UUUUUUUGH!" he grunted, panted, and then collapsed on my back for a quick moment. Then very quickly, he jerked up as if he had been burned. At the same time I immediately turned around, curled up in the corner of the couch, and stared daggers at him as he slid his member back into his unzipped pants. He avoided eye contact with me, but didn't move away from that couch as he fixed himself. And still never laying his eyes on me, Leon stood up and said, "Go get cleaned up for bed, O'Zella." Then he walked off, went to his room, and closed the damn door.

So, this bastard did know my name!

The morning after my birthday was a day that I hoped would never begin. I figured that even if I was awake, as long as I didn't leave my room it didn't count.

"O'Zeeella!" I could hear the man that was supposed to be my flesh and blood walking to my room, sounding like he was singing my name. Was he really going to act like he hadn't given me dinner and dick for my fifteenth birthday? Suddenly, the door to my bedroom burst open and there he was with a huge smile plastered on his face as if the world was great and life was grand.

"Wake up, sleepy head," he said in a cheerful voice. "It's time to get our weekend started. I was thinking we could go to the public market and get the kettle corn you like."

"I don't feel good, Leon," I mumbled in a voice that revealed the depression that was covering me like a heavy blanket. "Can I just stay in bed?"

"Uh, well," he spoke as if concerned, "I suppose. Do you need anything like ginger ale or Tylenol?"

"No," I refused to even look at him. "I just need to rest."

"Ok, well, yell if you need me, sweety," he spoke like a loving and caring father.

When he walked out and closed the door behind him, I was even more confused than I had been the night before. Leon was acting as if nothing had ever happened. And I wasn't sure if he thought I'd forgotten, but I figured that telling him I didn't feel good would let him know that he was the only one that was blacked out drunk. After that, I sat in my room that whole day just staring at the walls and having the same one sided Q&A conversation in my head that I'd had all night. *If he is my dad, why did he do that to me? Why did he keep saying my mom's name? Was it because he was drunk? Does he really not remember? Why? Why? Why? AAAAAAAAAHHHHH!* I screamed within myself, completely unable to understand why he would do something so terrible. Unable to come up with any answers, I spent the whole day in my room blocking the entire world out. Leon didn't say much to me that day, at least not until it was time for dinner.

It appeared that my father was a thoughtful man since he'd made me chicken noodle soup to help me recover from being raped. I sat at the table pushing my spoon around in my bowl but my appetite was long gone. When he finally sat down at the table with me, he started doing the same thing I was, moving his silverware around in his food. We both were avoiding talking to each other, but the difference between me and him was that I didn't have a damn thing to say to him.

The way he started to clear his throat told me that he was clearly gearing himself up to say something. "So, O'Zella," he began in a voice I really didn't want to hear at that moment.

"Yes?" My own voice was void of emotion.

"About what happened last night! Listen, I've been under a ton of stress and that wasn't supposed to happen…" he trailed off as if unsure of what to say before he continued, "not like that anyways. What I mean is that I work really hard to make sure you have everything you need. You're too young to work and contribute to the house yet, so the least you can do is make sure I'm taken care of while I take care of you." By the time that man was done talking I was staring at him with my mouth wide open and my jaw on the fucking floor. That nigga just couldn't be serious.

"Excuse me?" I was barely able to get the words out of my mouth.

"You heard me," he said as his voice went from buttery smooth to monstrous. And as I watched Leon, he looked at me as if he had lost patience with me, as if he was done coddling me. "It's clear you ain't no virgin, so you can make sure I'm satisfied in one way while I make sure you're satisfied with the things I provide for you. Don't act like you don't know what I'm talking 'bout. And if you think you gon' tell anybody anything about what goes on under the roof of the house that I pay for, I swear you won't be going nowhere good."

"Leon," I snapped hard at him, "you must have lost yo fucking mi..." Before I could finish my statement, he reached across the table and backhanded me so hard that I fell off the chair and onto the floor.

"Watch yo tongue, little girl," he warned. My eyes widened in horror as I looked up at him and saw in his eyes that he was no longer the same nice man that had been taking care of me so far. He was different, everything about him was different, mean, scary. When he'd watched me long enough to be satisfied that I'd gotten the point, he went on as if everything was perfectly fucking normal. "Now, like I was saying," his voice had gone back to buttery smooth again, "I'll make sure you're taken care of, but you will learn what it is to be a woman that takes care of me."

He paused, watched me long enough to see the moment when I understood his meaning, then continued "And If you ever talk back to me again, Imma do more than knock your ass on the floor, I'mma make sure you lose a damn tooth next time. Because as long as you're under this roof, you gon' do what I say." I kept looking up at him, unblinking and in absolute shock as I held the side of my face. As I lay there, he towered over me, staring daggers at me with spit flying from his mouth as he chastised me. "Now, go clean ya self up and get ready for bed!"

I lay absolutely still, wondering how I was going to handle this new abusive situation in my life. I wondered if I should tell somebody, if I should run away, if I should just kill him and take my chances in jail for the rest of my life. However, the answer to all of those questions was no. The feisty, fiery, take no shit girl that I had been when Jazz was alive no longer existed. That girl had died behind the dumpster with Jazz that night. And whatever backbone I had left after that ran away the day my father pinned me to a couch and violated me like I was some whore on the street instead of his daughter.

At that moment there was no more fight in me, no more fire or feistiness in me. All that was left was extreme exhaustion and resignation. So, without saying a single word, I picked myself up off the floor and got ready for bed just as I had been told. I was in shock, but didn't show any emotion until I was in my bed later that night, all by myself. And that's where I cried a silent cry that also doubled as a prayer. That night I had a talk with God as tears of pain, anguish, and emotional and mental exhaustion ran down my face.

"God, I don't know what it is that I've done to deserve this life, but please be done. I've learned my lesson, whatever lesson it is that You're trying to teach me. I know You work in your own time, at least that's what momma used to say, but this is one of those times I hope you put a rush on it because this is just too much for me to bear. Thanks. Amen."

Then I closed my eyes, curled up into a ball, and tried to fall asleep, hoping that when I woke the next day my prayer would be answered. Focusing on escaping the madness that had become my life, I stared at my closet door handle, counting until I fell asleep. Last thing I remember was getting to number five thousand, six hundred and twenty-three before I was startled out of my sleep by a knock on my door right before Leon stuck his head in.

Fourteen

"Zell, get dressed," he called out to me. "We going out for a ride!"

I was still so in shock that I didn't even bother to ask where we were going. I just got up, took a quick shower, and was dressed in less than thirty minutes. I had just finished brushing my teeth when I looked in the mirror above the sink and noticed that I had a bruise forming on the side of my face. I needed to cover it but knew nothing about makeup. From the rage that Leon showed me the previous night, I knew that if I kept pissing him off, I would need to learn a whole lot about cover up and concealer. Feeling as if I had reached a new low in the lows of my life, I washed my face and hoped my bruise wasn't noticeable.

Leon took me on a ride to the Big Mall on the east side of town. I was in the mind state to just mope around and window shop, but then we walked to Old Navy and went in. As I was just barely glancing at things because I was too depressed to really care about anything, my eyes landed on the new sandals that had just come out. They were the exact ones that I had secretly wanted so bad. Leon, noticing that I was staring at the sandals, gave me a cool gaze as he told me to check for my size. Without me having to ask for anything, we ended up leaving the first store with my sandals in three different colors and some jeans.

I knew that he was trying to buy me, trying to buy my body, my silence, my emotions. And even though I would never be able to truly forgive him, I let him spend as much money on me as he wanted to.

Why Would I Love You?

What else could I do? I believed there was nothing I could do to stop him that wouldn't make my life worse. I had been assaulted in one way or another in each place I'd lived, and in every place where there was a male, I had been sexually assaulted. So, I couldn't open my mouth and allow myself to be put back into the system where it was likely that I would end up being sexually abused again, and this time maybe worse. So, I didn't even try to stop Leon from buying me, I just went with whatever. Besides, the abuse would only last until I was eighteen, at that point I would be free to leave and never be forced to put up with shit again.

We walked the mall for a good while, hitting up a couple more places that Leon thought I wanted to check out. Then we went to the food court. I sat down at a table with all of my bags while Leon went and grabbed us some food. He came back to the table after a short while and placed food in front of me, and without hesitation he dug into his plate. I sensed he was building up for something like he'd done the night before at dinner, so I braced myself for whatever bullshit he was about to throw my way.

That's when he cleared his throat and went for it. "Uhm, so, Zell, you done getting everything you wanted today?"

I didn't look up, just moved my fork around my plate, "Yeah, I guess so," I said, somewhat confused because he'd been the one taking me places he thought I wanted to go to and buying me whatever I so much as looked at. I hadn't asked to go one single place, neither had I asked for one single thing. I was too much of a wreck to do that.

"Ok, good. Well," he looked at the table as if he knew he was wrong for what he was about to say, but he said it anyway, "there's one more store I'd like to go to before we leave."

"Okay," I said, not thinking much of his words and not daring to disagree with him and piss him off. The only thing I thought was how I wasn't in a rush to be behind closed doors with him again, so to avoid that, I would have agreed to just about anything. And from the way his eyes lit up, my agreement seemed to satisfy him a lot.

Leon seemed so happy that he rushed through lunch. As soon as we finished eating, he grabbed most of the bags and practically took off while I followed behind him wondering what was going on and where our last stop would be. Finally, he slowed down as we got close to FYE, the music store. However, instead of making a right, he made a left turn. My heart instantly dropped to the bottom of my stomach and I stood frozen, watching Leon cross the hallway and making his way into Victoria's Secret.

Now I might have been afraid of him by that point, but I was far from dumb and I wanted no parts of picking my poison for his twisted sexual pleasures. I also didn't want to piss him off, so I kept my face blank, kept my mouth shut, and followed him into the store. I was extremely uncomfortable with what was going on and hung back a little as I watched him walk from section to section acting as if he was just killing time while his significant other was shopping. Then something caught his eye. I couldn't see what it was because I didn't leave the doorway, but he snatched it up real quick and damn near ran it to the cashier. Once he was done, he came strutting out of the store with a big ole goofy grin. When he was a safe distance in front of me, I rolled my eyes and just followed him out of the mall.

When we got back to the house Leon told me to go put my stuff away and get started on dinner. All of a sudden, it was like all those years of programming in the system really worked because I didn't put up a fuss at all, I just did as I was told. The night went smoothly, there was no anger and no attempts to get at me. To keep it that way, as soon as dinner was over, I washed the dishes and ran to my room. And the whole time I lay in bed, I was hoping to be asleep before he got any ideas to come into my room and teach me a lesson about what it means to be a woman.

Why Would I Love You?

Thankfully, I made it through the week without so much as a side glance from Leon. It was almost like he'd intentionally kept his distance to see if I would tell someone from school or even worse, the police would come knocking to take him away. My suspicions were confirmed when I got home from school that Friday and Leon was waiting on the couch with a stupid smirk on his face. To this day, I don't understand how God could let this monster be anyone's father.

"Hello, Zell," he gave me that voice that let me know he was ready to teach me what I didn't want to learn.

"Hello, Leon," I couldn't help but to roll my eyes at him.

"Don't roll ya eyes at me," he warned. "And what happened to daddy?" His stupid smirk turned to an evil snarl. He hopped up from the couch making his way to me as his words dripped off his lips like venom. "I see you kept ya mouth shut all week. For that, I'm gonna take it easy on you and reward you."

"Okay!" I spoke quietly, refusing to remove my gaze from a spot on the floor.

"Go wash up and put on the outfit I set on your bed."

I gave him no back talk whatsoever. I simply walked away from him, went into my room, and surprise, surprise, there was the bra and panty set that he'd been so eager to purchase from Victoria's Secret. I put on the inappropriate attire and made my way back out to the living room. One thing I learned about Leon was that he never got loud, not unless he was absolutely furious. Despite his quiet demeanor, you could still tell what he was feeling by his tone and the moment he opened his mouth, I knew he was very displeased with me.

His annoyance came through loud and clear when I entered the room and stepped into his line of vision. "Who told you to put on a robe?" I didn't even bother saying anything. I just slowly untied the robe and let it fall off my shoulders. My skin was crawling as I watched him squirm in his seat, watching me with hungry eyes.

"Come here, Zell, baby?" he spoke in a voice that was filled with lust and excitement.

With all the reservations in my soul, I slowly made my way across the living room floor, looking up to see him licking his lips with sick desire in his eyes. Once I was within reach of him, he pulled me so close that his nose was touching my crotch. I heard him inhale deeply and then moan as I cringed. Slowly, he leaned back and eased my panties down. He never took his eyes off of me as I stepped out of my panties. Once they were off in one swift movement, Leon lifted my left leg, threw it over his shoulder, and placed his tongue on my hotspot.

As much as I wanted to fight him off of me, to kill him, to make sure he could never touch me again, my first instinct was to gasp in sheer pleasure. That was the first time in my life anyone had gone down on me, and for a split moment my body reacted before my mind could. In a move that went completely against my every inclination, I closed my eyes and imagined that what was happening to me was being done by the man of my dreams instead of Leon. My pulse raced, my blood thickened. I threw my head back, absolutely hating the fact that my body was betraying me so viciously.

This was not supposed to be enjoyable. I was not supposed to be moaning. But it was enjoyable, and I was moaning because it felt good. I stood there, frozen, giving in to him, my legs going weak while a blazing trail of tears ran down my cheeks. I was so torn and confused and shaken. I wanted to shove him away and pull him closer at the same time. I hated him with a deep passion, hated what he was doing to me, yet I had one hand on his head to keep him there, and the other hand covering my mouth in an attempt to stifle the cries of pleasure soaring from me. I felt sick to my stomach when all of a sudden ripples of orgasms exploded through my body. Those were the first orgasms of my life, and although they pleased my body like nothing I had ever experienced before that, mentally and emotionally they ripped me to shreds. I was scared, confused, and on the verge of a nervous breakdown.

When Leon had tasted enough of me, he put my leg down, sat back as he wiped his mouth, and still couldn't wipe that dumb look off his face. Just seeing the sheer satisfaction on his face, the smug look that said he knew that he'd brought me pleasure, brought me back to reality. Now, in addition to every other emotion I was feeling, instant rage showed up. I hated him even more at that moment than I ever had. But I didn't move, I stood there frozen, waiting for my next orders even though I knew what he wanted.

"You like that, baby?" he had the fucking nerve to ask me.

On the outside, I just looked at him as the tears continued to fall from my eyes. I hoped with everything in me that what I was thinking wasn't written on my face. Inside of my mind, however, I was screaming, *Bitch, you know I liked it! You know you fucked me up with that! But that don't change shit, I still hate your disgusting ass!* Instead of saying any of that, though, I just responded with, "Yes, Leon."

"All this week I've been thinking about how you're gonna call me daddy from now on," he began in that smooth voice. "Now, I just rewarded you for being a good girl by keepin' ya mouth shut about our little arrangement, but," his mood and his voice changed mid-sentence as he quickly stood and grabbed my face, " if you call me Leon again, you gon' know what it feels like to be punished." He was less than an inch away from my face now, snarling and talking in his low, intimidating voice, breath smelling like pussy. "You understand me, baby?"

"Yes, Daddy," came my quick and obedient reply.

"Good," he smiled a charming smile, changing his mood at whim once more. "Now, go get cleaned up. If you got homework, do it now. I'mma order us up some Chinese for dinner."

I'd have sworn that man was gonna rape me again. When he didn't, I learned a serious lesson about Leon that night. What he was doing was never about the sex, it was and always would be about control. He was fighting to control the two people inside of him, and was forcing me to give up my control to them both. Just as he was one person fighting two demons, I was only one person playing two roles. I was his daughter and his lover. He was my dad and my daddy. Things for me had gone from sick to twisted to downright demented.

For the months that followed, Leon continued doing that to me, continued making me like some of what was happening to me. He had taken me from hating the thought of him touching me to enjoying him touching me in certain ways. After a while, I began to hate myself, to hate looking in the mirror and seeing the sick monster I was becoming. It would have been so much better if he had just raped me without caring about how I felt. I could remain distant that way, neutral to everything. I could stay separated from what was happening to me. But now, he was no longer just fucking my body, he was fucking my mind, fucking *up* my mind. He was mentally and emotionally beating me to death. And that was so much worse.

Leon had effectively taught me to hate myself as much as I hated him, to despise myself and to often wish death upon myself as much as I wished it upon him. He had taught me that the monster in him also resided in me, taught me that the monster could be passed down from parent to child. And each time he touched me and made me like it, I saw the monster in me emerge, a monster that was greedy and selfish and that was more than willing to indulge in sick and twisted pleasure even while knowing it was dead ass wrong. I began to see myself as ugly and evil and that broke me more than the actual rapes did. It was then I learned that there were some things that were far more ugly and tremendously worse than physical abuse and rape. Pleasure. Pleasure could be a mean and evil bitch all by herself.

For the first year that I lived with Leon, he had me following a very strict schedule. I went to school and when the weekend came, I would only leave the house with him. I had to have dinner ready by a certain time every day and if he was gonna be late because of work, I had to make sure it was warm and ready whenever he walked in the door. The good thing was that he always called before he left work, so the time that I should've had his dinner ready was never a guessing game for me.

Then there was the sex. Leon had very specific days that he would fuck me and outfits I had to wear on those days. To make my horrendous situation bearable, I convinced him that I liked to be blindfolded during sex. I told him it turned me on, which he seemed adamant about doing. But truth be told, I just wanted to pretend he was anyone other than my father, and if I was blindfolded, my covered eyes wouldn't open, fuck up my imagination, and force me to face the nightmare that I was living through.

Then, maybe because he felt guilty, maybe because he was trying to make things up to me, and definitely because he was trying to buy my silence, he would take me out every weekend on shopping sprees. He kept me in the latest clothes, the nicest jewelry, and the freshest kicks. That was the crazy life I was living, the life that had me feeling as if I was going insane. In fact, things were so fucked up in my head that after a while I stopped fighting it, taught myself to stop hating it so much. Then I taught myself to embrace it. I learned what to do to make Leon happy and what not to do to so that I wouldn't piss him off. Because of that, the rapes were hardly ever coupled with violence.

Fifteen

After some really long months, the end of my school year was coming, and I was extremely happy. I was going to get away from Leon for a few months because Aunt Lori invited me to spend my summer with her. Since it was taking her so long to relocate from down south, she wanted me to visit her down there. I believed my vacation was an escape for me, but things for me never went that smoothly. In fact, it seemed as if anytime there was a light at the end of the tunnel, there was always some asshole behind me with a slingshot, aiming the muthafucka right at the bulb.

Like I was saying, I went to take my last class of the school year and then Leon and I would be on our way to meet Aunt Lori at the airport. As I sat watching the clock tick away, my other classmates were struggling to finish their test. I guess I had an unfair advantage because this was my second time going through the tenth grade. Me being left back a year was due to the way I'd behaved after Jazz had died. I hadn't even tried at school back then, and when I did bother to show up, I did no work, so it was like I wasn't even there. They failed me and I didn't care, so I definitely wasn't thinking about making it up in summer school. It was for that reason that I was a grade behind and learning the same shit twice.

"Pencils down," were the last words I heard as the class erupted into a dull roar and we all made our way out of the school. Most of the students were celebrating their freedom from one jail while I headed to another with hopes of escaping real soon. Obediently, I stood at the main entrance watching the cars pass by until I noticed Leon pulling up. I made my way to the curb before the car was all the way there and there she was, smiling just as bright as ever when the car pulled up in front of me.

Why Would I Love You?

"Auntie!" I yelled. I was so happy to see her face that I ran to the car, snatched the door open, and dove in, giving her the biggest hug ever.

"Girl, you so happy you gon' end up breaking my neck," she said, laughing and hugging me back.

Since losing my mom, Aunt Lori was the first consistent female family member in my life that I knew loved me and wanted the best for me. Ms. Linda had been the first woman to fit that role outside of flesh and blood. As promised before she'd left the first time, she stayed in touch and we talked several times a week. And whenever she called, Leon didn't bother me, it was like she had him punked and I loved every moment she spent making him cower.

"Sorry, Auntie. I thought you were coming in later," I spoke through my own huge smile.

"I know you did, but I wanted to surprise you."

"Well, color me surprised," I said as I eagerly hopped in the back seat and sat down comfortably. Then, before he decided to become pissed and punish me after Aunt Lori went to bed, I leaned up and kissed Leon on his cheek. "Hello, Daddy," was my obedient greeting to him.

He pushed his cheek toward me to receive the kiss. "Hi, sweetie."

"It is so refreshing to see how far you guys have come in such a short time," Aunt Laurie exclaimed, still smiling and with a twinkle in her eye as she gushed at our natural display of affection.

If only she knew why I acted like we had such a good relationship. She would probably have cringed inside if she had known that I was more afraid of being beaten by him than I was of being raped by him.

"Anyways, I have good news and bad news," she spoke and had my undivided attention. "Which one do you want first?"

"Ugh," I groaned, hating the idea of bad news coming from her. "Auntie, how you come into town with bad news?"

"Girl, hush and pick," she laughed.

"Bad, I guess," I whined.

"I can't keep you the whole summer like I planned," she blurted the word out and broke my heart. I was so ready to get away from her demon brother.

"Aww, man," I expressed my heartbreak in the safest way I could with Leon sitting right there. "How long am I gonna get to spend with you?"

"Well, that my dear is the good news," her bright as the sun smile was back. "Me and you are going on a roooaad triiiip," she sang, the excitement in her voice making me forget that the time I had outside of the dungeon had been cut short.

"Yaaay! Where are we going?" I bounced in the back seat like the kid that I actually was.

"Well, I was thinking maybe a trip to see the falls, Luray Caverns, and the Columbus Zoo." Her plans had my curiosity fully piqued. "We're gonna take an RV, learn some camping songs, roast marshmallows, and find some small watering holes to get into. Lil Mama, I hope you know how to swim cause I'mma get you in a lot of water over the next two weeks."

"Yesss, I do," now it was my turn to sing my words. "Daddy, can I go get a new bathing suit?"

Before Leon could answer that, Aunt Lori chimed in. "Don't worry about any of that, Auntie's got all that covered." Leon gave Aunt Lori a look, but she knew how to handle him. "Don't look at me like that, Leo."

"Like what, Lo?"

"Like I'mma spoil this young lady."

"I thought no such thing. Plus, Zell is a good girl, she deserves to be spoiled by her only and favorite Auntie." They both broke into laughter because Leon was talking in a weird voice that I only heard from him when Aunt Lori was around.

Why Would I Love You?

Aunt Lori stayed at the house for a couple days, finalizing all our plans and taking me out shopping, shopping, and shopping. Anyone watching us would've thought that we were in the process of starting all over in life with the way she bought stuff for us. I was in my glory because this wasn't like when Leon took me shopping with his ulterior motives. I was actually having the time of my life, ripping and running the streets, trying on outfits, and just being unconditionally loved, hugged, and kissed by someone that wasn't trying to harm me.

The day had finally come for me and Aunt Lori to hit the road, I was so excited that I could barely think straight. She had left the house to pick up the rental RV and I was in my room getting dressed. My back was to the door and I had music playing out of my phone. I swear I had almost forgotten where I was and what my role was because I was surprised when I heard my room door creak just before Leon walked in. I caught sight of him in the reflection of my mirror, but I didn't turn around abruptly or say anything smart. I knew exactly why he was slinking in my room and I didn't want to piss him off moments before I was going to be free.

Slowly, I turned around to greet his hungry gaze with a smile. "I'm gonna miss you, Daddy," I lied, more than ready to get away from the monster that was my father.

"Don't lie to me, girl," he snapped, just a little annoyed. "I can tell you been happy that our schedule has been thrown off. But it's ok, have your fun. When you get back, though, you're all mine."

The lust filled look on his face literally made my stomach turn. Then he leaned forward, placed a hand on the back of my head and pulled my face to his. The next thing I knew, he was tongue kissing me as he gripped and then patted my ass. Then without another word, he walked out of my room just as fast as he had entered. After that, there was nothing that could slow me down from getting my bag packed and heading to the door to wait for Aunt Lori.

On our first road trip together, I sat shotgun in the cab of the RV. The radio was blasting some good music while Aunt Lori and I bopped our heads. We had been driving for an hour already and I was glued to the window, enjoying the scenery and the feeling of freedom. I was hellbent on not speaking of or thinking about Leon the whole time I was on the road. I was deep in my thoughts about what life would have been like if Aunt Lori was the family member who'd found me.

When I was done with my original thoughts of Aunt Lori, I had an even better thought about what my life would've been like if my mother hadn't died a junkie, leaving me to this cruel, cruel world. After that, I started to see a Leave It to Beaver scene play out in my head, a scene in a completely different world from the one I was living in now. *'I was coming home from school and my mom had a plate of cookies ready for me when I walked through the door. Leon was actually a decent doting father who took his cigar pipe into the den. I was a cheerleader, and it was spirit week and on and on and on.'*

I must have been quiet for too long because in the middle of my daydream I was interrupted with a, "Heeeello! Earth to Z!" I snapped out of my fantasy land and looked over at Aunt Lori. "Hey, kiddo, what lala land were you in?"

"None, Auntie. I was just enjoying the view." I had been zoned out for so long that by this time we were in the Pennsylvania mountains and they were the picture of tranquility.

"Mhm, girl it is beautiful up here, isn't it?" She spoke in appreciation of the gorgeous scenery all around us. "Our next stop will be at a spot I picked that has the best view you ever want to see," she said as she reached out and touched my hand. Before I could help myself, I was flinching from her touch just as an instant feeling of embarrassment came over me. My cheeks felt flushed and warm. "I'm sorry, I didn't mean to startle you," she spoke with concern and sincerity in her voice.

Why Would I Love You?

I was so ashamed that I couldn't even look into her eyes for fear that the horrible secret I was holding onto would be seen when she looked into mine. Instead of looking at her, I kept my gaze fixed outside the window and whispered, "It's ok, Auntie." I knew for a fact that it wasn't ok because Auntie was like a bloodhound once she sensed something was wrong. I knew for certain that if it wasn't me jumping at her touch then my dry answer was the scent that told her something was wrong with me. That conversation was definitely not over.

We rode in silence for another couple hours before pulling onto a trail that led to the entrance of a hidden RV park. It was pretty neat how the RV's had their own spots and private areas that looked like camp sites. I was so ready to experience something new, hell, something plain ole normal, like campfires and smores and all the shit you see on Tv. Once we parked and settled the RV, it took Aunt Lori no time at all to build a fire and start teaching me how to make something called a box pizza. We sat around a campfire enjoying ourselves as I took in the scenery and enjoyed the freedom of not having any expectations or wife-like duties forced upon me. I looked at the night sky as I listened to the crickets chirping and the fire crackling. I was finally, after a very long time just being a child. I was able to say I was at peace.

As I stared at the millions of stars that could be seen from the campground sky, I could feel Aunt Lori's eyes on me, but she didn't say anything. She just sat watching me as I watched everything else. Because she was making me just a little uncomfortable, I decided not to pay her any mind, until she took a deep breath and as cool as cool could be she asked, "O'Zella, when you gon' tell ya daddy you pregnant?"

If I'd had water in my mouth, it would have gone flying everywhere. In a heartbeat, my head snapped her direction and I looked at her like she had lost her ever loving mind. *One, there is no fucking way I'm pregnant, and two, the only man that I've been having sex with is my daddy*, were the thoughts that were flying through my head.

"What?" is what exited my mouth. "Why would you say that?"

"In the day or so that we've been together, you have been either eating, peeing, or sleeping. You've been complainin' about being nauseous a lot, and you've thrown up several times. As much as I hate to scare you, sweetie, this is just something I am never wrong about."

"Well, there's always a first," Auntie, because there is absolutely no way I'm pregnant," I assured her even though I was nowhere near sure.

"Ok," she began in a kind and calm voice, "well, you either have a baby or a bug, and I want to make sure we know which one it is. So, in the morning we'll stop and get a test on the way to the zoo."

One thing I knew for sure about Auntie was that when she spoke, there was nothing else to be said. So, instead of putting up a useless protest, I just let her word be that and we finished up our night like the conversation had never happened which was just fine with me.

Back inside the Rv, we readied ourselves for bed. There was a small sleeping area in the back for Auntie and the dining area converted into a comfortable little bed that was all mine. As much as I craved peaceful sleep, I spent most of my night tossing, turning, thinking, and peeing. Halfway through the night, I went from being uncomfortable to being completely stressed with questions floating through my head that couldn't be answered at that time. *What if I am pregnant? Will Leon make me have it? Is this even possible? Will Auntie believe me if I tell her the truth about how I became pregnant?* Needless to say, with my mind moving at a hundred miles an hour, I didn't get a wink of sleep.

"Rise and shine, baby girl. We have a zoo to get to," is how Aunt Lori woke me the next morning.

I rolled over, fake rubbing my eyes even though I hadn't gotten a wink of sleep. "Mmm, what time is it?" I asked in a groggy voice that came more from exhaustion than from deep rest.

Why Would I Love You?

"Six-thirty, but we still have about two more hours of driving to do. If you want you can sleep the rest of the way, I just thought you could keep me company and teach me some of those teeny bopper songs you listen to," she spoke cheerfully, as if she'd had the best night of sleep ever.

"I would love to keep you company," I spoke truthfully. "Let me just go to the bathroom and brush my teeth."

"Mhhm!"

I caught that shit, but I wasn't about to say a word. I just got up, got myself together, and hopped in the front seat where I proceeded to play as many ratchet songs as I could think of. Lil Kim started it off and I saw Aunt Lori's face the moment she realized that she'd signed up the wrong damn DJ.

On our journey, we made one stop for gas and snacks because Auntie said that buying food at the Zoo was way too expensive. I didn't care about any of that, I was on pins and needles just anticipating seeing the zoo. After she'd told me where we were going, I decided to google it, and what I saw I liked very much. The place was huge and it was like half zoo and half amusement park. The child in me emerged and I was ready to do and see everything.

When we turned that last corner that would lead us to the parking lot of the zoo, I could hear angel harps playing. My eyes darted everywhere. The zoo looked just like the picture on its website, and I was glued to the window taking it all in. It felt like we took forever to just make it to the parking lot and because we were in the big ass RV, it took even longer to park. But that didn't dampen my spirits, this trip was a big one for me and so far I was not disappointed in anything.

Finally, we found a spot, packed up all our stuff and were off. The walk from the back of the lot was difficult because it was first a long walk and then it seemed that the closer we got to the front gate of the Zoo, the more the smells coming from the zoo got to me. I didn't want Auntie to start bringing up being pregnant again, so I swallowed hard and tried to act cool. But then all of a sudden, it was like some kind of switch had been hit and my cool was thrown out of the window. As soon as I was close enough to a garbage can, I ran for it and began puking my insides out. Even though all the food I'd consumed that morning was out of my system, I still kept going, throwing up so bad that it felt like my intestines would be coming out next. My legs were shaking, my body was sweating, and I felt hella weak.

"Come on, baby," Auntie spoke in a soothing voice, "let's get you back to the Rv for a minute." Auntie helped with holding up my weak frame and together we walked back while I dry heaved the whole time. Once there, Aunt Lori helped me into the RV. I slowly slid out of my pants, and she told me to go rest on the bed in the back. When I climbed into the bed, she covered me up. "I'm gonna get you some water and you rest up. We can try it again in a little while. After getting me some water, she walked up to the front, turned on the reserve power, started the Air conditioning, and that was the last thing I remembered before I drifted off.

Sixteen

The faint rustling of a bag was what woke me from the deepest sleep of my young life. My eyes were heavy and it took me a couple of tries before my lids began to flutter. As my sight slowly came into focus, I finally saw Aunt Lori sitting on the side of the bed with a box in her hand. She held the hand with the box in it toward me. Her look was neutral, but I could still see the concern etched in the corners of her eyes.

"Here, you need to do this," she spoke softly.

"Why? I asked when I saw that it was a pregnancy test. "I told you it's not possible. Why don't you believe me?"

"It has nothing to do with believing you, Zell. I have a feeling, and to ease my own worry, I'm asking you to please just take it."

She was lucky I had to pee anyways. Irritated, I snatched the box from her hand and mumbled, "Fine." The RV from front to back was all of ten steps, but the walk to that bathroom was like walking a marathon with a broken foot. It was excruciating. To get things over with and get on with our day, I quickly read the box, followed the directions, and then left the tube wrapped up on the little shelf above the toilet. Without looking back, I nervously left the bathroom.

If there was one thing I could be certain of, it was that my Auntie was a cool ass G. So, I knew that no matter the results of that test, she would still be my biggest fan. I stepped out of the little bathroom like I had just been released from a twenty year bid at a max penitentiary. At this point, she was in the dinette area putting on a pot of water for a cup of tea.

Without looking up, she spoke to me. "Come sit with me, baby."

Nervously, I crept over to her and sat down. When I did, she put out her arm and let me lean my head on her shoulder. In that moment, she proved my thoughts about her to be true. I sincerely believed that no matter what the results were, I was safe with her.

"I'm not accusin' you of nuthin but, baby, something is going on with you and I'd like you to tell me what it is."

"I can't tell you," I blurted the words out without even thinking about them first.

Aunt Lori leaned up in one smooth and swift motion. Before I realized it, she had my chin in her hand and we were nose to nose. With clenched teeth and a stone cold look in her eyes, she breathed, "What do you mean you can't tell me?" Her grip tightened just slightly, not enough to hurt me, but enough that I knew she would hurt whoever dared to hurt me. Her next words only served to solidify my thoughts. "If someone is hurting you, you tell me!" She kept her eyes on mine, searching them for the answer that I'd told her I couldn't give her. I stared back at her for only a second, but it felt like that second was long enough for her to see my whole life story in my eyes. Even though I didn't utter a syllable, I knew she felt my pain because she just grabbed me and hugged me as I lost control, sobbing into her bosom. "Sshh, child. Everything's gonna be ok," she whispered as she stroked my hair.

Once I had calmed down, she let me go so she could go into the bathroom and read my fate on a little pee stick. As she entered the bathroom, I watched her back while I bit and practically chewed off my nails. The possibility of me being pregnant wasn't truly real in my mind until I saw Aunt Lori's head drop.

Instantly, my body began to shake and tears welled in my eyes once more. This time it wasn't because of fear, but out of anger. I knew the shit Leon was doing to me wasn't right, but I never said anything because I knew no one would give a damn one way or the other. I also knew that opening my mouth could have gotten me taken away from him and placed in another situation that was far worse. Since my mom died, I had yet to come across one adult whose major concern was me. Now that the pregnancy was in my face and I finally had an adult that gave a damn about me, I knew I needed to play my cards right. Aunt Lori didn't know it yet, but she was gonna help me get rid of her sick ass brother. I just didn't know how I was going to pull it off yet.

With a somber look on her face and an extremely concerned look in her eyes, Auntie sat down with me, and in her lowest and most compassionate voice she said, "Baby girl, it's positive. Now, I need you to tell me what is going on. Maybe we can just start with who this boy is. I mean, I thought we talked about everything, so I don't understand why you never mentioned a boy before."

I inhaled and exhaled deeply, slowly coming to accept the latest hardship I was to endure. "Auntie?"

"Yes, Zell?" her face held no judgment as she watched me.

"I promise I will tell you everything," I assured her, "but I need you to promise me something first."

"What is it, honey?" More concern presented itself in her eyes.

"Can I tell you when we get back home? And will you promise to let me tell my dad?"

She grumbled and groaned a little, but after a moment she agreed to hold off on everything until the trip was over.

We never made it back to the zoo that day and I was okay with that. Aunt Lori and I ended up spending the rest of the week hosting our own rendition of the show 'Diner's, Drive-Ins and Dives'. Auntie let me google local restaurants that weren't big chains, and then we would order their specialty and rate its deliciousness. There were a couple times that the food didn't agree with my stomach and I got to throwing up like crazy, but for the most part we had a blast. Every once in a while,

I would catch Auntie staring at me, but she didn't say a word just as she'd promised.

The day came when we were leaving our final stop and heading back home. It was like there was some kind of shift in the environment and the tension in the Rv was so thick you couldn't cut it with a knife. We had been riding for about an hour when the silence finally became too much for Auntie.

"Zell, can I ask you something?"

"Sure, Auntie."

"Do you want me to be there with you when you tell ya daddy that you're pregnant?"

There was a long pause as I sat in that seat and thought about what I was going to do. I went over and over the different scenarios that could've played out between Leon and I when I revealed to him that I was carrying his seed. And the more I thought about it, the more I became angry. This sorry ass nigga was supposed to protect me, but instead he took advantage of me like I wasn't his flesh and blood. With a sneer curling up the corner of my lip and a snarl ready to be released from my throat, I answered, "I want to go up and get it over without you."

"You sure, baby?" Aunt Lori asked in a way that let me know she would have my back if I needed her to.

"I'm positive, Auntie," I assured her that my mind was made up.

I don't remember how I got to the front door of the home I shared with my monster, when we arrived at the house, or what I was going to say when I got inside. All I knew for sure was that I was not going to hesitate to let out whatever this new rage was that was stirring inside me. I had been angry before, very angry, but never to that degree. I'd wanted to harm someone before, very much so, but never with murderous intent. This rage was different, this new sensation felt more like a furious hurricane than just my regular angry emotions.

Why Would I Love You?

It was like there was some kind of beast in me that had been suppressed throughout the years, throughout all of the abuse, and it was determined to no longer be held back. She finally wanted to get out and I was not stopping her. She was a beast that no one ever even knew was inside of me, especially not me. And the stealthy way she was moving through me at that moment let me know that when she did emerge, no one would see her coming.

Turning the key, I let it jingle a little as I put a smile on my face and then pushed the door open. There he was sitting on the couch watching tv. Hearing me enter, he looked my way and a huge smile climbed across his face,

"Hey, baby!" he said, opening his arms to me. I closed the door behind me. "Where's your Auntie?"

"She had to run to the store, Daddy." I said as I walked to him and sat on his lap.

"How's my sweet girl been?" he asked as he leaned in to kiss me on my neck and then on my lips. My body was cringing and the beast within me was infuriated. "Why you so stiff, baby? You need Daddy to take care of you?" he offered, and before I could respond he was already moving me in the direction of where he wanted me to be. "Stand up?" I did as he said because with every word he spoke I was slowly suppressing the beast and losing my nerve to fight back.

Leon unzipped the front of my jeans just enough to pull my panties down and expose my bush. Leaning into my crotch, he was close enough for me to feel his breath as he talked. My skin began to crawl and more of my nerves disappeared.

"Were you a good girl while you were gone?" he asked as his voice began to fill with the lust that I despised. I didn't say anything. Usually when I didn't answer, he took my silence as a challenge to make me scream either in pain or ecstasy. "Ah, you playing quiet, huh?" his voice was taunting, I could tell he really missed having me as his sex slave while I was gone. "Don't worry, Daddy missed you," he continued, "and I'm gonna show you just how much."

As he began to grab at my pants to pull them down I was so filled with anger and disgust that I blurted out, "Leon, I'm pregnant!"

That turned out to be a very successful way of getting him to stop touching me. Suddenly, he froze, pushed me away from him and stood up.

"What the fuck did you just say?" He was furious, and it showed all over his face,

"Daddy, I'm pregnant," I repeated myself as we looked at one another eye to eye.

"FUUUUCK!" he was having serious trouble containing his rage. "What do you mean? How do you know?"

"Auntie got me a test 'cause I was throwing up a lot."

"This is some bullshit!" he shouted as his fury took over and he lost all control.

I saw it happening in slow motion, and since I had already blurted out all of my confidence, all I could do was stand there frozen, unflinching as the back of his hand came down hard on my face and knocked me to the floor. Once I landed, I scrambled backwards, trying my best to get to my room, to get to some kind of safety.

"Oh, no you don't!" he spoke angrily as he reached down and grabbed me by my hair.

The grip he had on my hair was so tight that it brought on an instant headache. The pain from that headache was devastating, I began to see stars, bright, blinding stars. The next thing I knew, Leon had flung me toward the small kitchen/dinette area. My back hit the leg of a chair, sending a sharp pain up my spine to go with the devastating pain now in my head. Before I could even think of making a move of any kind, I was given a swift kick to the stomach. I let out a yelp like an injured dog, but that didn't stop him. His next vicious move was to kick me one more time and then stand over me screaming like a rabid dog as spit flew from his mouth and onto my face with each of his words.

"You tryna get me caught? You think you fuckin' slick?" he had completely transformed into a demon. "You little bitch, ain't gonna be no baby around here even if I got to cut that motha fucka outta you my damn self!"

Leon then grabbed me by the hair once again and snatched me to my feet. He yanked me to the other side of him so that I was facing the counter in the kitchen. Then he slammed the side of my face into the countertop, causing me to lose focus for a quick moment. The man that brought me into this world then leaned over my back and with gritted teeth whispered into my ear, "Ain't gonna be no baby when I'm done with yo ass, you little bitch!"

He then clutched the back of my unzipped pants and ripped them down. Before I could get my focus back and even try to fight him off of me, he rammed his dick into me so hard that it felt as if he had torn me in two. I let out a pain filled shriek, but Leon quickly used his big hands to cover my mouth to muffle the painful screams I let out every time he mercilessly thrust into me.

"You ain't gon' be bringing no babies into this world and getting me locked up for the rest of my life. Bitch, you ain't worth that! You got me fucked up!" he raged as he tore through me so hard that I screamed for dear life.

That only pissed him off more, made him hurt me more, made him tighten the hand that was covering my mouth and spread his fingers so that it was covering my nose too. Now, not only did it feel like he was shredding my insides with a razor blade, but I was struggling to breathe. Under the pressure of the hand that was covering my mouth, I tried begging him to stop. My screams of protest and my incessant pleading made him thrust more feverishly. It was like he was feeding off of his power and his control over me, becoming angrier as he went on. Leon was in a zone I had never seen him in before and his only goal was to hurt me and to make me lose that baby.

My tears of shame and pain turned to tears of rage as he plowed through me as if I were nothing. As much as I wanted to get him off of me, to destroy him, I couldn't move. His own fury was bigger than mine and it had me pinned to that counter while he did everything to make it so that there was no way I could ever carry a baby for him or anyone. Trying to get up, trying to move so that he would get away from me was wearing me out, especially since I couldn't breathe. I was beginning to lose consciousness. I knew it was only a matter of time before I blacked out and I truly feared what he would do to me when I was no longer conscious. Everything in me told me that he really would cut that baby out of me just as he'd said he would. Fear ran through me like a hot knife through butter.

Then I heard it, the sound of my salvation. "Leeeeoooonnnn!" Aunt Lori screamed from somewhere deep inside of her soul. She had appeared out of nowhere and was at the door, frozen, watching in total shock as her brother viciously raped her niece.

Shocked down to the bone, Leon jumped out of his skin as he got off of me, took a step away from me. Then he released the hold he had over my nose and mouth and I began to gulp for air like a fish out of water. My lungs stopped burning and my vision began to clear. Slowly but surely, I was coming back from the brink of death as my father pulled up his pants and began to cover his ass.

"Lo, it's not what you think," he lied as he started to plead his case. "She made me..." he began to lay all of the blame on me, began to make it seem as if I was the aggressor. That man was trying to destroy my world after he'd already destroyed my world. "And then she..." he continued.

That was all I needed to hear. With energy that suddenly came from nowhere, I lifted my head just high enough to make eye contact with the knife block. And before I could think or stand there as a victim being labeled a villain, the beast within me took over. Every single time in my life that I had been abused flashed before my eyes, scene after scene of repeated abuse roared through me and left me shaken with madness. Every instance of the rage I had spent years suppressing showed up and showed out. I was tired, done with people taking advantage of me and fucking me over. I wasn't going to be anybody's victim anymore.

The old me would have cowered and watched the scenario play out as usual, would have allowed myself to be victimized and then damn near punished for being a victim. But my inner beast wasn't having any of that coward shit, she was all about action and this was her final straw. As Leon continued talking, lying, placing all of the blame at my feet, I grabbed a knife from the butcher block and in one swift movement, I twirled around and sliced his fucking throat.

Blood gushed from him, warm and thick as it sprayed my face. I didn't even flinch, I stood there, keeping my eyes on him as he grabbed for his neck and fell to his knees. I watched as he gurgled and gasped for what little air would make it to his lungs. Just as he had tried to take my life, I had succeeded in taking his. And as he lay on the floor dying, I stood over his body, gripping the handle of the knife for dear life until he took his last breath.

His eyes rolled into the back of his head before coming forward again and fixating on one spot, everything began moving in slow motion.

From behind me I heard Aunt Lori scream my name as if she had lost the entirety of her mind. Even that sounded as if it was hallow and in slow motion. "O'Zeeeeeeeellllaaaaaaaaaa!"

Once I heard her scream, I let the knife go and my eyes watched as it slowly tumbled to the floor making this clanging sound that I would never forget. Whatever trance I had been in was broken by the sound of the metal blade tinging on the floor. Everything went back to regular speed, and Aunt Lori made it to my side just in time for me to collapse in her arms. The beast in me had done what she came to do, after that she checked back out and I was left to face the reality of her actions.

There was this big blank spot where I really don't remember anything that happened. It was like the computer of my mind hit control, alt, delete and eliminated any memory of me leaving the house I'd been imprisoned in for over a year. After staring at Leon while he lay in a slowly growing puddle of blood, the next thing I remembered was my Aunt tucking me into a bed at a hotel as she hugged me and kissed me.

I didn't remember the police being there, or being questioned, I didn't remember being violently raped, I didn't even remember killing my own father. I didn't remember the ride to the police station or being in the police station where I was formally questioned. I didn't even remember Aunt Lori being questioned since she was the only witness to everything. All I remembered was waking up and seeing my aunt sitting on the bed beside me praying.

When she felt me move a little, she turned her head in my direction and I saw that her eyes were filled with tears. "Zella, baby," she sounded so relieved that I was awake. "I am *so* sorry. I wish I had known."

"I didn't tell anybody," my throat felt raw, my words sounded gravelly and hoarse.

"Why not?" she asked as she caressed my face, looking at me with eyes filled with sorrow and love.

"Honestly because..." I started to speak but trailed off. I had no answer for her. "I don't know." Suddenly I felt every emotion I'd ever felt since my mom died all come rushing into me. I opened my mouth to speak more but no words would come, only emotion. Unable to do anything else, I buried my face into my aunt's shoulder and bawled like I should have done the day my mom died.

Aunt Lori squeezed me and stroked the back of my hair. "Sshhhh, baby. It's ok, I got you now. I promise," she comforted and assured me.

Why Would I Love You?

Sobbing into her shoulder, I finally remembered that there was more than just me now. "What about the baby?" was all I could say.

"Hush, baby," she soothed me. "We'll talk about all of that tomorrow. You just rest yourself."

Seventeen

The next morning, I woke up feeling like a ton of bricks were sitting on my chest and head. As I opened my eyes and turned in the bed, I let out a groan that was loud enough to wake up Auntie who was sitting in the chair next to me.

"Hey," I called out to her, "Were you in that chair all night, Auntie?"

"Chile, don't worry about me," she said as she sat up and began to stretch. "How are you feeling?"

"I don't know," I answered honestly.

"I'm here for you, ok?" she said as she reached out, grabbed my chin, and forced me to look at her. She wanted me to see the truth in her eyes. "Nobody, *and I mean nobody*, is going to ever hurt you again as long as I have breath in my body. You understand?"

I sat up in bed to get a better look at this woman who'd just come into my life. Up until that very moment, it hadn't occurred to me that the man she saw raping me, the man whose throat she saw me slice was her brother. She'd made no mention of it, just watched over me and made sure I was okay. Once the realization hit me, I felt the tears begin to well up and I started to repeatedly apologize while sobbing uncontrollably.

"I'm sorry. I'm sorry. I'm sorry. I'm sor—"

She sat next to me on the bed, hugged me, and cut off my words. "Hush. What do you have to be sorry for?"

Why Would I Love You?

"Auntie, he was your brother. I killed your brother!" I sobbed more.

"And *you* are my niece! I loved my brother with everything in me, but I will not let you shed tears for defending yourself against someone that was hurting you. He was raping you and you were defending yourself." She squeezed me tighter and then said the words that I will never forget as long as I live. "I'm just sorry that it wasn't me instead. I was supposed to protect you."

Shock hit me, had me pulling back from the hug so that I could look at her face. "What do you mean?" Her statement sounded strange to me, as if there was a story behind it.

Then I wiped my tears, blew my nose, and sniffled while listening to her fumble through words I would have never expected her to say. "Well, when we were younger, my brother was somewhat of a ladies man," she began. "And he had a way about him, a way of turning girls' no's into yeses. When he was in college, a girl with a reputation came forward and said that he raped her, but Leon, cool as ever, denied every bit of it. Needless to say, the girl left school and he got away with it because she was slut shamed." She paused as if she was currently experiencing what had happened back then.

"I had a feeling that he'd done exactly what the girl had said he'd done, but it couldn't be proven so there was nothing anyone could do about it. Unfortunately, that wasn't the first or the last time that he had gotten away with it. But since no woman could ever show proof, my brother just kept moving through his life tearing the lives of others apart. Then one day the accusations stopped, and I assumed he'd stopped," she said as she shook her head in shame. "I am *so* sorry, Zell," she told me. "I knew he had a problem, but no one had come forward in more than a decade, and never in a million years would I have thought that he would do something like this to his own daughter."

"Auntie," I began in a voice that sounded much more grown than my actual age, "I know I'm young, but since mommy died, and maybe even before, I learned that you should never put anything past anyone. People will let you down or hurt you every chance they get."

For the longest time she just looked at me, several emotions crossing her face until she finally spoke. "You are such a strong, inciteful, and amazing young lady and I hope you never lose that."

I don't know how long we were there in that room talking and hugging, but that day I learned something else. Aunt Lori was a safe place for me, and I cherished that thought as she held me, rocked me, and hummed to me while she stroked my hair.

I finally felt safe again.

Fast forward four months past the incident and I was actually starting to be a happy teenager. I still didn't trust people, still didn't like myself much, but I was happy at home and that was what mattered most to me. After the police had questioned and requestioned me and Auntie about what happened with Leon, they finally ruled it self-defense and left us alone. I was thankful every day that I hadn't stabbed him repeatedly like I'd wanted to. Doing that would have made it extremely difficult to claim self-defense. I guess my inner beast knew exactly what the hell she was doing.

After everything with the police and Leon was all wrapped up, Aunt Lori and I sat down and had a talk about whether or not I was going to keep the baby.

"Baby, I know that at the end of the day this is your choice, but you are running out of the time to make your decision."

"Auntie, I'm scared," I admitted. "I'm scared to have a baby so young. And I'm scared that if I keep this baby, I will not only be raising my child, I'll also be raising my sibling."

"I know, baby," she said, and that was exactly what I needed at that moment. "And what do I keep telling you?"

"That you are here for me every step of the way."

Why Would I Love You?

"Right. So, if you choose to keep this baby, I will be here for you and him or her. And if you choose not to, I will still be here for you."

"I know... but..." I trailed off, decided not to say what I was thinking. "I know, Auntie."

"But what, Zell?"

I was quiet for a long time, a really long time. I knew what had been inside of my father, had both seen and experienced what had been in him. I had also come to realize that the same monster was inside of me. My father's demon seed was just incubating inside of me, waiting to come out. After all, look at the murderer that came out of me when I was pushed. It had been sitting in there just waiting for its moment to strike. What if that evil had spread to my child? What if, by agreeing to keep the baby, I birthed another Leon, another me? And then there was the child's medical condition, which could turn out to be terrible by the baby being the spawn of two people so closely related. "What if my baby comes out with problems because—" I blurted out.

"Stop right there! I know I'm not the most spiritual person, but baby, I have prayed for your heart and that baby's health every day. And I know it is a tough decision, but just take time and think about it. You aren't alone. I promise."

"Ok, I'll think about it," I said the words I had begun to say a lot lately. I would think about it. However, while Aunt Lori was praying for the baby's health because she thought I was only worried about that, I was going to pray about its soul. I was far more concerned with that.

At first, I didn't want to have the baby, but I knew it would break Aunt Lori's heart if I had an abortion. The deciding factor came for me when I realized that even though the child was a part of him, it was also a part of me. And yes, I truly believed that Leon's monster was lurking inside of me, just waiting to emerge, but I also knew that I had seen neither hide nor hair of the monster in me until Leon's wicked actions invited it to come out and play. Other than that, I was not a monster and had never been one. The only time anything truly bad came to life within me was when someone truly bad pulled it out and since Leon was dead, there was no chance of that ever happening again. So, feeling confident in that, I decided to keep the baby and just focus on the positives of becoming a mom.

When I made my decision known to her, Auntie took me out of regular school and put me in a program with other young mothers. She didn't want me to be judged or ostracized. I found that school to be a real experience because those chicks had no clue as to what a real struggle was. I mostly stayed quiet because I didn't want anybody asking me questions about my baby and the father. I did do a lot of listening though, and I personally would have preferred their problems over my own any day.

"Girl, this nigga, Darnel, came over to my house drunk again, saying the baby's not his and that I should have gotten an abortion."

"Bitch, at least yours is acknowledging your baby. When I told my baby dad I was pregnant, he bounced and ain't been back. That was seven months ago."

That was the chatter I heard each day and sometimes it made me feel as if I didn't belong there. To my way of thinking, that program was for bird bitches who were chasing a check from a street dude and had bit off more than they could chew. I hated the program but because I wanted to please Aunt Lori, I stuck with it.

When I was five months along, we were assigned to write a poem for literature and present it before the class. The day had come and when it was my turn I didn't want to go up. I had made it my business to damn near be a mute when I was at school, but we had to share our work with everyone so I was unable to sit this one out like I wanted to. The poetry was supposed to be about our experience going into motherhood. Had I known that we would have to share our poems with the class, I wouldn't have been so transparent, but because class participation was required, I got up in front of the class anyway and shared my thoughts about motherhood so far.

My palms were sweaty and I couldn't stop crumpling the corners of the paper I held in my hands. I was scared to share my thoughts about how I felt about this baby of mine, but I braved up, cleared my throat, and began to slowly read the words that had been written.

"Mama's Baby," I said aloud as nervousness settled over me. Then I took a few moments to relax my mind and my body and to just breathe. When I finally felt settled, I began again.

"Mama's Baby

It's said, Mama's baby, Daddy's maybe.
Maybe I don't want to be a mama.
Maybe I want to be a maybe.
My fear of the future sometimes hurts me,
Cause I see a child that I might fail.
It could be a doctor or end up in jail.
Sometimes, I don't want to, but keeping it is my fight.
My skin is feeling as cool and clammy as a mid-summer night.
Mama's or maybe's,
I'm still scared because I'm having this baby.

By the time I finished the poem, standing in front of a class full of pregnant, emotional, crying girls, I was even more nervous than when I'd started. I said a very quiet, "Thank you" and went to my seat. Then the room began to clap, slowly at first, and then louder. And as they continued clapping and looking at me, I realized that it was truly nice to be noticed by my peers. However, I still didn't want to talk to any of them, so I smiled and then went back to writing so they would get the hint that I was done.

"Ladies, Ladies, settle down," the teacher said as she got everyone to stop clapping. Then she turned to me, "O'Zella, thank you so much for sharing your piece with us." I shook my head in acknowledgement of her words, then I went back to trying to be invisible. That was the first time I'd been honest about how I felt about my journey since my mom left. The best part was that even though I had been transparent, I'd done it in such a way that nobody knew exactly what I was talking about but me.

When I got home, I was in a good mood and ready to tell Aunt Lori about my day. Since she was the one that was with me when I was writing the poem and had listened to every version of it, I was anxious to share with her how the reading turned out. At that time we were living in a side by side house that was spacious enough for both of us. So, I rushed in the door, kicked off my shoes and went running up the stairs. It took me a second to get to her bedroom, but when I did, I was yelling like a kid in a candy store.

"Auntie, Auntie! You won't believe what happened tod…" Then all of the blood drained from my body and all I could do was open my mouth and let out a blood curdling, "Aaahhhhhhhhh!" God had a hell of a sense of humor. When I walked around the corner of her bedroom door, Aunt Lori was lying on the floor. I ran to her side in a panic. "Auntieeee!" She was face down on the side of the bed, looking as if she wasn't breathing. I kneeled down next to her and began shaking her shoulders. When she didn't respond, I hung my head with tears streaming from my eyes falling on her shirt. "Auntie, please get up," I pleaded through my sobs.

After a few seconds, I heard a groan and then her body began to move. "What happened? Why am I on the floor?" she asked as I sat her upright.

"Don't move, I'm gonna call an ambulance!" I said as I started to head out and get my cell phone.

"No, girl, don't make no fuss!"

"I just found you unconscious on the floor. God knows how long you was down there before I got here," I spoke, unable to believe she was blowing off something I thought was so serious. "What do you mean don't make a fuss?"

"I think it was just my sugar," she said, then paused to get her thoughts together. "I just need to get some juice and I'll be fine."

"Auntie, I respect you, but please don't make me curse you out. You're not okay!"

She looked at me with a smirk on her face. "I'm too weak to even threaten you girl."

"That's what I thought," I told her, my nerves as bad as ever. "Now, don't move," I commanded as I left her room and headed in search of my bag and my phone.

I rifled through my bag looking for my cell phone, for some reason it was hiding from me. I was panicking and needed to calm down. Even though I knew she was alive and talking, just seeing her laid out like that shook me to my core. I was quickly losing control of my emotions, and just as I was on the brink of having a mental breakdown, my hand touched the phone. Immediately, I snatched it out of my bag, dialed 911, and put the phone to my ear.

"911, what's your emergency?"

"It's my Aunt," I began speaking quickly, trying to get the words out as fast as I could. "I came home from school and she was passed out on the floor."

"Is your Aunt still nonresponsive?"

"No, she woke up and started talking to me, but she's weak."

"What is her name?"

"Lori."

"Can you put her on the phone?" At that request, my once solidly planted feet began to move at lightning speed. I ran in the room and found that Auntie had sat up. She was hardheaded, but she wasn't crazy. I put the phone on speaker and held it near her ear.

"She can hear you."

"Hello, Lori?"

"Yes," she responded, her voice as weak as her body.

"Can you tell me what happened?"

"I'm not sure. One minute I was fine, the next I was dizzy, and then I was on the floor."

"And where are you right now, Lori?"

"I'm in my room, still on the floor."

"As long as you're comfortable, stay right there and ask your niece to go downstairs. Someone has to let the EMT's in, they're on the way."

"Should I keep the phone?" Auntie asked.

"Yes, Lori, stay on the phone with me, ok?"

"Ok."

Aunt Lori looked my way but she didn't have to say a word, my feet were already heading to the door.

The fourteen steps I had to take down were the longest ever. It gave my heart time to play a fearful beat in my ear. I took that time to think about what I would have done if she never woke up, I just couldn't seem to shake the fear of possibly losing her. Although I made it to the porch very quickly, under my current circumstances that journey felt like forever. Rocking back and forth holding my stomach, I thought about the small family I had acquired after being in hell for six years. For the first time in a very long time, I bowed my head, closed my eyes, and prayed.

"Listen, God," is how I began. "I know you and me ain't talked in a while, but my Aunt, she's a good one. I've had a long, hard road since momma died and she's the first person, the first adult, to come along and make my road easier and lighter. I don't wan—" The thought running through my head was far too much to bear and I had to cut myself off from even verbalizing it. However, the need to complete my prayer pressed me and I continued. "I can't lose her. Please, let her be ok, God. She is literally the only good thing I got left. I'm begging you, pleeea—" My begging and pleading with God was put to a halt when I heard the sirens from the ambulance coming up the street. In a heartbeat, I stepped to the top of the porch stairs, waving my arms. Although I knew they had the address, I needed to make sure they stopped.

It took no time at all for them to get to Aunt Lori and to get her into their ambulance. Not even ten minutes later, she made it to the hospital in one piece. After she was examined he doctors said she had an issue with her diabetes. Apparently, her sugar dropped too low and that was why she passed out. I was so scared and didn't know what I would've done without her. So, while she fussed over me about the baby, I fussed over her about making sure she was doing everything she was supposed to with her health. Thank God she was released from the hospital that same night and we were back at home, back at our routine. Only this time I was now keeping as much of an eye on her as she was keeping on me.

Eighteen

At the end of my second trimester, Auntie convinced me to find out what I was having during a routine ultrasound. Up to that point, I hadn't even considered the sex of the baby, I'd been too focused on accepting my decision to keep it. I had actually come to enjoy being pregnant during the second trimester. I'd started to go for walks with Aunt Lori where we talked about any and everything. Then I started sharing the baby's kicks with her, grabbing her hand and placing it on my belly each time my baby moved. Aunt Lori and I would then rush to the computer, looking up the baby's development along with picking out names. I was finally at a point where I didn't constantly think about who my kids' father was and started enjoying the fact that I was going to be a mother and a damn good one at that. So, when Aunt Lori brought up finding out the sex of the baby, I was completely caught off guard.

This was it, the day for me to get my six month checkup which included the ultrasound. I lay on the table with my legs in stirrups while Aunt Lori held my hand as the doctor examined me. My OB, Karen, was a nice lady with pretty brown hair. She was very gentle, but I think that was the result of her being told about some of my past. When she was done with the exam, she sat up from her bent position between my knees, pulled her gloves off and gave me a genuine smile.

"O'Zella, everything is looking good, and because we are at the six month mark, we get to take more pictures of the little one today."

Why Would I Love You?

"I know!" I was excited and nervous. "I was wondering if you could tell me what I'm having this time," I inquired as I put my legs down and covered up my exposed nether regions.

"That shouldn't be a problem at all," she smiled at me. "I'll put that in my notes right now." She rolled her stool over to the computer, clicked a few keys and looked my way. "Done! Now, what are you hoping for?"

"I'm not sure." Hearing that question sent a lot of emotions through my body, a lot of negative emotions, but before I could sink all the way into a trance, Karen's voice brought me back. She looked over at Aunt Lori who had been standing by me quietly, "What about you, Great Aunt?"

"Oh, chile, I just want that little peanut to be healthy."

"That is all we can hope for," the doctor agreed with a smile just before she headed for the door. "Well, you ladies have a great weekend, and I'll see you in about two weeks."

"Ok, Dr. Karen. Thank you."

"You're welcome," and with that, she left.

As soon as the door closed I got dressed and Auntie and I headed to my ultrasound appointment. It was only right across the hall, so we went to the window, signed out and signed in. Two birds, one stone. It didn't take long before I was being called to enter the back. I started following the lady in scrubs down a small hallway, tightly holding onto Aunt Lori's hand. I knew it was just a routine ultrasound, but the thought of finding out the sex of my baby was a bit nerve wrecking. We made it to the spacious room with a regular table for me to sit on like in the doctor's office, and then the ultrasound machine. They were big and somewhat intimidating, but hell, I was already scared so they weren't doing much. The attendant gave me a towel, instructed me to pull my pants below my stomach and told me to tuck the towel in my waist band to protect my clothes. She then left the room.

It wasn't my first time in that room, but something was hanging over my head that I just couldn't put my finger on. I lay there, belly exposed, when I heard, tap, tap.

"Hello?" they called out to me.

"Come in," I answered.

"Hello, Ms. Grife," the ultrasound technician said as she entered the room. "So, I hear we're not only making sure the baby is doing good, but that we get to determine the sex too."

"Yes, we are," I admitted shyly.

"Ok," she smiled big and kindly, "well, this is gonna be a little warm but it's better than it being cold." As she talked, she put warm gel on my stomach and then put a T shaped probe in the gel. She moved it around on my belly while we all kept our eyes glued to the screen. First, we heard the heartbeat. "Baby Grife has a strong heartbeat," she commented just as the baby came into view. I was busy staring at the screen, trying to figure out what we were looking at when it suddenly became clear. Then she started pointing out body the parts on screen. "There's little baby's arms, legs, we have ten toes and fingers. There's baby's face. The head is measuring at just the right size for where you are in your pregnancy. Everything is looking good and the baby is developing well."

"So, everything looks good," I repeated her statement, surprised because I'd been worried from day one that the baby was going to be a Mongoloid.

"Yes, Ma'am, the baby is looking great. Now, let's find out if it is a baby boy or girl. You ready?"

"Let's do it."

"Here we go," she said as she moved the probe back to the bottom of my stomach, sliding it back and forth slowly, pressing and pressing until finally she stopped. My heart raced, my nerves were very high. Then, "Congratulations, Mom, you are having a bouncing baby boy!"

Why Would I Love You?

When Aunt Lori and I got back to the house, I headed straight to my room without so much as a word. In fact, I hadn't spoken at all since I'd broken down at the doctor's office, so Aunt Lori had no idea what was wrong with me. She was so cool about her shit, though, that she always got information out of me with little to no effort at all.

Once I reached my bedroom, I stormed inside, slammed my door, threw myself on the bed, and buried my face in my pillow. I could hear Aunt Lori slowly making her way up the stairs as if she was the tortoise and I was the hare. Slow and steady was her pace. She made it to my door and knocked. I didn't even bother moving. She knocked again. I rolled over with an attitude.

"Yes?"

"Can I come in?"

"Yes, Ma'am." I sat up in bed and adjusted my attitude a little bit, how I was feeling had nothing to do with my aunt. When she heard my agreement of her entering the space she had blessed me with, she opened the door just as slowly as she had been climbing those stairs, walked into my room, and sat on the edge of my bed. No one spoke for a while, not me and not her. In that room, the silence between us became as thick as London fog until she finally let out a loud, long sigh.

"Zell?"

"Huh?"

"Don't huh me, girl. You gonna tell me what all of that was about?"

"I don't know!" I folded my arms across my chest and pouted.

"What you mean you don't know? Something clearly upset you."

"Well... Uh..." I wasn't ready to talk, not even sure if what I had to say was serious enough for me to have freaked out the way I did. But if anyone was going to give it to me straight, it would be Aunt Lori. So I sat there, contemplating whether or not I was ready to tell her.

"It's ok, Zell. You know you can talk to me," she spoke in that loving tone and with those kind eyes. Before I even knew what was happening, I broke out into tears again, throwing my head on her shoulder.

"What if my son grows up to be like him. I read that things like that are hereditary. I don't want my baby to grow up to be a pre... pre... predator!" I said as my sobs became worse. Aunt Lori said nothing as she wrapped her arms around me and started to rock back and forth.

"Baby, don't put that on you. This baby, no matter the evil he came from, is a blessing." She put her hand on my stomach and began to rub in a circle motion, knowing that was calming to me. And when I had quieted down a little, she put her hand under my chin and lifted my face so I could look her in the eye. "Don't worry your mind about things like that. He will be loved and taught right and wrong. We cannot worry about the path he will choose. We just have to show him the love he needs so that he will want to make the right choice."

"I know you're right, but I'm still scared."

"You wouldn't be a real mother if you weren't scared of what type of person your child will grow to be."

I heard what she was saying, but there was still this sad tugging at the bottom of my stomach that wouldn't let my mind rest. I did come to grips with the fact that there was nothing I could do. If my son was going to become a monster predator like *our* dad, then it was just destined to be. I shook my head for the moment, wiped my tears, and looked at the ultrasound pictures with Aunt Lori. Then I held my breath and said a silent prayer, asking God to not allow the fears about who my baby would be consume me.

Another few months had gone by and things had been as good as expected. My due date was around the corner and both Auntie and the baby were doing great. I loved watching my stomach rise and fall whenever the baby moved, the feel of him kicking me in the stomach and in the ribs were both amazing and painful. To this day I couldn't tell you which one was worse, but I enjoyed every moment of it.

Why Would I Love You?

Those last three months of my pregnancy were the least stressful of all because after the ultrasound, I stopped worrying. Every night Auntie would make it a habit to come into my room and rub my belly for no less than thirty minutes while she sang to my stomach and told me and him stories. I knew she was doing it for the baby, but I enjoyed the attention, especially since it was nothing like what I had been getting.

One day, Aunt Lori and I were out for our afternoon walk when suddenly I had this rush of pressure in the bottom of my belly just before I felt like I was peeing on myself. Immediately, I let out a loud groan before doubling over and grabbing my stomach.

"What's wrong, chile?" Aunt Lori looked at me, concern all over her face,

"I think I just peed on myself," I said as embarrassment washed all over me.

"Oh, Zell!" her voice hitched up a notch as excitement filled her. "I think your water just broke!"

"What am I supposed to do?" I shrieked as I tried to stop panic from setting in.

"Come," her voice was much calmer than mine had been when she said, "let's sit on this bench, cause I don't think you're going to make it back to the house." I did as I was told and when my stomach tightened and pained, I started breathing through a wave of cramps that were slowly creeping up on me. Trying to remain relaxed, I leaned my head back and closed my eyes as I listened to her give directions to the 911 operator. It wasn't long after that phone call that I heard sirens wailing and felt contractions building. Trying her best to make sure that I kept calm, Auntie whispered, "Breathe, baby, breathe." That's all I remember.

Everything after that was a little foggy up until I was in the hospital with my legs in stirrups, with a doctor between my legs coaching me to, "Push!"

It was time to have my baby and even though Aunt Lori was with me every step of the way, I was too scared and didn't even have time to think about it.

"Ok, O'Zella, relax. When you feel the contractions start, we're going to start pushing again, okay?" That was what I heard from the doctor every five minutes for almost an hour. Finally, everything changed and she said, "Ok, this should be your last time. Your little one is crowning now, so when I tell you to, you're going to push as hard as you can, ok?"

"Yeeeeeeeees!" I was hit with a contraction as the doctor was between my legs and Aunt Lori was at my side holding my hand.

While I felt as if my body was going through some kind of torture, they were both telling me to, "Push, push, push!"

After that last push, I knew for sure that my baby was finally out. All of the pressure that had been in the bottom of my stomach had eased up and all of the nursing staff started to move quickly.

The first one to say anything was Auntie. "Doctor, why isn't the baby crying?" There was silence for just a moment before Auntie spoke once more, "Doctor?" she called out.

When no one responded to her, she let my hand go and started walking toward the crib that was surrounded by the doctor and several nurses. There was only low voices now, whispering and hands moving feverishly over my son's body as Auntie took more steps toward them. My heartbeat began to pound in my ear, my nerves began to shatter. With every step Aunt Lori took, it sounded as if a hammer was slamming into cinder blocks. Thinking back on it now, I think I loved my baby before I'd even seen his face, and the moment I heard him scream for the first time, it was like the ceiling had detached from the building, letting birds, butterflies, and bright rays of sunshine come flowing through the room.

Auntie came over to me and hugged me. "Baby, he is so beautiful and healthy."

"Is he ok?" was all I wanted to know.

"Yes, he's good. He's really good, baby. They just had to clear his airway."

"Really?" I let out a deep sigh of relief. "Oh, thank God!"

Aunt Lori smiled at me, then kissed me on the cheek before saying, "I'm gonna go check on my great nephew. I'll be right back. Ok?"

"Ok," I smiled at her.

It wasn't long after the baby and I had been cleaned up that the room started to empty out. It had taken them a while to bring my son to me, but when they did, once I had him in my arms, I never wanted to let him go. My first instinct was to check out everything, his fingers, his toes, his entire body. For a long time, Auntie and I just sat and looked him over as we oohed and aahed about every little thing. He was perfect, and when his little fingers grabbed my finger and held on, I knew then that I would never want to let go.

When Aunt Lori had enough of me hogging my son, she reached for him, picked him up from my arms, and sat down just rocking and humming to him. In that moment, I didn't see him as a product of incestuous rape or as an unwanted mistake. He was a little person that had grown inside of me. I'd spent months feeling every kick, following every craving, having his head full of hair give me never ending heartburn. He was mine, all mine, and I stared at him in a daze, falling deeper in love with the small human being that'd I'd finally had the privilege of meeting face to face.

Never taking her eyes off of her great nephew, Aunt Lori broke my trance when she asked the question I had never given any thought to. "What are you going to name this little fella?"

"Honestly, Auntie," I said, completely off guard, "I never even thought about it."

"Baby," she finally looked up from his face and into mine, "what do you mean you never thought about it?"

"I know you've asked me about it, but I never picked a name," I admitted.

"Well, we can't have him going home with no name, now can we?"

"I'll have one for him before we leave," I assured her as for the first time I began to allow some names to flow through my head, "but for now, the hospital can keep calling him Baby Grife."

I felt myself becoming really short with her, so to keep from being disrespectful, which she did not deserve, I told her I was going to close my eyes and that if she was going to leave for any reason, she should call the nurses to get the baby. I could hear in her voice when she responded that she knew I was frustrated, but she respected me enough to allow me the silence and the space I needed to deal with my feelings. That was one of the great things about Aunt Lori, she always knew when I needed space and when I didn't.

Before long, I found myself actually drifting off as I ran through every boy name I could think of in my mind. I hadn't realized just how tired I was, but I must have really needed that sleep because when I woke up, an entire fourteen hour block of time had gone by. I started to stir and flutter my eyes, and before I could get them opened all of the way, there was Aunt Lori like a guardian angel.

"So, I guess you weren't playing about being tired, huh?"

"I guess not," I groggily giggled.

"Listen," she began in a gentle voice, "I know everything about this situation is hard and different for you. And I'm genuinely sorry if I've added stress about naming the baby."

"I'll admit I was frustrated, Auntie, but not because you asked me to name my child. It was because I'd had nine whole months to do it and I still didn't think to pick a name for him."

"Oh, baby..." she whined as she made her way to me, sat on the side of my bed, and guided my head to her shoulder. "It's gonna be ok, "she whispered as she rocked a little bit. I was back in the comfort, safety, and love of my aunt and those were things I never took for granted since she'd come into my life.

"I think I have one," I told her, never moving my head from her shoulder.

"And?" she questioned, excitement running through her.

"Samael," I said as I tried the name out on my tongue.

"Samuel?" she questioned as she did the same.

"No, like Sam and ale combined Samael!"

"Hmm, it could be way worse," she said as she processed the name. "But, sweetheart, where did you come up with that one?"

"It's a spin on Samuel. In my class, those other girls were naming their boys things like Semaj. S-E-M-A-J, Auntie. That is just James spelled backwards." I know that the way I said it made the name sound crazy, which actually made her laugh, but I was serious. I hadn't done much talking when I was in class because those little thot boxes had been willing participants of the underage pregnancy epidemic, but I did listen. And some of the shit they'd said shocked me and at times even made my skin crawl.

"Hello, earth to Zell," I heard Aunt Lori calling out to me again.

"Oh, um, huh?" I asked as confusion hit me hard. I'd gone back to school in my mind and was now struggling to come back to the present.

"It looked like you were lost in a daydream. What's on your mind?"

Before I could come up with a lie, which I really didn't want to do, there was a light tapping on my door. "Hello," someone sang out all cheerfully, "I'm bringing baby Grife back." The nurse on shift pushed Samael in the door gently and parked his bassinet next to my bed.

"How is mommy doing?" she asked as she looked me over. "Is there anything I can get for you?"

"No, I'm fine," I assured her, "but thank you."

"Ok, well the photographer is making her way around and will be here soon if you want to pick out an outfit."

"Ok, thank you," I repeated myself as I looked over at my sleeping baby and couldn't help but to smile. As I stared at him in complete silence for the longest time, I learned that it was true that you fell in love with your baby from the moment you set eyes on them.

Nineteen

After giving birth to Samael, I was in the hospital for an additional three days and I was ready to go. I'd gotten pictures, diapers, and had named my baby, I was killing my check off list. Next on that list was to go home and take care of my little person where there would be no nurses to give me a break. To say I was afraid was an understatement.

I was looking out of the window of the moving car, and with every house we passed my anxiety kicked up a little higher. The destination itself wasn't scary, because I loved the place I called home. What had me anxious was what that home represented. That would be the place where I was to officially exercise my responsibility for another human being and I had to make sure that none of the stuff I'd gone through would happen to him. That level of responsibility felt tremendous, and I felt my eyes welling up with unshed tears when we pulled up to the house.

Auntie, who seemed calm and relaxed, turned to the back seat with the biggest smile on her face said, "We're home, my two babies." Seeing her face and her huge smile seemed to ease all of the reservations that were running through my head. When she reached back, wiped my eyes, patted my leg, winked, and whispered, "You got this," I began to believe that everything was somehow going to be alright. By the time she'd helped me and Samael into the house, even though I was still a little frightened, I was also ready for whatever challenges that may have lay ahead.

It didn't take long for me to get into the routine of taking care of Samael. He moved like clockwork most of the time, which was helpful to me because it enabled me to plan naps sometimes. He was a good baby for the most part, but being a mom was hard. It always seemed like everything was never ending, like laundry, making bottles, cleaning bottles, changing diapers, feeding him. Auntie was always trying to give me a break, but I would decline her help. I wanted to do this on my own. She was quiet and observant, so she would step back and let me do me until one day she couldn't ignore what she was seeing.

"Zell?" she called ever so sweetly.

"Yes, Auntie," my tone dragged and my patience had become real thin. I wasn't even sure why I was mad most of the time.

"Come with me to the porch while lil' Sam is sleeping."

Without a word, I dropped the dishes I was elbow deep in and walked out behind her. When I got to the door, she was already sitting on the top step looking back at me. Patting the spot next to her, she told me to sit. Her tone had changed from ever so sweet to firm and demanding. So, I did as I was told. I may have had an attitude, but I wasn't crazy.'

"Yes, Auntie?"

"What has been going on with you lately?"

"What are you talking about?"

"Let's start with something small like how you have been responding to me this last week?"

"I don't know what you mean, Ma'am."

"Ok, fine! Let's try something you know for sure, when is the last time you ate something?"

"I... uh... uh... I stumbled over my words, unable to recall the last time I'd eaten. "I'm sure I had a little something this morning."

"I don't think I've seen you eat anything solid in days."

Why Would I Love You?

"You leave the house to go to work, so how would you be able to track every morsel I consume?" I felt the last word burn my lip as it left my mouth. That was the attitude she was talking about and it was written all over her face from those raised eyebrows and her tilted head.

"Excuse me?" she looked at me as if I had crossed a line that I'd better uncross as soon as possible.

"I just meant that I eat, just not at regular times."

"Mmm, hmm," she hummed as she looked at me as if she didn't believe me. "Well, I've noticed a lot more than just that, and because I'm not a doctor I'd like for you to make an appointment with your primary. Soon," she said it in a way that let me know that there was no room for negotiations.

With a huff and a puff, I spoke through gritted teeth. "Yes, Ma'am."

The porch grew deathly silent when, as if right on cue, Samael began to cry from the living room. Immediately, I hopped up and ran to tend to him. As I went through the motions of taking care of him, it seemed like nothing I did would calm him down. I changed his diaper, he still cried. I gave him a small bottle and he spit it out. I even put him in the bouncer, and nothing was working. I felt myself becoming so overwhelmed, like the roof was caving in on me in slow motion. I just wanted to run away, but my feet wouldn't move.

Not knowing what else to try, I stood in the middle of the room and it felt like my head was spinning. I felt my cheeks getting hot and my shoulders feeling heavy. I wasn't sure what was happening, it was like my body was back on auto-pilot. I sat down, threw my face in my hands and began to sob right along with Samael. The waterworks wouldn't stop flowing. I couldn't hold it. I don't know what came over me, all I knew was it wouldn't stop. Auntie was upstairs when she heard and came rushing down when my sobs turned into uncontrollable cries that turned into a shriek.

"What's going on?" She came to my side and wrapped her arms around me. I was so overwrought, overworked, and overwhelmed that I couldn't even respond. I just put my head on her shoulder and kept crying. She rubbed my back and whispered in my ear repeatedly, "It's ok, baby, just let it out," while keeping an eye on both me and the baby the entire time.

It took me a while to finally compose myself, but when I did, Aunt Lori finally released her loving hold on me and went to tend to the baby. I was so depleted that all I could manage to do was curl up into a ball on the couch and eventually fall asleep.

Because my meltdown was a clear indication that I was on a downward spiral, Aunt Lori took some time off of work. A week later, she took me to see my primary care physician and I was diagnosed with severe postpartum depression. It turns out that I had lost almost thirty pounds in a matter of weeks due to my lack of appetite. Worst of all, I didn't want to even touch my baby. It was like the more he began to develop, the more he looked like my dad. He became a constant reminder of what my father had done to me and what he had left me with. I hated myself for feeling that way, but I hated my three month old son even more because of what he stood for in my mind.

Auntie signed Samael up for daycare as soon as she could and would never leave him alone with me. It got so bad that any room he was in, I would make sure not to go in or I would avert my eyes away from him and walk the fuck out. I knew I seemed like a piece a shit, but I couldn't help it. Anytime I caught a glimpse of his face, all I saw was Leon and seeing his face always ended with me having a panic attack.

One night I was sitting outside on the porch, Aunt Lori had just finished putting Sam down for the night, and she came out to join me on the steps.

"Uggh, these old bones!" she said as she took a seat.

"Hi, Auntie," I spoke quietly.

Why Would I Love You?

"Hey, Zell, baby. How are you feeling today?"

"You ask me that every day, and I don't know is always my answer."

"I know, but I still wanna make sure I ask because even though Sam's safety is a priority, your mental health is important too."

"I know, and I am so thankful to have you here to help me while I'm broken."

"Oh, Zell, baby, you're not broken. You're hurt and you have every right to be."

"Auntie, my son is almost six months old and I can't even look at his face without breaking down into tears and a cold sweat."

"You still haven't told me, or anyone for that matter, why that is," she said and made me realize that she was speaking the truth.

It had been three months since I had so much as been in the same room as Sam, and this lady hadn't questioned me or pushed for me to give her an explanation as to why I had left her to take over being his mom. I looked my aunt in the eye, took a deep breath, and before I even said a word, I felt the tears begin to slowly build.

"I know, and I am so grateful for your patience. Honestly," I began to finally let her in on my truth, "every time I look at him, all I see is L... Leon." There, I finally said it out loud. "And then all the things he said to me and did to me plays back in my head and I start to freak out." She reached out and hugged me.

"Oh, my Zella baby. I'm so sorry you felt like you had to fight that all alone. And I know I've been so into getting Sam settled that I hadn't given you as much attention as you needed."

"It's not like I was letting you in, Auntie," I couldn't allow her to shoulder that blame alone. "You're amazing."

"I am, aren't I?" she let out a giggle. "How about this, when you're ready, I want you to make sure you also acknowledge the parts that have nothing to do with Leon. Focus on all the parts of us that Little Sam has, like my nose and your smile. And I want you to try looking at things this way," she said as she looked me in the eyes, "it's not Leon that you see, it is our family you're actually looking at. Your grandmother's lips and your own mother's eyes. He is not a curse, baby, he's a blessing just like you."

"Really?" I was surprised as I smiled at her, "he has my mom's eyes?"

"He absolutely does."

You would think that after a heart to heart like that, things would just jump back in line and my perspective would change, but it didn't. I honestly think it got worse.

My doctor said that the way I was feeling was normal with some new moms, but it was still unnatural to me. How could I treat my own son like he had the plague? It was like walking alone in a fog while trying to find my emotion for just one person. As time went by, I began locking myself in my room and didn't eat for days. The only time I emerged was when I needed to pee, and that I would hold off until the very last minute. I was so determined to stay away from everyone that I would walk to my bedroom door, hold my ear to the door, and wait to make sure I heard nothing before I stepped outside of my room. I didn't want to open the door and run into anyone.

In my bedroom, I kept the lights off and the curtains drawn so that when I did finally come out, the light that hit my eyes was damn near blinding. Then I would tiptoe to the bathroom and slowly close the door so as not to alert anyone that I was out of my room. However, as luck would have it, just before the bathroom door was fully closed, there would be a loud *creeeeak!* Damn! I had done a good job of avoiding Auntie and Samael, I didn't answer any of her knocks, didn't answer my phone if she called it, and she hadn't seen my face since that heart to heart. I was successfully staying away from them and anything that had to do with Samael, but after about a week, Aunt Lori had had enough and was on high alert.

Why Would I Love You?

"So, why are you avoiding me?" is what she said when I opened the bathroom door. She scared the hell out of me when I saw her standing there looking like a stealthy ninja waiting for his target to be in the right place.

"Uh, I'm not avoiding you," I lied. She just cocked her head to the side and gave me the look that only an old soul who 'don't play that' could give. "Ok, ok. I *was* avoiding you, but I don't know why."

"I think I have an idea why," she said as she kept those ninja eyes on me. "It might have to do with me attempting to get you back to bonding with Sammy."

I let out a deep sigh and shook my head. "It's not that I don't want to bond with him, or that I don't love him." I let tears fall down my face as I stood there for a moment lost for words. "I just, I just... I just don't know what to do."

"I know it's hard, baby," she cajoled as she let me cry, while she stepped closer and hugged me. In my quest for solitude, I had denied myself the relationship with her that I had come to love. I really missed talking to Aunt Lori, she was like my best friend. Truth be told she was my only friend. "Zell," she went on when we released the hug and stepped back a little, "you are not alone in this. Even though I have never gone through what you are going through, I imagine it can't be easy and I'm here for you."

"It's *not* easy, Auntie" I admitted, fear and frustration running through me. "And I don't know how to control how I'm feeling."

"Then I'll work with you, baby," she did her best to assure me. We can do the exercises the doctor showed you together." I looked at her, the expression on my face blank enough that she couldn't read it. "I'm here to help you, Zell," she reached out, laid a hand on my shoulder, tried connecting with me in some way. "You don't have to fight this battle by yourself. You're not in this by yourself, so you don't have to avoid me. Okay?"

I shook my head up and down as I kept wiping the snot and tears from my face. I was willing to work with her, I was willing to try the techniques the doctor had given me. However, I still wasn't sure if I was ready to be a mother to a child that looked just like my abuser, my tormenter, my father.

It had been weeks and both Auntie and I were finally making a breakthrough. I followed the exercises the doctor had given me, and slowly I was reintroduced to my son. Being around him wasn't the same as it had been before, but I didn't freak out whenever I was in the room with him. I was trying, really trying. Auntie and I worked on breathing exercises and even started yoga, I was finally evening out.

After giving birth to Sam, I took a maternity break from school and never went back. For the first time in a long time I mentioned going back to school. Auntie was so happy and couldn't stop telling me how proud she was of me.

As the months went by, I began to take on more responsibility with Samael but there was still something that kept me from getting emotionally involved with him. He was now about to turn one and I was still very detached. I performed my motherly duties with him, cared for him and his safety, but I was not cuddly and kissy with him like Aunt Lori was. My lack of attachment with him showed in his behavior toward me. He would freely run to Auntie, cuddle with her and call her Ma while I would only be around to assist like I was a nanny or the hired help. As bad as I knew it was, I was honestly ok with that.

As a family, we had fallen into a routine that worked well for all of us. To outsiders, I'm sure it seemed really weird but I didn't care because we were all content. I would've loved to say that we were all happy, but there was always this black cloud looming over my head that kept me from experiencing that complete joy that should have come

Why Would I Love You?

with motherhood. I had become great at putting on a smiley face when necessary, I was a mastermind at hiding my true feelings.

    I had finally changed my mind about being out of school, had gone back, and found that it was great to be back to some sort of normal. I didn't want to go into the young mother's program even though the girls that were there before were long gone. I just chose not to associate my full school day with being a mom. I was going to a place that allowed me to take regular high school classes half day and take up a trade the other half. I decided to go for my CNA. There was a daycare on site, so I was able to continue relieving some of my responsibilities from Aunt Lori by taking Samael with me and putting him in the school daycare program.

    Things were finally on track. I was adjusting to taking care of Sam and not feeling like my connection with him needed to be rushed. He was two at this point and his development was moving along well. That was one of my fears for him. It was great to see that he wasn't affected in any way. I was also doing great in school. The year was half over, and I was getting damn near straight A's. Grades were never a problem for me if and when I applied myself.

    I had also made a friend or two, but never got too close because I didn't want to ever feel the loss like I felt with my best friend Jazz. One day, I was walking down the hall with them toward class. I'll never forget, it was a Monday and I had just finished a major Algebra exam when the program counselor came running down the hall yelling for me. I told them I would catch up with them and walked toward the counselor. At the time, I chuckled in my mind because the counselor's name was Mr. Sacc and he was a hefty guy. The way he came bounding down the hall with his jowls jiggling back and forth like a set of balls hanging from his chin made me think that his name was fitting.

    When he reached me, he put up a finger, signaling that he needed a minute to catch his breath.

"Ms. Grife, I need you to come with me to the office."

"Can it wait, Mr. Sacc? I am on my way to my trade"

"I'm afraid not." He had finally caught his breath and with that came a look of seriousness that made me follow him without another word. Once we got into his office, he closed the door behind him and began to fill me in. "Ms. Grife, we received a call from the hospital that your Aunt had been rushed in with some type of complications. You are her only family listed so they called us. We've arranged a ride for you to go and be with her."

I sat there listening in total shock. This couldn't be happening, not again. All of the worst case scenarios I could think of began running rampant through my mind as I began to shake my leg and let tears fall from my eyes.

"...O'Zella?" Mr. Sacc's voice jolted me out of my thoughts. "Did you hear me?"

"Yes, Mr. Sacc. I'll go get Sam from the daycare and I'll be ready in fifteen minutes."

"Ok, just come back here and we will have a ride for you."

"Thank you," I said as my whole body and my entire mind went numb.

Twenty

Quickly, I piled out of the car with Samael, his stroller, and both our bags. I did a juggling act with everything until we got through the first set of sliding glass doors. I strapped Samael in his stroller and handed him a toy that would keep him preoccupied until I found Auntie. Once I got myself situated, I made my way to the information desk.

"Hello, how can I help you?"

"I'm looking for Lori Grife. She came in by ambulance."

"Hold on one moment, let me check." I stared a hole in that lady's forehead the entire time she was trying to locate my aunt. She was on her computer just clicking away and my nerves were becoming worse and worse by the second. Then, as if she wasn't moving slowly enough, she picked up the phone and repeated my aunt's name about four times before hanging up and going back to clicking. I was just about to click her if she didn't come up with some damn answers when she said, "Ok, Ms. Grife is on the third floor by the green elevators. When you step off, make your way straight down the hall, make a right, and the unit is straight ahead of you."

"Ok, thank you," I said politely but I really wanted to whip her slow ass.

Moving as quickly as I could with all of the baggage I was carrying, I followed the signs all the way to the green elevators. The ride up the elevator was eerily quiet and had me going mildly insane. I took a glance down at Sam and he was just as content as could be with his toy and his sippy cup. *Ding*! The doors of the elevator opened and everything turned into a movie scene. The hallway became a mile long and my feet felt like I had cement shoes on. I actually had to stand still and breathe so that I could get myself together. After the fear wore off a little, I made my way down the hallway and to the right where I pushed an intercom button.

Scchhhhk, came the inevitable static just before I heard, "Yes, can I help you?"

"I'm here for Lori Grife."

"Yes, come in," the voice was entirely too pleasant for the anxiety I was feeling.

After a moment, there was a beep and some clicks before the door automatically swung open. As swiftly as I could, I walked to the desk and was greeted with a friendly face. The fact that she wasn't looking at me with pity or sorrow put me at ease a little. I assumed that maybe I had been thinking the worst when it really wasn't that serious.

"If you and your little one will have a seat in the family room for a little while someone will come and get you."

"Why can't I see her now?" I wanted to know.

"She just got up here. We have to get her over to her bed and make sure she is all set before having visitors."

"This all seems a little crazy, but ok. How long do you think it will be? Actually, can you tell me what is going on and why she is here in the first place?"

"Ma'am, can I ask your name?"

"O"Zella Grife, I'm her niece and family contact."

"Oh, yes, we were expecting you, Ms. Grife. I'm going to have a doctor come speak with you in the consult room."

"Why? What's wrong?"

"I'm sorry, I can't fully say. But if you follow me, the doctor will be in shortly."

Why Would I Love You?

I was pissed, but I sucked my teeth and followed behind her. Being led into the room felt like I was heading to impending doom. My anxiety was at an all-time high and honestly, I was scared to death of whatever news the doctor would be delivering. I sat in that little blank room with my leg bouncing a mile a minute, keeping tempo with the beat of my heart. Next to me was Samael, just as content and low maintenance as ever.

Tap, tap, tap, I heard and whipped my head in the direction of the sound.

"Hello?" It was a male voice that called out before opening the door. He was tall with salt and pepper hair. When he greeted me, he didn't give me a big friendly smile like everything was gonna be ok. Instead, he gave me a half smile and a don't get your hopes up eyebrow raise. Well at least that is how I read it.

"Hello, Ms. Grife."

"Hello."

"Ok. It says here that Lori Grife is your Aunt?"

"Yes."

"She was at work and had a stroke," he just blurted the words out like they were nothing, like they wouldn't hit me hard and shatter my whole world. And then he kept on talking as if he was discussing a recipe for Cotton Candy. "She is currently in stable condition, but there is no telling how long. I am so sorry to have to deliver this news, but because you are her next of kin, you will have to make medical decisions for her until she becomes responsive."

"Responsive?" I said as I tried to maintain a hold on my sanity. "You mean *if* she becomes responsive?"

"Yes," he said and continued delivering blow after blow to my psyche.

I sat there quietly, listening to that man tell me that every bad thing I'd thought was actually true. I felt it in my soul, felt the pain and the shock all the way down in my bones. I knew in my heart that the bad shit was happening again because I was too happy. That was the story of my fucking life. As soon as I found someone who loved me and I was happy, boom! Just like that it was all taken away from me. I swore I was cursed, but the truth of the matter was that I just was an unlucky mothafucka!

I won't drag it out. My Aunt was in the hospital for all three days without once regaining her consciousness before she went into cardiac arrest and the staff was unable to resuscitate her. I was at the hospital when it happened, but Samael was at daycare. After they were unable to revive her, they let me come back in and say goodbye. I wanted to go in and feel her spirit's hand on my shoulder giving me this wave, a feeling telling me that everything was going to be ok while a low soothing song played in the background. Unfortunately, none of that happened in real life. Instead there was a chill in the air, the sounds that could be heard were the beeps and clicking from the machines that were once hooked up to her now lifeless body. I stood over her and watched as her chest didn't rise or fall. She simply looked like she was sleeping.

I sat there for almost an hour in the loud silence of uncertainty, looking at her still body, waiting for her to say something. Her voice never came, her smile never came, her comforting hug never came. And whatever the color was on the walls of that room became my least favorite color. The brightness from the monitor started to burn my eyes. I wouldn't wish that feeling on my worst enemy, hell, at that point I wouldn't have wished anything about my life on my worst enemy. In complete silence, I walked out of the front doors of the hospital and felt like all sense of direction had escaped me.

What am I gonna do? Where the fuck do I go from here? Shit, I'm not working, how am I going to pay these damn bills? Those thoughts overwhelmed me, as well as the loss of my aunt and the unknowns that I knew were to come. Unable to take it anymore, I fell to my knees and started to cry like I had never cried before. I felt like I had just lost my mother all over again, but this time I was well aware of what was happening and I knew that Auntie Lori wasn't coming back.

A few people had gathered at first because they thought I was hurt. Everybody wanted to be a good Samaritan. When they realized I was ok, a security guard helped me to my feet and got me to the nearest bench. Another guard rushed over with some water. I had muffled my sobs enough to say, "I'm ok!" However, the guard that helped me up didn't believe me, so he sat with me and gave me silent company until I pulled myself together.

"Fuck!" I whispered under my breath.

I hadn't given much thought to it while everything was happening, but now that my mind was beginning to process everything, I realized that Aunt Lori hadn't just left me, she'd also left Samael. She'd left me by myself with Samael. For a split second, I contemplated running and leaving him to the state, but then I remembered how that felt and even though I had no deep connection with him, I wouldn't dare leave him to be a ward of the state. Again, I wouldn't wish my life on my own worst enemy. So, I decided then and there to suck it up and made my way back to school to gather my things and my kid. I wasn't going back for a while, at least not until I figured out how I was going to get by in life without her.

The bus ride home with Samael was an awful one. I kinda resented him. He just sat next to me without a care in the world while I spent every moment of the forty five minute ride holding back my tears. Honestly, I had already cried so much that I was damn near out of tears by that point. In my mind, I did the worst thing I could possibly do, I decided to recap my life. I'd lost my mom and cried. I was first touched by Mr. Bill and I cried. Then I'd promised myself never to cry again until Tyler touched me and I cried, and then I'd lost Ms. Linda and the only mother figure I'd had until that point. Then there was Jazz and all of the crying that came with losing her.

However, the icing on the cake was Leon, just Leon because I could never even refer to that mothafucka as my dad, my father, or my sperm donor. He was none of the above, he was just punk ass Leon. After I'd cried because of him and his cruelty, I'd finally gotten rid of him and was able to sit back and think, *'Ok, Zell you done made it through all of that and now Aunt Lori's got ya back!'* Wrong! She got taken away from me too. It was just another hard ass pill for me to swallow.

Walking into the house didn't give me the light loving feeling it usually did, and I was fighting to hold it together as I put our stuff away. As I was heading to the kitchen to make Sam something to eat, all I heard were his little feet running past me and his voice yelling, "Momma!" in his playful sing song tone.

A wave of anger flowed through me and before I could stop myself, I grabbed Samael by his arm mid stride, and yoked him up. His little body dangled there in shock as I held him by his wrist. I started shaking him and screaming, "Shut up! She's gone!" Then I threw him in his playpen and walked off. It all happened in less than twenty seconds, but I'm sure to him it felt longer. Unable to take it anymore, I sat in a corner on the kitchen floor crying my eyes out. I didn't know what I was going to do and I definitely didn't know how to take care of this boy by myself. Hell, I didn't know how to take care of my damn self by myself.

Even in death, Auntie Lori was looking out for me. I had gotten a letter in the mail about three days after she'd passed. It was from a lawyer telling me that she had a life insurance policy and a last will and testament. When I met with him, he broke everything down. She'd left me all of the money she had in savings as well as a twenty-thousand dollar life insurance policy. After following her burial wishes, I was left with a little over ten-thousand of those dollars.

When I first saw numbers like that I thought, *Oh, I'm good for a minute unless I shit all the money away doing dumb shit.* Well, that was partially true. It took a few months for me to get the check from the insurance company. While I waited and stressed, I was able to get a part-time job and what I brought in from that went out for a babysitter and keeping food in the house. Auntie's death damn sure didn't stop the bill collectors from coming. I used the savings she left me to pay for the next month's bills, but when the following month came, nobody cared that I was still learning how to be an adult or that the money was on its way. By the third month, I was getting letters and calls from cable, electricity, water, and especially the landlord. By the end of the third month, Sam and I had been evicted. I still had to pay the back rent, and I couldn't find anyone who would let me get an apartment with no money down.

    The following months came with a real learning curve. Being alone with Sam was like living with a dependent, noisy stranger. I never neglected him, but he did spend a lot of time in his playpen or in his crib. I wasn't into hugging and kissing him. I don't think I even told him I loved him. I did, however, get very creative though. When he would cry or reach for me, I would figure out how to satisfy him without even holding him. On top of all of that, I had to figure out how to be an adult. I'd never had to worry about bills or how they got paid. I'd just settled back into high school after taking that long break, but when the past due and final notices came, I knew I had to figure something out or I was gonna be on the streets.

    This wasn't like when me and Jazz were running the streets. It wasn't easy to go out without dragging Sam with me, and that was a lot when he yelled, ran, and cried everywhere. Ok, maybe not everywhere, but his ass usually yelled when I needed him to be quiet. Needless to say, I wasn't able to get out and do shit. We were good for the first month because Aunt Lori left a decent savings, and her burial was fully paid for by insurance. When all the money was gone, I did what I could by tapping into my inner hustler and selling whatever I thought had some type of value around the house. Ebay became my best friend when it came to paying off a bill or two even if it was late, but in the end the landlord didn't care. Eventually I ran out of stuff and the money just wasn't there.

I remember it like it was yesterday, walking behind the sheriff while he dragged all our shit out onto the porch. "Please, I just need another week or two to get the money together," I pleaded with him.

"I'm sorry, Ma'am, but that's not up to me."

"You the one movin' my shit to the curb, what you mean? Just put it down!"

"Ma'am, I'm just doing my job."

"Well, your job sucks because you are putting me and a little boy on the street!" I spoke angrily. The whole time I was trying to convince those people to let me stay in the house, Samael was just as quiet and content with a stick on the side of the porch. I looked back at him for some sympathy assistance and he was no help.

"I'm sorry, Ma'am!" the sheriff said again, "but we're done here. So, if there is anything of value that you want to get out, we will give you a few minutes."

I was so defeated after staring him down for a minute and he still didn't change his mind that I finally walked back in the house looking for anything that I may have wanted to hold on to. I went to Auntie's room and got her favorite picture of us from vacation and left the rest. No clothes, no pictures, nothing. Walking out of that room had me feeling like I was nine years old again and in my old house getting the last of my belongings before saying goodbye to all the memories my mom and I ever had. There I was again saying bye to another woman in my life, not knowing what was ahead of me and it was scary. I looked back one more time as I got to the porch and watched the Marshall board up to the door. I was on my own again.

Nine months had come and gone with me trying. That was all I could do besides being a statistic. After the marshals locked the doors, Samael and I sat on the porch. I really wasn't sure what to do. We were homeless, so that night I found a women's shelter and they admitted us. It was strange how much nicer people were to me when I had a kid with me while I was begging them for help. That actually helped me find my way around the social service system quickly. It only took me six months to get on my feet. I got a place of my own, Sam was in daycare and I finally got into a program to get my GED.

Life was not the greatest because even though I had my own place, it was a small one bedroom. However, I didn't have to share it with a bunch of other catty, ratchet bitches like I did in the shelter. I was so determined to make something of myself that I finished my GED prep and passed it in three months. Then I decided that I wasn't just going to be another statistic like I heard people say under their breath when they thought I couldn't hear them. So, I signed up for the nursing program that started at the end of summer and I made it up in my mind that nothing was going to stop me from finishing.

My first day was like a dream, I functioned off of routine for the most part. I would drop Sam off to his daycare provider and then take the city bus across town. I would get off a stop early so I could stop by the corner store and get a coffee and some snacks before class. That was my routine. I would keep my head down, focus on work and then go home. As long as I was in school, the rent and daycare was paid and I was given food stamps, so there was always food in the house. I was working the system and getting ahead of the game.

At home, everything was normal, but that wasn't a real normal. Samael was three and half years old and smarter than your average three year old. On some days he would just go on about his business, reading and playing with his toys. I would call him for meals and make sure he was bathed. It was just motions with very little emotion. He was still a happy kid nonetheless.

I found myself looking at him from time to time and seeing Aunt Lori in the bridge of his nose and my mama, what little I could remember of her, in the corner of his eyes. In those moments, I would smile, but only for a moment. Then he would look up at me and I would see Leon in his eyebrows and his wrinkled forehead and just that quick the moment was over. It happened like that a lot. His face made it hard for my heart to soften and fully accept him as my son instead of Leon's.

In between those moments, I continued my routine. Every day I would get us both dressed, feed him, walk up the street to the daycare and drop him off. Then I'd hop on the bus and ride it across town. Most days I would have my book out, doing some last minute studying for a test. There was always a test in my class. I would make it through the day, pick Samael up, and go home just to get ready to do it all again tomorrow.

One night while we were finishing up dinner, Samael looked up from his plate with Leon's wrinkled forehead and asked me, "Zell? How come you never hug me?" The question took me by surprise, and I was curious as to where it had come from. So, I kept looking at my plate as I probed him for a reason.

"What do you mean, Sam?"

"When Andrew mom pick him up, she hug him and she spin him and her kiss him. How come you don't hug me?" he asked, his eyes boring into me as he waited for an answer.

I almost felt bad, but then I looked up from my plate and saw that forehead and that was enough to ice my tongue over for my response. "Because I just don't want to hug you, Sam." With that, I stood up and walked away from my innocent not quite four year old.

I dropped onto my bed when I made it to the back room and I fought the urge to cry. Then I started to think of why I would be crying. Maybe for the first time since Aunt Lori died it was being brought to my attention that I was still physically distancing myself from him even though I had convinced myself that I was doing a great of job hiding it. I was a mixed bag of emotions because I cared for Sam, but there was always that underlying disgust that made me keep him at arm's length.

Why Would I Love You?

He was so young, but the trauma of his features erased any fucks I could give about his age.

I lay in my bed waiting for him to finish eating. When he did, he came into the room, got in his toddler bed, and went to sleep without a word. From the outside looking in, one could say that my lack of emotion was going to lead him to a lack of emotion and that essentially, I was raising a serial killer. I wouldn't have been able to disagree with them even if I tried.

Twenty-One

The next day we were back into our same routine. It was like the previous night had never happened and I was thankful for that. I hopped off the bus and made my way to the store to get my usual snacks and head to class. As I walked in the little corner store, it was mad empty, so I went on a scavenger hunt for a Kit Kat because I had been wanting one for a minute.

"Excuse me, Miss," I heard someone say, but I didn't talk to people so I didn't even bother looking. "Excuse me, Miss," the voice got louder. I jumped and turned around as I felt a hand touch my shoulder.

"Oh, I'm sorry, I didn't mean to frighten you."

"Well, you did!" I said, grabbing my chest in shock.

"I just…" he took a deep breath. "I see you every day, and you are so beautiful I just had to know your name."

I was not the one and I didn't even have the energy to go off on him. I was not in the market looking for another man to abuse me, so I turned, grabbed my kit-kat off the bottom shelf and excused myself as I walked past him. I headed to the register with a couple of items and placed them on the counter. That's when I heard his footsteps behind me, but I was determined to ignore him.

"My name is Delroy and I hope to know your name one day," he said as he dropped a five on the counter to pay for my things and then left. I scoffed at the gesture. Like who the fuck did he think he was paying for my shit like I couldn't pay for it?

Why Would I Love You?

After leaving the store, of course I headed to class, but for most of the day I was distracted with thoughts of Delroy. I had to admit that he was handsome with smooth skin and one dimple that showed when he flashed his pearly white smile. His six foot something frame was thick and muscular. He wasn't dressed like a street dude, and even though I was rude as hell, he'd still been respectful. I began to realize that I'd never noticed him in the store before, but then again, I didn't notice anyone. I just kept to myself and stayed in my own world. Seeing that I was completely unfocused on my class work, I actually had to shake the daydreaming out of my head and focus because we were learning new material that day.

The next day I went to the store again as it was a part of my routine, and when I went to the back to get my snacks, there he was at the cooler. He noticed me and gave me a wave. I quickly looked away, grabbed my Kit Kat, and made my way to the counter where I threw my money down and quickly left. This time I'd paid attention to how handsome he really was with his clean cut and low beard, but I still wasn't trying to get to know him. However, it was nice to have someone tell me they saw me but wasn't being pushy or disrespectful about it. Either way, I wasn't interested so that was that.

I would see him all the time after that and all he would do was say, "Good morning, Kit Kat," and keep it pushing.

I'd done such a good job at keeping my distance from him and then one day we ran into each other at the door on the way in. He grabbed it, opened it, and stepped to the side.

"After you," he said and allowed me to walk in first.

All I could think about was how good he smelled when I said, "Thank you."

"You're welcome, Kit Kat."

"Why do you call me that?"

"Because you never gave me your name."

"Ok, but why do you call me Kit Kat?"

"When I finally got the nerve to talk to you, you were picking up a Kit Kat."

"Zell," I finally told him my name, and after I did, I quickly grabbed my stuff and hustled out of the store.

"Aye, Zell, wait up," I heard him calling after me. Even though I didn't slow my stride, he still caught up with me and walked next to me. I could smell his cologne. "Zell?"

"Yes?"

"Will you let me take you on a date?"

I stopped and finally looked at him. His smile was captivating. "No, I can't do that."

"I respect that. I'll see you tomorrow, Zell." I didn' say anything, just turned and walked away.

I didn't know what his motives were, and I didn't want to find out. Honestly, if I learned anything in my few years on earth, it was that people were disappointing. So, if I had to, I was going to shut him down all together because he was causing me some major anxiety. Not because I thought he was a danger to me or anything like that, but because he was the first guy I had actually looked at like I had an interest in him. Whatever this feeling was that he was giving me, I didn't fucking like it at all.

I headed home that day thinking about this man and the fact that he'd asked me out on a date. However, those thoughts were brought to a screeching halt when I showed up to get Sam from daycare and the director of the center asked to speak to me before I picked him up. With curiosity filling my head, I followed her, watching as her heels clicked down the hall. I didn't like the feel of her fake smile, but I was an adult so I had to face whatever conversation she wanted to have. All I could do was hope this conversation didn't take long.

"Please grab a chair, this won't take long," she said as she closed the door and took a seat on the other side of her small desk.

"Can I ask what this is about?"

Why Would I Love You?

"Today while playing at free play, Samael began to cry in the play house area. It took us quite a while to calm him and when we asked what was wrong, he wouldn't answer. We did a physical check, and he had no injuries. So, I just wanted to have a talk with you to see if there were any changes or issues at home that we should be aware of." I watched her mouth move and couldn't give her an honest answer other than he was probably upset that I didn't want to hug him. But I wasn't going to tell that bitch that, I had to come up with something quick to appease her.

"Well, he hasn't shown any signs at home, but it is coming up on the one year anniversary of his great Aunt Lori's passing and they were close. He did ask about her because I put a picture of her up that I recently had printed."

"Oh, I am so sorry to hear that," she spoke sympathetically. "I'm sure that is a hard thing for someone his age to talk about with everyone."

"Yeah, we had a talk about her being in Heaven, but he didn't seem to grasp the full concept of her not coming back."

"Well, that does make sense," she said as she pondered on my words. Then, "If there is anything we can do for you, please let us know. We do have some resources for some highly recommended children's counselors."

"I appreciate that," I replied noncommittally. "I'll most definitely let you know if I see anything that makes me feel like he may need that. Thank you!"

"Absolutely!"

"Can I get Sam now?"

"Sure, and thank you for taking time to talk with me about this. Again, I am truly sorry for your loss."

"Thanks," I replied, glad the conversation was over.

I knew the lady was only trying to help, but the mention of a children's counselor made my skin crawl. I was being raped repeatedly at home while I met with a counselor weekly. So she had to forgive me if I didn't exactly jump at the mention of her resources. And even though I didn't say anything about the abuse to my counselor, I still didn't trust the fact that she wasn't able to figure it out.

Once I got to the room that my son was in, I put on a face that said I was a loving supportive mother, even though Samael and I both knew that I was anything but. I was his caretaker and his provider. That's it.

"Sammy, your mom is here."

I put on a joker smile and reached out my arms to him. The way his face brightened up as he ran to me made me feel so bad because although he was ecstatic to receive a hug for me, my heart was not in that hug at all. I just knew why he was crying and knew that I needed to make it better so those people would stay off my back about his meltdown. When Samael reached me, he eagerly jumped into my arms and I did everything he said Andrew's mommy did. I did the spin, the hug, and even the funky ass kiss on the cheek. I even walked out with him on my hip until we got outside.

"OOO, Sam," I said once we got outside, "you are so heavy. You're a big boy so you gotta walk for me, ok?"

"Ok, Zell," he spoke happily. Whenever he and I were walking, I would always have him walk in front of me so that I could see him, but that day he did something different. Instead of walking ahead of me, he grabbed my hand and walked next to me. As we were walking, he whispered under his breath, "I love you, Zell." I heard him, he was clear as day, but I just couldn't bring myself to respond. I just squeezed his hand, looked down at him, gave him a smile and continued on our way.

That night while I was giving him a bath, Sam, with his little boat in his hand, spoke in a casual voice, "Zell?"

"Yes, Sam."

"Thank you for hugging me like Andrew's mommy."

"Is that why you were crying in class today?"

"Yes, but I won't do it again."

"Hmm."

"Are you mad at me?"

"No, Sam. I just wish you understood that I care about you."

"I know."

"How do you know?"

"'Cause you give me baths with toys, I have lots of toys, and you make my favorite food. You don't yell at me like Sarah's mommy yells at her."

"Oh, ok," I spoke as I completed the process of bathing him. "Well, it's time to get out of the tub. You ready?"

"Yes."

Somehow the conversation with my toddler made me feel better about my parenting. So even though I still distanced myself from him, picking him up from daycare with the works made him happy and made my life a little less stressful about all the questions from him and his daycare.

It was about a week after the daycare incident, and everything was running smoothly. To avoid Delroy and the situation he was putting me in, I'd decided to start going to the corner store near my house and then taking the bus straight to the school. The less I saw of him, the better. I had a great routine going on and my grades were stellar, the last thing I wanted was any distractions that could mess that up.

Two more weeks had gone by and I was on my way to school, sitting in the back of the bus with my nose buried in my book as usual. The bus had made the stop close to my old favorite corner store and I looked up. In fact, every time I passed by that store, I would look just to catch a glimpse of Delroy, but he was never anywhere in sight. On this particular day, I saw him and by chance he looked up and saw me as well. There were thousands of pounds of steel, double paned windows, and at least thirty feet between us. That knowledge is what gave me the confidence to not look away until the bus had driven far enough away for him to be out of sight. Even though we had been nowhere near one another, I could smell his cologne and that made my heart flutter.

The next day, I made sure that I had a spot by the window in anticipation of seeing him again, but he wasn't there. I was kind of disappointed, but I figured there was always tomorrow. Putting Delroy in the back of my mind and school in the front where it belonged, I began packing up my books and papers because my stop was coming up next. When it did, I headed out of the crowded bus with all of the other students that attended the school. I was making my way up the sidewalk when all of a sudden a voice stopped me dead in my tracks.

"Kit Kat?" Slowly, I turned to see Delroy and had to fight to keep my jaw from dropping. The man was wearing a light blue button up with the top two buttons undone, navy blue slacks that hugged him just right, some white dress shoes, and in his hand was the most colorful bouquet of flowers. I could feel my heart pounding through my chest and even though I kept my face stone wall blank, on the inside I was smiling big enough for it to have covered my face.

"What are you doing here and why are you still calling me Kit Kat?" I snapped.

"Well, hi," he responded, not even slightly bothered by my attitude, "nice to see you too."

"What?"

"I don't buy this act."

"What act?"

"This mean girl act you put on," he told me. "But either way, I can't get you out of my mind. And I thought I would never see you again until I saw your precious face yesterday."

"So, you followed me?"

"Yes, but I only did it because you were avoiding me."

"No, I wasn't."

"Well, it doesn't matter now because I found you."

"So?"

"Go on a date with me. Just one and I promise I will never ask again!"

I looked at him, took a deep breath and acted as if I was annoyed. "Fine!"

"Do you like Jamaican food?"

"I guess, I've never really had much more than curry chicken," I admitted.

"Hmm, well can I show you more than curry?" he bragged.

"I guess," I hunched my shoulders.

"Great, how about Friday? Six p.m.?"

"Make it seven. I'll text you my address."

"Ok, have a great day!" Then he handed me the flowers just as cool as a cucumber and flashed me his million dollar smile. That's when I caught a whiff of that cologne. "See you tomorrow at the store," he said as he gave me a wink and walked off.

The day dragged on as I tried to focus on the lesson. Everyone was preparing for our internship placements that were just a month away. While they were all talking to each other, I was at my table alone, daydreaming. What would our first date be like? What would we talk about? Would we even have anything in common? I would find out soon enough because our date was only two days away.

Friday finally came and I was a ball of nerves. Thankfully, I had a little nest egg of cash saved up, so I was able to pay for a babysitter. She came highly recommended from one of the teachers at the daycare, and she was right in my price range. I took Sam home, gave him a bath, and made him dinner. I put cartoons on and went to the bathroom to get ready for my date.

I stood looking at myself in the mirror, wondering what I could do to make myself look cute. My usual attire would be some loose jeans or sweatpants and an oversized t-shirt, however, that wasn't what I was planning for this occasion. I dipped in my cash stash and bought myself a cheap dress and matching sandals from a little shop downtown. I usually wore my sandy brown hair in a bun, but that night I blow dried it out and straightened it. I took my time going over every inch of myself, lotioning my skin, putting light makeup on, and even painting my nails. When I was done, I looked at myself in the mirror one last time, seeing a brand new woman. And for the first time in a long time I smiled because I wanted to be seen. Not just seen but seen as a woman.

When I finally came out of the bathroom, I stopped at the end of the hallway. I peeked in at Samael and saw that he sat playing with his toy truck and watching Spongebob. This was one of the sweet, stolen moments I remembered, but like with all good moments in my life, they were often followed with the bad. I still had thirty minutes remaining before the babysitter came, and another hour before Delroy was supposed to pick me up, so I sat down on the couch with Sam.

When he looked over at me, his eyes grew big like saucers. He was usually a pretty laid back kid, so big reactions from him meant he was surprised or passionate about what he was seeing.

"Zell, you look really nice," he spoke truthfully.

"Thank you, Sam."

"And I like your hair like that."

"Do you?"

"Mmhmm!"

"I think I like it too. In a little while, Brenda, the girl that volunteers at daycare, is going to watch you while I go out tonight."

"Yaay! I like her. She is nice to me and she tells me stories."

"Oh, she does?"

"Mmhmmm!"

"So, that means that you're gonna be good for her? Eat all your dinner, brush your teeth and go to bed when she tells you?" I questioned him.

"Yes." He replied. Then, "Zell?"

"Yes, Sam."

"How come I don't have a daddy?"

That question came like an unexpected punch to the chest. It knocked the breath out of my body. My smile fell from my face like a head rolling after the swift drop of a guillotine blade. I froze, not wanting to think about that subject much less talk about it.

Ding, Dong. I was literally saved by the bell.

"I think that's Brenda," I said as I jumped up and headed for the door like I was on fire, anything to get away from that unwanted conversation that Samael was trying to have.

As quickly as I could, I walked to the door, took a breath to calm myself, put on my Stepford Wife's smile, and opened the door. I had never been so happy to see somebody in my whole life. It took me about fifteen minutes or so to give Brenda the complete rundown of Sam's routine for the night. Then I used the excuse that I was going into my bedroom to put on some finishing touches, when in all reality, I was going to finish swallowing that hard pill Sam had served me. Once in there, I plopped down on the edge of the bed trying to catch my breath to stop a building panic attack. That's when I heard the doorbell ring.

Twenty- Two

Quickly, I pulled myself together, looking in the little mirror hanging on my bedroom wall. Then I sprayed myself with the one perfume I owned and headed up front. Delroy was stepping through the doorway just as I turned from the hallway.

"You look amazing," he gasped as I reached the door and met him with a coy smile.

"Thank you," I managed as he handed me another beautiful bouquet of flowers.

"Are you ready?"

"As ready as I'll ever be." I looked back and said goodnight to Brenda and Samael while handing the flowers to Brenda.

Once the door was closed and I heard Brenda click each of the locks, I was comfortable that they were safe for the night. I then turned to face Delroy, nervousness running through me. Outside of my fifteenth birthday with Leon, this was my first date. Ever. I had no idea what to expect or of how I was supposed to behave. Deciding that the only way I was going to relax was by going with the flow, I gave up any preconceived notions about dating I'd had and willed myself to just let Delroy lead unless or until he tried to lead me somewhere I didn't want to go.

The ride to the restaurant was mostly a quiet one until Delroy turned the radio on to kill the dead air. Even though neither he nor I were saying much, every once in a while, I would catch him looking over at me. That made me think that maybe he was just as nervous as I was and knowing that helped me to relax even more for the remainder of the ride.

It wasn't long before we pulled up to a place that was clearly proud of being Jamaican owned as there was a huge graffiti image of the Jamaican flag painted on the side of the building. Delroy parked and quickly jumped out of the car to come around and open my door. He then held out his hand and helped me out of the car even though I was more than capable. His actions were very chivalrous which was obviously all new to me. Once I was out of the car and he had closed and locked the doors, he gently took my hand and we walked up to the doors of the restaurant which he also opened for me.

Inside, were the sounds of smooth Reggae playing through unseen speakers and people enjoying food that smelled oh so good. From the back of the room there flowed a loud voice that carried to the front. "Blu boi, from long time me nuh see you." Apparently that person was talking to Delroy because he tightened his grip on my hand and led me back to the counter.

"Wha gwan, Uncle." Hearing him speak with an accent took me by complete surprise because in the times we spoke he never once gave any hints of an accent.

"An is who dis pretty gyal yuh ave pon ya arm?"

"Uncle, a mi fren Zell. Zell, this is my uncle Verly."

"Hello!" was all I said.

"Nice fi meet yuh, Ma'am."

"Uncle, wi a go sit an eat fi a spell."

"Alrite, gwan an sit, mi a sen Tan ova fi tek yuh awda."

"Yes, mon."

Delroy then led me over to a table in a cozy little corner. As I got comfortable, I began looking around my environment more, taking in the sights and the delicious smells. There were pictures of people from

Jamaica on the walls and the decor wasn't tacky. Although there were many images that lined those walls, the only person I recognized was Bob Marley. The place was small and very inviting with only seven tables total, and each of those tables had candles and place settings with cute decorative menus. I had to admit that it was a nice little spot.

Once we sat, Delroy was the first to speak, maybe he'd noticed the look on my face when he spoke to his uncle. "My parents were from Jamaica, but I was born here."

"Oh, so that is where the accent is from."

"Pretty much when you grow up around Jamaicans you tend to learn it and switch up when it's not your native tongue." He chuckled and then picked up a menu. "Is there anything you want to try?"

"Honestly, I'm not picky, so you can order for me."

Delroy signaled for the waitress and when she came over, he ordered for us both. I watched him, taking notice of how friendly and sociable he was, which was the exact opposite of me. Once the waitress walked away, he turned his attention to me in the form of a stare.

"So," he said as he looked at me and smiled.

"So?" I replied while fidgeting with my fingers under the table.

"I have been dying to have a chance to get to know you. I see that you have a little one?"

"Yeah," I replied tersely. The moment he mentioned Sam, I tensed up a bit. Remembering what he'd asked me before made me realize that this date may have been a big mistake. I was ready to go home but since I didn't want to just get up and walk off, I decided that I was going to show him exactly who I was. To my way of thinking, that would make him end the date, drop me back off at home, and never look for me again. "Why do you think you want to know me?"

"I work an overnight shift and go to that store every morning. Out of the blue one day I see you and I'm hooked. You have this natural beauty about you and I see that you stay to yourself, you stay out of the crazy stuff. Something about the way you carried yourself made me want to get to know everything about you," he shrugged when he was done talking as if what he said was a given. He saw me, he liked what he saw, he wanted to get to know more of what he saw. In his mind it was that simple, but my life was far more complex than the simplicity he thought he saw.

"There is nothing to know." I told him a partial truth. There was a lot to know, but since all of it was bad, I was sure he didn't really want to know it.

"I highly doubt that," he kept that sexy stare on me. "It took me damn near a month of seeing you day in and day out to get the courage to stop you and ask for just your name. So, tell me about yourself?"

"What do you want to know?"

"I don't know, maybe we can start with how old your son is." I tried not to but I think I rolled my eyes. "Is that a touchy subject?"

"What! No. Honestly, you keep asking me to tell you about myself, when in reality you don't have the stomach to hear my story," I assured him. "So, why don't we just enjoy this date with some superficial convo, ok?"

"Try me," he persisted with a straight face, almost as if he were daring me to try him.

Delroy just didn't understand. While he grew up playing UNO, I was learning Poker and I was about to use my Poker skills to call his bluff. He wanted to know me? Cool. I was going to let him get to know me, but I was about to give his ass the Cliffs Notes version while showing him the kindness of sparing him the gory details.

"My name is, O'Zella. My mother died of an overdose when I was nine. I was put into a group home where the man of the house molested me for months until I was moved to a foster home in the suburbs. Once there, I was eventually raped over and over again by that woman's thirteen year old son. When the rapes were discovered and I was subsequently moved out of there, I was then sent to another home where I met up with my best friend Jazz whom I'd met in the first group home. Jazz and I were inseparable 'til I was fourteen years old, at which time I helplessly listened to her being murdered on the phone. But wait, it gets better," I spoke sarcastically just before I paused, waiting for him to tell me to stop or that he'd heard enough. When he did neither, I continued telling him the saddest tale I was sure he'd ever heard.

"Shortly after losing my best friend in this cold and cruel world, the state proudly reunited me with my father, you know, the one who'd abandoned me and my mother when I was an infant. Well, this dude was so great that for my fifteenth birthday he got drunk and raped me while calling out my mother's name. After that, he turned me into his housewife and sex slave while he used sex as both a reward and a punishment. It was all a punishment to me, but he didn't seem to care too much about how he was torturing the fuck out of me." The retelling of my story was getting to me, but I refused to allow any emotions to stop me from telling Delroy what he seemed so determined to know. When he still gave me no comments, I continued giving him what he wanted.

"The day that I told the man that was supposed to be my father that I was pregnant with his child, he became furious, physically attacked me and raped me once more until his sister burst in, saw what he was doing to me, and distracted him with her screams. When he was busy explaining how everything was all my fault, I managed to slit his throat and kill him. I moved in with his sister after that, was investigated by the police for months until they finally concluded that my murderous, patricidal act was self-defense. Then I had his baby, and that was almost five years ago."

As much as I wanted to pause, wanted to stop retelling the story of my life so that I could stop feeling dirty and unloved, I was determined to get it out of the way so that Delroy could bring me home and we could put an end to the fakeness of this damn date. So, even though it was killing me, I kept talking.

Why Would I Love You?

"My aunt, who was actually the only person who genuinely cared for me besides Jazz, died nine months ago. I was homeless for a little while after that until I figured out how to get on my feet. Now that I'm on my feet, I just want to figure out how to actually love my dad's son and live." There, I'd told him. Now I was just waiting for him to announce that he was done.

I was so sure that the cynical tone with which I'd spewed that whole thing out had taken Delroy by surprise. And the fact that he just sat there, staring at me with blank eyes, solidified my thoughts that I was way too much for him to handle. As we sat in complete silence, just staring at one another, the air between us grew so thick you'd have needed a chainsaw just to break the surface. The only sound that registered to me at that time was the low hum of Bob Marley singing, "Every Little Thing Is Gonna Be Alright'. When the anticipation became too much for me, I raised my brows at him expectantly.

Delroy started to kind of snicker. I then widened my eyes at him, very much offended. With no words, I removed the napkin I'd previously placed in my lap and threw it down. I started to get up so that I could leave when he reached over and grabbed my hand.

"Please sit?" his voice was calm, soothing.

"Why?" I snapped. "You need to laugh a little more?"

"Trust me," his voice was very serious at this point, "I wasn't laughing at you. Please," he directed his eyes toward the chair, "just sit for a second?" Hesitantly, I eased back into my seat, fiddling with my hands in my lap as I waited for him to continue. He didn't make me wait long. "I chuckle when I'm nervous or don't know what to say. But honestly, I think it's funny that you thought telling me your story was gonna drive me away. If anything that shit makes me want to love you."

He looked at me, eyes as serious as could be. "I can't imagine going through half the shit you've been through in your life, yet you've been through all of that and you still keep going. That shit makes me admire you and think that you're the most incredible woman I've ever met."

His words were making me hate myself. I had opened up as a way of defending myself, but instead of running away from me, I had unintentionally helped him to break down my walls. For the first time in a long time I was actually letting out tears of fear and pain. I'd thought that I was the only one that could see and feel where my wounds were, but the way he looked at me made me feel like he could see them too. Not only that, but he made me feel as if he was ready to carry the burden for me.

Without words, Delroy got up, came around the table, and hugged me. And for the first time since I'd known him, my instant reaction wasn't to push him away. Maybe it was his cologne that always mesmerized me. or maybe it was his big arms wrapped so snugly around me, but whatever it was, something about that man made me feel safe, like Auntie Lori safe. So, instead of running away from him, I burrowed myself deeper into his chest, and as he stroked my hair and slightly rocked me back forth, I cried a silent waterfall.

When Delroy whispered, "Don't worry, Zell, I got you now. I promise," I could feel in my heart that every word he spoke was true. I was truly safe again.

Delroy Blu St. James was twenty-two years old with his head on straight. He had a good job as an overnight foreman at a local factory. He didn't have any kids, and he owned his own house in the nineteenth ward across town, a good neighborhood. He was born in Maryland, but had come to live with his Uncle when his mother and father were killed in a house fire when he was thirteen. He was loved from the moment he was born, so it was second nature for him to show love and to be affectionate, something I wasn't too comfortable with doing.

Everyday for the first two weeks after our date, Delroy and I would meet at the store and he would drive me to school where we would sit in his car and talk until it was time for class. I really came to enjoy those times with him, especially since he was so cool and so funny on the low.

Why Would I Love You?

The man kept me laughing. He was also serene to be with, easy to open up to, and it was uncomplicated to share my life with him. My life may have seemed like it was filled with nothing but tragedy for me, but there were happy times that I was able to share with him. He'd had such a wonderful life with his family that I would sit and listen to him talking about his childhood for hours while imagining what his life was like in my mind. Those were some of our most precious times together, some of those happy times in my own life that I loved so much.

Even though he worked the overnight shift and it threw his schedule off, Delroy would not only bring me to school, he would also pick me up from school and then drive me across town to pick up Sam. I always told him that I would walk Sam home and he didn't push the issue. One day when he was taking me home from class, I asked him what his plans were. He told me he was just going to go home and sleep because he had the night off, so I finally invited him over for dinner. He eagerly accepted. On the walk home from daycare, I told Sam that I was having a friend over for dinner. We had never had company over except for Brenda when I went on my date, so he was really excited.

When we got home, he was still so happy that he started to clean up his toys and put them in a bin. "Zell, I'm going to clean up so that the house can look spotless," he said as he smiled up at me.

"Sam, I tell you, you have quite the vocabulary."

"Thank you," was all he said before busying himself with getting the house ready for our guest.

I had taken enough chicken out the day before just in case Delroy, who now wanted me to call him Blu, agreed to come over. I was in the process of cleaning the chicken when Sam came running into the kitchen.

"Zell, what is your friend's name?"

"His name is Blu."

"Like the color."

"Mhm."

"Coooool."

I got busy in the kitchen making fried chicken, green beans, biscuits, and mac-n-cheese. Not that Macaroni in a box bull either, Aunt Lori taught me a few things about getting down in the kitchen, so my macaroni was being made from scratch. I even had enough time to make a pineapple upside down cake. I had just taken the cake out of the oven when Blu rang the doorbell.

"Zell, your friend is here!" Sam yelled excitedly like he was the one that actually had friends coming over.

"I hear it, Sam," I said as I wiped my hands on my floured up apron and then answered the door with Sam two steps behind me.

Twenty-Three

"Hi," I said to Blu the moment I laid eyes on him. "Please come in."

"Thank you, and this is for you," he said as he handed me a bottle of wine. Then he turned to Sam, extended a small gift bag in his direction, and said, "Hello, I'm Blu, and I bought this for you."

Sam took the bag from his hands and thanked him before digging in to see what he had. "Wooow! Thank you, Mr. Blu," he said as his eyes lit up.

"You're very welcome, Sam."

"Thank you, Blu," I also expressed my appreciation, "but you know you didn't have to bring anything, right?"

"Oh, but I did," he corrected me. "It would be rude of me to show up empty handed," he explained.

"Ok, well again, thank you for your kindness. Now, please excuse me while I get cleaned up and then we can eat."

"Take your time, beautiful."

As I ran to the back to change, Blu took a seat on the couch next to Sam. He had bought Sam a mini Transformer and the two of them began talking about its many features. Hearing their discussion made me feel absolutely comfortable leaving Sam alone with Blu for a few minutes. So, I took my focus off of the fellas and put it on what I was going to wear. Because I knew I would be getting a little messy in the kitchen and would have to change after cooking, I put away my dinner outfit, quickly shimmied out of my clothes, freshened up, and slid on my summer dress. I'd been keeping my hair straight lately and the new look had been giving me a new attitude to match. I didn't do anything to my hair as I already liked it the way it was. Then I sprayed myself with my only perfume, looked myself over in the mirror and approved of what I saw.

Once fully ready, I exited my bedroom, slowly walked down my short hallway and peeked into the living room to see how Sam and Blu were getting along. It warmed my heart to see that they were playing and laughing. It was like getting a beautiful view of what a normal life could have been like for me.

Hating to interrupt their time together, I cleared my throat so they knew I was there. "What are you two out here laughing about?"

"Sam was showing me the Transformer he got for his birthday last week." Blu got close to me and whispered, "Why didn't you tell me he'd had a birthday?"

I shrugged my shoulders, responding nonchalantly, "I don't know, we didn't do too much." I brushed his question off and headed to the kitchen area. "Are you guys ready to eat?"

Sam hopped up because he was ready. "Yes, I am!"

Blu and I chuckled as we headed to the dining area. Even though my table was small, it was big enough for the three of us. After I made our plates and we were seated, everyone dug in. As I looked around the table, I had to admit that it was really nice to feel like I had a complete family. I happily watched as both Sam and Blu ate like they were starving. In fact, all at the table was silent except for the fact that they both kept going, "Mmmm," every time they bit into something. That didn't bother me, though, it actually made me smile knowing that they were enjoying the meal I'd slaved over. When I brought out dessert, they went even more wild. All in all, it was a great evening for everyone.

After dinner, I lay Sam down for bed and joined Blu in the living room. When I walked in, he patted the couch next him, an invite for me to sit beside him. I did as he silently requested, but I was kinda nervous about it. Even though he and I had been spending almost every day together in his car, getting to know each other, there was always that small distance that the front seat of the car created. We were together but still separated by those two bucket seats, on my couch, that distance did not exist.

Up to that point, Blu had been so respectful of me and my reservations that we had never even kissed. However, this time I feared that he might finally try to go for that kiss, or for some gentle form of intimacy. Anticipating that made my nerves as bad as they could get. So, ensuring that no part of my body touched any part of his, I reached for the remote and put on a movie that would distract us.

Quietly, Blu and I sat, looking straight forward at the TV. I was nervous about what he might want to happen now that we were alone and in a more comfortable setting and I could feel him watching me. Nervously, I began to fidget with my hands, trying so hard to avoid eye contact. He cleared his throat as if he was trying to get my attention or get up the nerve to break the awkward silence I know I had created.

"Zell?" I damn near jumped out of my skin at the sound of his voice.

"Yes," I braved up enough to look his way.

"Dinner was amazing. Thanks for having me over."

"You're welcome. Thanks for coming."

"Sam is a pretty amazing kid."

"He is, despite me and my issues." I looked away from him because my statement was filled with so much shame. He reached over and grabbed my hand.

"He's amazing *because* of you," he complimented me and I was so uncomfortable with that compliment that I gave him a weak smile and went back to watching the movie. "I'm serious," he spoke once more, determined to get me to see what he saw. "We've talked about the feelings you're fighting and even with all of that you're still kind to him and you take really good care of him."

"Thanks, that means a lot," I told him as his words had me relaxing and scooting closer to him, closing the space between us on the couch.

Blu wasted no time lifting his arm and I laid my head on his chest. *Oh, God*! I thought as I discovered that his cologne was a secret weapon. It took everything I had in me not to drool all over him as he wrapped his arm around me while we watched the movie together. When the closing credits were finally rolling, I looked over at Blu who already had his eyes on me. "You are so beautiful, Zell," he said and his words caught me completely off guard. But what shook me even more was when, without warning, he leaned down and kissed me.

At first, I tensed up, but slowly I began to melt at the touch of his soft, supple lips against my own and at his gentle hand caressing the side of my face. Then I surprised myself when I kissed him back and realized that for once it was nice to be kissed. Blu then shifted his body and gently moved his hand to my hips. Immediately, I realized I wasn't ready and let out a pained moan as I pushed him off of me and jumped to my feet with my arms wrapped across my chest.

"I'm sorry, Zell," he pleaded instantly as he hopped to his feet.

He reached out to touch my arm, but I flinched. "It's not you," I spoke truthfully. "I'm just not ready." I couldn't even look at him.

"Are you ok?" the concern was clear in his voice.

"Yes, I'm fine," I lied. "I think we should just call it a night."

"I understand," he admitted sadly, but he didn't force the issue. Quietly, I walked him to the door and as he stepped into the hallway, he looked back with a questioning expression on his face. "I'll see you tomorrow, right?" Even after all of that, he still wanted to see me again.

"Yes, I'll see you tomorrow," I rushed the words out and with that I closed the door.

Why Would I Love You?

You know how in the movies when a girl is sad she puts her back to a door, slides down to the floor, and cries loudly into her hands? Well that is exactly how my scene played out. I was embarrassed and scared that my scars and reservations would run him away. I wasn't the average girl who could cast my fears aside and give myself to him. I had been taken by so many men, that the thought of sex didn't even sound like a thing of pleasure to me. But I knew that men had needs, and if I wanted to keep him I would eventually have to fuck him or lose him. PTSD was mothafucka, I swear.

The next day I woke up contemplating whether or not I should go to the store. I wasn't sure if it was fear of facing Blu, or fear that he wouldn't be there because he finally had realized he had bitten off more than he could chew with me. Deciding not to let any of that change my plans, I threw all of that to the back of my mind and got my day started. I decided that I would figure everything out after I dropped Sam off to daycare. Going with my normal routine, I got both of us dressed and we headed out the door.

Once we stepped outside, Sam suddenly squealed, "Zell, look! It's Mr. Blu!" I closed the door to our home and turned around to see Blu standing by his car with coffee for me and orange juice and a donut for Sam.

"Hey," he said, offering us a smile. "I was wondering if I could take you to school today?" I smiled back at him, relieved that all of the worrying I was doing had been for nothing.

"That would be nice," Sam said, not hesitating to hop in his car and bust down his donut.

"Sam, did you say thank you?"

"Thank you, Mr.Blu," he said through big chomps and chews.

"You're welcome, little man," was Blu's kind reply.

We got to the daycare and dropped Sam off, when I got back into the car, Blu had a big smile plastered on his face.

"Why are you looking like that?"

"Like what?"

"Why are you smiling at me like that?"

"Because whenever I am with you, I'm happy," I could hear the honesty in his words. "I know last night ended a little rough, but I don't want you to think that I am rushing you. Did I mention I am sorry?"

"Honestly, you don't have to be sorry. I've never had sex with someone by choice so this is all new to me."

"I know, and I want this to be a great experience when you're ready. No sooner."

"Hhm."

"What?"

"Nothing, it's just that you're too good to be true."

"No, beautiful, you're too good to be true." It was crazy how every time Blu called me beautiful it made my heart flutter, but once upon a time if anyone had done that it would have made me nervous. Funny how times and circumstances changed.

Having Blu in my life and in Sam's life was so wonderful. He was affectionate with us both and all of the affectionate things I was incapable of, he took over. It was like Auntie Lori had sent him into my life to give me the same love she had been giving me and Sam. Day in and day out, Blu did whatever it took to earn my trust. Not that my trust was anything special, but the way he treated me and made me feel, let me know that to him it was special. His relationship with Sam was instant, they had taken to each other immediately.

Blu was so mindful of things concerning me. He was understanding of the fact that if we went somewhere, I had to find a babysitter, and he was fully understanding of the fact that being alone with him still made me nervous even though I trusted him. So he would plan dates at the park, or picnics on the beach. It was always crowded places and places that we could bring Sam with us if we chose. He kind of made us his instant family and I didn't mind that at all. We would look like the happiest family too. He would have Sam on his shoulder, laughing and talking, while I would be walking along holding Blu's hand, just enjoying the moment. He had become a part of our routine.

It was a late night and Blu had just laid Sam's sleeping body down after we tired him out at a local amusement park. He came to the kitchen where I was washing the Tupperware from the day. He walked up behind me, gently hugged me, and then sat at the dining table.

"I take it he didn't wake up, huh."

"No, Ma'am. He is out like a light."

"Well, he was running nonstop through that place."

"Zell, I was thinking. It's been over three months and I know for a fact that I don't want to ever be without you or my little Sam man."

"Ok?" I questioned cautiously, not sure of where he was going.

"You said your lease is about to be up," he spoke carefully, "so why don't you two just move in with me? There's plenty of room."

I froze, stopped what I was doing and sat down at the table with him. His request took me by surprise, so I didn't answer right away, "Why?" I asked when I could finally speak.

"Because..." he paused for the briefest moment, "I love you, O'Zella." That was the first time he'd said that he loved me and even though those words sounded amazing rolling off of his tongue, I still wasn't sure if moving in with him was a good idea at that time.

"Blu, you have been a blessing in our life, a big one," I began, "but I don't know if I'm ready to take such a big step."

"I understand, but I just was thinking that you're about to graduate and I want to be close so that I can help you with my little Sam man."

"It's not that I don't want to move in with you, I think I'm just scared," I admitted the truth. Blu reached out, grabbed my hand as I contemplated. "How about we give it a month and me and Sam can spend the night a few times. If things keep going well, we can go from there."

I could feel him squeeze my hand as my words pleased him. "I like that idea. Whenever you want, my doors are always open."

"Thanks, babe," I said, still scared of taking such a huge step.

I decided that on Blu's next night off, we were going to take him up on his offer. He and I picked Sam up from daycare as usual, but instead of heading home we went to Blu's house. I had our clothes already packed, so we didn't have to stop at home for anything. Even though I was a little scared, I was happy that we were all off to experience something new. I know it may have sounded crazy, but Blu and I had been dating for four months at that time and I had never been to his house. Going there felt too much like I would lose home court advantage, so I avoided even the mention of it until I was ready. Blu beat me to the punch and became ready before I even had the chance to.

When we finally made it there, I was very surprised to see that his home was a two story, brick front place with all the rooms that people with money have. Once inside, he gave Sam and I a tour. The house was beautiful, the gorgeous decor made me think a woman lived with him. There was a fireplace in the living room, a wall separating the dining room and the kitchen. There were sliding wood doors that lead to a huge den. He even had an enclosed back porch with a huge back yard. Needless to say, I was in awe of his living situation. That was until we went upstairs where I found myself dumbstruck.

The second story was huge. It had three bedrooms with two bathrooms. One of those bathrooms was in the master bedroom which had a large tv and a king sized bed, the other bathroom was in the hall. I guess when Blu found out that we were coming, he set up one of his spare rooms to accommodate his Little Sam Man, a name that I though was so cute every time he said it.

"WOOOW! Papa Blu," Samael called out when he saw it, "the bed looks like a Transformer. This is so cool!"

"It's specially made for you, my Little Sam Man."

"Blu, when did you have time to do that?" I asked as surprised filled me.

"Babe, I've been working on his room for over a month."

"What if we never came over?"

"Then I would have brought it to you," he said as he shrugged his shoulders.

"You are a trip," I said as a huge, appreciative smile covered my face.

"You love it though," he teased playfully as he kissed me and headed down the stairs.

While Blu was downstairs getting our dinner started, I stayed upstairs and unpacked our clothes. When I was done, I followed Blu downstairs to help him in getting dinner underway. Halfway down the stairs a smell hit my nose and it smelled like our first date. I made it into the kitchen to see my man, with his fine self, slaving over a hot stove and chopping up all kinds of vegetables.

"You cook too?"

"Well, you know, when you're the complete package you gotta flex."

"Talk that shit, boo!" I said and we both broke out laughing.

When dinner was done, I lay Sam down while Blu cleaned up, then I went to the bathroom to get ready for bed. I looked at myself in the mirror, trying to give myself the pep talk about finally having sex with him. I felt myself tearing up just thinking about it, I fought hard to try and push the fear and shame about sex away from me. To ease my worried mind about what I was going to do, I also thought about how much I loved this man how I wanted to share myself with him. That helped a little, but not much. Because I didn't have anything sexy in my wardrobe, I put on my usual oversized t-shirt, climbed into bed, and waited.

For just about an hour, I lay in Blu's big bed alone, but he still hadn't come up. I knew he was done in the kitchen because I hadn't heard any dishes clanking in a while. Concerned now, I went to see what was taking him so long. It was dark downstairs except for the light from the Tv, but when I came down off of the last step, I saw Blu with a pillow and blanket, laid out on the couch.

"Hey, is the tv too loud?" he said the moment he saw me.

"No, I was looking for you. Why are you down here with a blanket?"

"I didn't want you to be uncomfortable, so I let you have the bed."

"Why would you have me over if you were going to sleep on the couch?"

"I just wanted you under the same roof with me." My heart melted at his words, the man just kept getting sweeter.

I blushed, giggled, and walked close to him. Then I grabbed his hand and pulled him up. "If I'm going to be under the same roof with you, I want to be in the same bed with you too." With that being said, I held his hand and led him back to his room. We both got in the bed and turned off the lights, then we lay there, in the dark, both on our backs holding hands. I could tell from the sweat on Blu's palms that he was just as nervous as I was. My heart was racing and all kinds of fears were marching through my head until a sudden calm came over me. I knew that I wanted this to happen, so I decided to just rip the bandaid off and get it over with.

Slowly, I turned to Blu and then scooted closer. As usual, he lifted his left arm so I could lay my head on his chest, but instead, I leaned up and started to slowly kiss him. He wasted no time kissing me back, but he didn't make any moves to advance us from there, he was following my lead. For the longest time we kept kissing, then as I relaxed a bit more, I slowly ran my hand down his chest. His left arm wrapped around my body and he grabbed my waist. My own hand kept traveling down his body until I got to the waistband of his shorts.

Why Would I Love You?

Quickly, he grabbed my wrist with his free hand and stopped kissing me. His aroused state had his breathing labored as he whispered the softest, "Baby, are you sure? We don't have to do this."

"Sshh! I want to." Then I pressed my lips back against his, reached into his shorts, and rubbed my hand up down his manhood. Blu let out a soft moan against my lips, a moan that let me know that what I was doing was very pleasing to my man.

When that became too much for him to bear, he pulled my hand out of his shorts and leaned up as he gently lowered me onto my back. He lay facing me and continued kissing me while his hand explored my body. Blu took his time as he rubbed my supple breast, making me feel things that I never thought I'd feel when it came to sex. Sliding his hand down my waist, he reached for the hem of my shirt and lifted it slightly to expose my trimmed vagina. Using one finger, he slid it across my pussy lips and my body jumped as I let out a soft hiss.

That concerned him, so he pulled back, looked down at me. "Are you ok? You want me to stop?"

I moaned, "No!" Then I grabbed his ears and pulled his face back down to mine so that he could keep kissing me.

Giving me what I wanted, Blu then lifted my shirt over my head and began licking and kissing a trail all over my body. Amazingly, my body was reacting to him in a good way and every kiss he placed on me set my skin ablaze. I felt as if I was finally free when my body and my yoni responded to his every touch with a wanting, an aching, and a needing I had never experienced before.

Twenty-Four

Life was good. Less than a month after our first overnight stay, Sam and I moved in and we couldn't have been happier. I was on cloud nine because I had found someone who was patient with me and my issues, someone that gave me control without blurring the lines of who wore the pants in the relationship. Things were going so well for Blu and Sam and me, that the time just flew by and eventually I started to relax and not always expect the other shoe to drop.

We were now going on three years together and there was no more routine. With Blu everyday was a welcomed adventure. Sam was seven, and he and Blu were inseparable. They were like best friends, and even though Sam was not Blu's biological son, there was no way anyone could tell because he was such a great father to him. I had graduated from nursing school and had gotten my LPN license. I was finally in a great place physically, financially, and mentally.

I had just gotten home from an eighteen hour shift and walked in to see my two men roughhousing in the living room. I was so exhausted that I just looked over at them and grunted, I was like the walking dead. Sam was bouncing on the couch as Blu made his way over to me.

He hugged me and kissed me on the cheek. "I'm going to take Sam Man to the park and maybe for some ice cream because he won't stop asking."

"Ok, sucker," I found the energy to tease him.

Why Would I Love You?

"Hey," he feigned hurt, "I'm not a sucker. I just won't tell him no," he chuckled. "When's the last time *you* heard no from me?"

"Touche," I said as I smiled at him, "but you still a sucka."

He then grabbed me and tickled me, causing me to giggle like a school girl. "Get some rest, when we get back I'm gonna make dinner."

"Ok, babe," was all I could say as I started to drag my tired body toward the stairs, but Blu held me in place. "Thank you," I said as I looked into his eyes to see why he was holding onto me.

"Love you," he said just before he kissed me and then released me. "And get some rest," he told me as I dragged my tired body up the stairs.

"Sam Man, get your jacket on," I heard Blu speaking. Then, "A'ight Zell, we're gone."

"Bye, Zell," Sam yelled out.

"Bye, Sam," came my groggy reply.

I listened for the door to close and lock, then I dragged myself to the bathroom. I was already tired from working the double but this was an abnormal kind of tired because I felt even more fatigued than usual. Plopping my purse on the counter, I began rummaging through it for my plastic bag. I found it and set it on the counter. As usual, my unit at work had been short staffed and I'd spent my night not only doing my own work, but also helping them out. As a result, my feet were extremely sore. I figured that all I needed was some Tylenol and a full twenty-four hours of rest.

After stripping my clothes off, I looked at the bag I'd set on the counter, then decided to hop in the shower first. I would deal with that later. I let the warm water fall over my hair and body, hoping it would ease my poor, aching muscles. I was so done with the day, but before I lay down to get some rest, I felt like I needed to get to the bottom of what was going on with me. I knew it was flu season, but I couldn't afford to be sick. Blu and I were working alternating doubles so that we could save up for a big family trip to Disney. So missing days would hinder that plan or possibly stop the trip altogether.

While I was rinsing off, I felt a knot form in my stomach and all of a sudden I began to heave. Immediately, I jumped out of the tub and ran to the toilet. I made it just in time to throw up everything I had eaten on the way home. I didn't want to believe what I knew it was, so I had to at least check, had to get it confirmed. When I finally felt settled, I splashed water on my face, rinsed out my mouth, then reached for the plastic bag. I pulled out the box, stared at it for a second, then taking a deep breath, I read the instructions. It was like déjà vu walking to the toilet with that stick in my hand, but this time the situation was completely different. Wasting no more time, I peed on the stick, set it on some tissue by the sink, then lay down in the bed. I wasn't in a rush to get any unexpected news.

After lying there thinking about what I was going to do if the test revealed what I already knew it would, I fell asleep. As my eyes fluttered open, I caught a glimpse of something out of the corner of my eyes. I rolled over just in time enough to see my phone light up. When I reached for it, I saw that it wasn't a number I knew, so I ignored it. Then, I checked to see what time it was because the house was quiet and it was dark outside.

"Oh damn!" I said when I realized that I'd been so tired that I'd slept for almost ten uninterrupted hours.

I was just about to get up and go look for Sam and Blu when my phone lit up again. It was the same number, whoever it was really wanted to talk to me. So, I cleared my throat and answered.

"Hello?" I listened as a woman from the emergency department told me that there had been an accident and that I was listed in Sam's medical records as his emergency contact. My heart hit my stomach. I screamed into the phone, asking her what happened over and over again but she was unable to give me any answers over the phone. As

Why Would I Love You?

fast as I could, I got up, threw on some sweats and slides and ran out of the door.

I sped to the hospital with tears blurring my vision, every possible horrible scenario racing through my head and, "God please," on repeat flowing from my lips. I was a mess, a complete mess. I couldn't have anything happen to Sam and Blu, I just couldn't. I finally had my good life, my good man. I'd finally found my comfortable place in the world, I couldn't have anything mess that up. As soon as I made it to the hospital, I pulled into the emergency entrance where I was met by a guard at my window.

"Ma'am, are you picking up or checking in?"

"My husband and my son are here. They came in by ambulance."

He noticed my panic and spoke quickly. "Ok, just pull over there, park, and the guard at the desk inside will tell you where to go."

I pulled off without so much as a thank you, parked my car, and ran inside. The first place I went was to the guard's desk and gave her Sam's name. She had me waiting for someone to take me back to him. As I paced the same three steps back and forth, it suddenly hit me. If they were calling about Sam, why didn't Blu call me? Why had they not even mentioned him? Why did the lady on the phone keep telling me she couldn't say? What the fuck? Where was Blu?"

"Ms. Grife?" I heard my name called and whipped my head in the direction of the sound.

"Yes, that's me." I rushed to her. "Where is Sam and Delroy?"

"Can we step into this office here for a quick second?" I followed her to a small room that was just past the double doors she had come from. My heart raced, my palms began to sweat. It was déjà vu all over again. Once she closed the doors, I felt the walls closing in.

"Where is Sam and Delroy?" nervousness had my words tumbling out of my mouth.

"Please sit?" she requested calmly.

"No!" I didn't give a damn about pleasantries or about being calm. I wanted my questions answered and I wanted them answered now. "Where are they?"

"Ms. Grife," she began again in that calm voice that was starting to irritate the fuck out of me. "Samael and Delroy were in an accident."

"Yes, I know that," I said as I shook my head up and down. "Are they ok? Why aren't you taking me to them?"

"I don't know how to say this, Ma'am, but," she paused and I snapped.

"Just say it!" I shouted, I was tired of the beating around he fucking bush. "Just say it!" I snapped at her again.

This time when she spoke, she got straight to the point. "They were hit by a drunk driver. Samael is ok, he sustained minor bumps and bruises. Delroy was pronounced dead at the scene."

All of a sudden, my ears began to ring. I could hear my blood rushing, swooshing in my ears. My head started to spin, my mouth dried. I felt as if I couldn't breathe, as if I couldn't pull in a single breath. I became dizzy, my legs gave out, and I fell to my knees. Those walls that had started closing around me finished their job and caved completely in on me. The world became black and all I could do was scream over and over and over, "Noooooooooo!"

Why was this happening to me again? I don't understand how every time I find love, it's snatched away from me. Those were my thoughts, my nightmares. *I don't mean like they move away or say they're in love with someone else. Noooooo!"* My mind screamed as I did. *I mean they leave as in death, instant and unexpected death. Whhhyyyyy?* My mind screamed again, from the depth of me, the core of me. *God, please tell me why I was going through this again.*

The pain was the same too, exactly the same. It felt like a spiked knife was being driven into my heart slowly while also being twisted counterclockwise. I don't know how long I was on that floor in that hospital, but somehow I managed to make it to my feet. I needed to get to Sam, he was the only one that could give me answers as to exactly what happened.

"Can you take me to my son?" I managed between sobs and sniffles.

"Of course, but there is the possibility that he may not be responsive yet," she informed me.

"Why not?"

"When we brought him in we weren't able to calm him down and he wouldn't let the doctors check his injuries, so we had to give him a sedative."

"Ok," I said as somewhere through the fog of my mind, I processed what she was saying. "Fine, just take me to him."

Just as she said, Sam was out like a light. His face was cut up and his neck and arms were blue and purple. I was so out of it that all I could do was walk up to him and trace my hand over a bruise on his arm.

"He's a lucky boy to have such minor injuries."

"Why would you say that?" I looked to her like she was crazy before looking back toward my child. "Look at him!"

"The crash was bad, Ms. Grife," she explained. "And he didn't have his seatbelt on." I looked at her like she had lost whatever mind she may have had. There was no way Blu would have let Sam ride without a seatbelt on.

"That's impossible," I immediately dismissed her words, I knew she had made a mistake.

She didn't bother to correct me, she simply said, "I'm going to let the police know you're here and they can give you more information about the actual accident than I can."

"Uhm, excuse me?" I said as I turned to her before she left the room.

"Yes."

"Is there any way I can see Delroy?"

"His Uncle is coming and will have to identify the body, after that I will see if I can arrange that."

I was about to ask her why that was when I was his woman, the woman that shared a house and a love with him. But then I realized that we weren't married, and that the hospital would not have looked at me as his next of kin. So I couldn't go off on her, couldn't tell her how stupid their police was. "Thank you," were the only words I allowed to flow from my lips.

I sat in the chair next to Sam's bed for hours. The police came and gave me just about the same answers that the nurse had given me. That wasn't enough for me, so the only thing left to do was wait for Sam to wake up and tell me what no one else could. I had to have wiped away a million tears while I sat listening to the mind numbing beep of the monitor checking his vitals when I finally heard a groan. My eyes whipped up to my child's face and I saw his eyes fluttering. I couldn't get to his side fast enough.

As intensely as I could, I stared at him, waiting for him to focus on me. As soon as he saw my face, he started crying and saying, "I'm sorry, Zell."

"Sorry for what?" I rushed to ask him. He didn't say anything for too long of a time, so I shook his shoulder and asked again. "Sorry for what, Sam?"

He was still crying when he said. "I... I... I took off my seatbelt."

"What!" I stated more than asked.

"I dropped something on the floor of the car and when I took off my seatbelt and got up to get it, Papa Blu reached over to push me back. Then there was a loud crash and he fell on me, and there was glass everywhere and I was scared."

I sat down and tried to wrap my head around what he'd just said to me, but I couldn't. And what the hell was so important that it couldn't wait? I was infuriated and ready to leave the room because if

Why Would I Love You?

I'm being completely honest, at that precise moment I was blaming Sam for Blu being gone. Not the drunk driver that crashed into them or even Blu for diving across the car. I was blaming Samael Grife. I can't tell you why I was doing that, but I always found a reason for my son and baby brother to be my arch nemesis. And there I was again, blaming him.

  I was so disgusted that I couldn't even stay in the same room with him anymore. So, I hopped up, keeping my back to him, and walked out. I wanted to see Blu, I needed to see Blu. Out in the hall, I walked up to the same nurse that said she would try and get me in to see Blu's body. I didn't want any excuses this time, I just wanted to see his body. I only had to ask once before she took me to see him. I couldn't touch him, couldn't get close to him, but I was able to see him through some glass. I was never really close with Blu's family, so not seeing them wasn't a big deal.

  "Can I be alone?" I asked.

  "Sure, I'll just be outside the door if you need me," she spoke in a soothing and understanding voice.

  Standing by the glass, waiting for them to uncover his body was like waiting for a punch to be thrown by a bully in a fight. You knew it was going to hurt, but you had to go through with it. My heart raced and a cold and angry fear encompassed me. There was someone in the room on the other side that gave me a nod of his head while asking if I was ready. I closed my eyes and nodded my head back. My eyes welled with tears as I forced them to open even though they burned. Then I looked at him, looked at the face of the man I loved. It hurt my heart to see that it was all cut up, that there was a huge bruise that completely covered his neck and shoulder.

  "You lied to me. You said you were going to be here for me. You lied, you fucking lied! Now, I'm alone again! You fucking promised!" Then I started gagging and ran off to the bathroom, still gagging and dry heaving.

When I was done getting myself together, I didn't even bother going back to Sam's room, I just needed to get out of that place, to get away from the location that held the sources of my current misery. So I moved quickly down that halls and more halls until I was free of that place. The walk out of that hospital was like walking away from happiness. I was angry, miserable and tired. It seemed as if I couldn't win at shit to save my life, and to be honest I was tired of trying to win when all of the fucking bets were always stacked against me. From that moment on, I decided that to keep from losing anyone else I was never going to let anyone into my life or my heart again. There was no way that this walk of doom was going to ever take place in my life again. Blu was the last person I planned on loving and I meant it.

Twenty-Five

When I made it to the house, I plopped down on the couch, curled up into a ball, and cried. I cried so hard and for so long that my body began to ache, and still I didn't stop. Eventually I cried and cried until I had no more tears left to cry. When I was finally in a muted emotional state and felt nothing, I realized just how surreal it was to be in that house and know that Blu would never be there again. There would never be a shared smile between us or another private joke. There would never be a playful back and forth for me to tell him he was crazy . Not in that house, and not ever.

There would never be a night of love making and exploring my body. No more nights of him holding me, him rubbing the back of my hand when I was scared, or even just him telling me he loved me. I was lost and broken, shattered and without a future to look forward to. I don't remember falling asleep, but when I found myself waking up, the sun was peeking through the blinds, beating on my face. My very first thought was that all that had happened the night before was just an awful dream.

Almost on instinct I jumped up, yelling for Blu and Sam. I walked to the kitchen wondering if they were in there preparing breakfast as they often did on my days off, but when I entered the kitchen no one was there. I looked in the den, it was empty. I ran upstairs and checked Sam's room first, nothing. The steps down our small hallway felt like they were never ending, and when I pushed open the door of our bedroom, things were just like I'd left them the night before. Denial tried to set in hard and fast, but reality fought hard and fiercely to keep itself in the forefront.

When I had no choice but to see that Samael and Blu weren't there, the fear and pain of losing him set in again, harder, meaner. I flopped down on the edge of his side of our bed and I hung my head in defeat. It wasn't a dream, this was more like a nightmare come true. I couldn't believe he was gone, really gone. I had no clue what to do. My first thought was to pack a bag and leave. Yes, leave without Sam. I was sure he'd be better off without me. I never loved him like he needed me to or wanted me to. As much as I tried, I just couldn't. This child was both my son and my brother, the product of repeated sexual assault at the hands of my father. Motherly love was something I just couldn't give Samael.

In the midst of my thoughts, I suddenly heard Aunt Lori's voice. "Oh, my Zella baby. You are so much stronger than you give yourself credit for. Don't let loss make you not love." At first I was shocked, but then I sat there, listening to her, seeing her appear before me as she told me that Sam was a blessing. And on the other side of her Blu appeared, he reached out and grabbed my hand. I was either losing it or they were showing themselves to me so that I could get my mind right.

"Zell," Blu said in that voice I knew I would miss for the rest of my life, "my Sam Man needs you. Don't leave him. I know I promised to be there, but it was my time. I didn't want to go, I swear and I'm sorry."

Then he released my hand and both he and Aunt Lori whispered in both of my ears, "I love you," just before they disappeared.

There was no way I was going to believe they had both been there, that was too much for me, especially when added to everything else that was going on around me. So, I chalked their words up to a manifestation of what I was sure they would say to me. After seeing them though, I knew I needed to pull myself together. When I chose to keep Sam, I knew it was forever. Therefore, I needed to get my head right and go to the hospital to get the child I'd promised to be a mother to. Finally, I got up and went to wash my face. Inside of the bathroom, I flipped the light switch on and stepped to the sink. And in that room I got the shock of my life. I'd completely forgotten that I had taken a pregnancy test, but there it was sitting there waiting for me to see what it had to tell me. Slowly, I picked it up, lowered my eyes to it and held my breath. And just as big and bold as could be, a bright pink plus sign was presenting itself to me. I was fucking pregnant!

I went back to the hospital with Sam where he was monitored for two days before he was well enough to be sent home. I didn't say more than two words to him the entire time we were there, but he was used to my silence when it came to him. His injuries were minor and he didn't need much from me once we got home, so I locked myself in my room and spent day after day crying. I barely ate, bathed or slept, I was a mess. I couldn't bring myself to care about anything and anyone, not even myself.

Sam was a kid that was wise beyond his years. I had known this about him before, but when he started taking care of me in my mental state instead me taking care of him, I knew his wisdom was even greater than I could possibly imagine.

"Zell?" he called out to me in a voice that sounded so adult.

"What, Sam?" I was groggy and cranky.

"I made you some soup."

"I'm good."

"You need to eat something. It's been a few days and you haven't even come out of this room."

"I said I'm good Sam."

"Zell?"

"What, Sam," I sighed exasperatedly.

"I know you're sad, but Papa Blu wouldn't want you to not eat."

"Just go away, Sam," I didn't want to hear a damn thing from him about Papa Blu.

I was miserable and in bed with no motivation. The only good thing I had going for me at that time was the fact that I was pregnant. And I wanted that baby, in fact, I wanted to have Blu's baby badly, because then I would have a piece of him still left in this world with me. I would still have a piece of his love that I could love. But I was doing nothing to nurture my pregnancy, nothing to ensure that the baby or myself was okay. I had no drive, no motivation to live. Every time I tried to push myself to get up, to move and be active, something would trigger a memory of Blu and I would start bawling all over again. I was sure it wasn't helpful that I was in a room full of things that reminded me of him, but those things were all I had left of him, there was no way I was willing to let them go, at least not at that moment.

It took me two weeks to finally get up and take a shower. I had to admit that it did feel good to let the warm water run over my head. I had been in bed so long that the shampoo in my hair felt refreshing. I'd just started to detangle my hair with my eyes closed, hoping that the heat would melt away some of my sorrow. I reached down to grab my soap and when my eyes looked at the bottom of the tub, it was all red.

I think I had gone temporarily numb because the amount of blood that was in the tub should have sent me screaming down the hall, especially since I knew exactly what it meant. I was losing my unborn child. And even that wasn't a surprise because everything in my life was looking like that. Nothing was going my way so why would I expect this pregnancy to be any different? I was at a point where I had given up on life altogether. So, needless to say I didn't even bother going to the hospital. All they were going to do once I got there was tell me that yet another being that I loved or had the potential to love had died, had been tragically taken away from me. I didn't want to hear that bullshit, so I stayed my ass at home and dealt with the bleeding until it eventually stopped.

Why Would I Love You?

Delroy Blu St. James had been a great man that died at twenty-six years old. I was so broken up about his death that I didn't even attend his funeral. His family liked me well enough, but we weren't close. When I didn't show up at his funeral, they all just wrote me off. And a short while later, they showed me exactly just how much they had written me off. I believe they'd been waiting for things to die down, but a little over a month later, they showed up at my door with papers telling me that I had ninety days to vacate the house. By that point, I had drank myself into a stupor and didn't even take their threat seriously.

Between my diminishing relationship with Sam and my growing relationship with vodka, I was batting a thousand in the deteriorating mental health department. I would wake up to a bottle on my nightstand and take a swig before I even thought about brushing my teeth. Throughout the day I would find ways to take swigs here and there from the secret little flask that I had become an expert at hiding. I was still a nurse, so I covered my day drinking up well at first, but after a while I was so out of control that the flask was too small for the amount of liquor I needed, and I stopped using a flask and started filling my water bottles with straight Vodka. My breath began to smell like a distillery and all the gum and mints in the world could not cover that up.

The straw that broke the camel's back came six months after Blu died when I left my water bottle on the cart I used to pass meds and a coworker picked it up. When I got back to my cart and noticed it was gone, I went the fuck off.

I was so distraught that I was screaming up and down the halls like a mad woman, "Which one of you stupid bitches took my damn water bottle? Don't make me fuck y'all up!"

Finally, one of the aides who never liked me spoke up. "I got your water bottle." When she said it, she threw air quotes up. She might as well have flipped me the bird because next thing I knew I was on her like white on rice. I mean I beat the brakes off of her and nobody wanted to stop me. Every punch I threw was seasoned with years of anger. That day, the stars had aligned or something because instead of her calling the police, I was only fired and escorted off of the property. I didn't care about that though, I just left, stopped by the liquor store, and went home.

Home was another story. Samael and I did get put out, but I was able to find a little two bedroom apartment on the west side. Sam had to change schools and didn't like the idea, but he wasn't going to say shit to me. In those six months, not only did I become a drunk, but I was a mean one. I still never put my hands on him though, but I damn near came close tons of times. He was getting taller and stronger as the days went by, but I didn't give a fuck. I didn't give a fuck about much of anything.

That day, I walked in and didn't say a word. I plopped down on the couch across from where he was doing his homework. I cracked my bottle of vodka open and threw it to my lips.

"Zell, how come your home so early?"

"Sam, leave me the fuck alone."

He knew what that tone meant so he picked up his books and papers and took it all to his room. I sat in the living room mumbling to myself while taking swigs until I fell asleep. That was what my norm began to look like and every day that norm seemed to get progressively worse. I needed an escape from the hell that had been my life since I was nine years old, and the alcohol gave me that. So I drank like there was no tomorrow.

After my outburst at work and all of the witness statements that had been provided claiming that I was drunk on the job, the licensing board revoked my nursing license which meant I could no longer work as a nurse. I had worked so hard for that license and I knew Blu would have been disappointed in me, but he wasn't there so I didn't even care that he would have been disappointed. I just collected unemployment and went right back to working the system like I did after Aunt Lori left. I had it so that I was able to get drunk every day and still have my monthly bills paid. I swore up and down I was a functioning addict, but Lord knows I was far from functioning at all.

There were plenty of times that I would stumble out of a bar where everyone knew my name and stumble down the street where all the neighbors knew me. Somewhere between the bar and home I would be slumped on the curb and someone would call Sam and tell him I was out there. Even through my blurred vision and slurred words I could comprehend that people were shaking they heads and talking about me, better yet, I was positive they were talking about me and about how they felt bad for Sam, but I never heard it. And even if I had heard it, I was suffering too much to care one way or the other.

My alcoholism didn't become a reality to me until I heard it with my own ears. Sam was twelve at that time and once again he had come down the street to pick me up off the curb while I sat there swaying back and forth, holding a bottle at damn near midnight.

My child came running up the street, "Thanks for calling, Ms. Jones," he said as he leaned down to pick me up. "Zell, let me help you get home, okay?" he spoke in a soothing voice as he helped me to my feet.

As soon as I felt steady on my feet, I snatched my arm away from him. "I don't need your help, get yo fuckin' hands off me!" He let me go, but kept walking beside me to make sure that I didn't fall again.

Then from out of nowhere that nosey bitch, Ms. Jones, put her two cents in. "You need to thank that poor boy for helpin' yo drunk ass!"

"Bitch, ain't nobody ask yo nosey ass!" I went back at her.

"Oh, but who asked my nosey ass to call him to scrape yo drunk ass off the curb every other damn night so you don't get arrested?"

"Ain't nobody ask you to do that either!"

"He did! Cause he care bout yo sorry drunk ass. I woulda been let the law haul yo sloppy ass off if it wasn't for him." A crowd had gathered cause they thought it was gonna be a fight. Sam stood in front of me, keeping me from lunging after her. "Get yo shit together, girl!" she said, and then walked back into her house slamming the door behind her.

"Fuck you!" I screamed as Sam pushed me down the street.

I snatched my hand away from him again and staggered the rest of the way home on my own. Once there, I walked into the house and plopped on the closest couch, hugging my bottle. I was drunk, but I remember seeing Sam standing in the doorway looking at me like he wanted to say something. Instead, he remained silent, shook his head, and walked off to his room. I sucked my teeth and went to mumbling nonsense as I rocked back and forth with my bottle until I fell asleep.

I woke up the next day with the scene from last night on my mind. I thought about saying something to Sam, but he had been off to school hours before. It didn't take me long to change my mind and forget the whole thing. So, I finished off the last of my bottle, went and grabbed a beer out the fridge, then headed out the door to go to the liquor store.

Something about what Ms. Jones said stuck in the back of my head. Not enough for me not to drink, but enough for me to get drunk at home that night and not in a bar. I made it back to the house around six o'clock that evening and saw that all of the lights were off. I knew I had my nerve being upset that Sam wasn't home from school yet when school ended hours ago, but shit, I was still his mother whether I acted like it or not. Quietly, I sat in my spot with the lights off, taking swigs as I waited for him to get home. He didn't end up walking his ass in the house until damn near nine. When he flipped on the light switch and saw me sitting there, I could tell he was startled.

"Where the fuck have you been?" I asked in a deadly voice. "School was over at three!"

"School was out at two and I've been at a study group for the mathletes team."

"What the fuck is that?" I demanded.

Why Would I Love You?

"A team for people who are in advanced math. We do competitions."

"How come I didn't know about that?"

"You haven't really been around for me to tell you."

I hopped up off the couch, bottle still in hand. "You better watch your mouth, boy, I am still your mother!"

Sam dropped his bag on the floor and took a step toward me, positioning his body in a challenging stance. "Are you?"

"What you say?"

"I said, *are you my mother*?" he boldly repeated himself. "Do you even know what today is?" I was shocked. I knew that little bastard hadn't just puffed his chest at me and got smart at the mouth.

"It's Wednesday, but it might be the first day I whoop yo ass."

"Nah, Zell, it's not *just* Wednesday. Today is my thirteenth birthday."

"So? What did you expect, me to be home with a cake and some gifts?"

"Hhm," he grunted as he looked at me crazy. "Nope, sure didn't expect anything from you." I didn't say anything, just looked at him with a blank stare while he continued. "All day I prayed for my birthday wish. You wanna know what it was?" he gave a disgusted giggle. "I wished that for once my mother would love me. Not because I've been a good son, or because I've been a straight A student, or even because I walk your belligerent, ungrateful, drunken ass home in the middle of the night at least four times a week, including on school nights. Nah, Zell," his voice had gone from disgusted to filled with contempt. "I just wished that you would love me because I'm your fucking son!" By the end of his spiel, Sam was yelling and I could see the tears forming in the corners of his eyes as his voice cracked.

I started to laugh, loud and crazy. Doubled over, I cackled and then in an instant I stood up straight and matched his tone. "Why the fuck would I love you, huh?" I asked as I stepped in his face.

He was young and confused at my words, at the meaning behind them. With his voice barely above a whisper and tears flowing down his face he asked the one question that he shouldn't have. "Why don't you love me, Mom?"

At first I glared at him, but when he looked back at me and all I could see was Leon's features, I lost it, completely lost it, and I decided then and there that it was time he knew why.

"Don't call me that!" I almost shrieked. "Do not call me mom!" I said as I took a step closer and covered the nonexistent space between us. "And you wanna know why I don't love you? I'll tell you why," I said as I geared up to tell him what I knew he wasn't ready to know, what I knew he would never be ready to know. But I spoke the words anyway, let them spew from my mouth regardless of how they would impact Sam. "Because every time I look at your face, I see him. Him! The bastard I fucking hate with everything in me!"

I stopped speaking for a moment, inhaled deeply, and let loose. "The truth is that when I was fifteen, my father started raping me and he continued to rape me for over a year. Then one day I found out that I was pregnant with you. When I told him, he beat the shit out of me, raped me again, and while he did it, told me that he would cut you out of my stomach. Huh!" I said as tears that I refused to let fall welled up in my eyes. "And I should'a let him cut you out of my stomach, but I didn't. Now, every time I look at you, every fucking time I see your face, I see Leon! I see the sick bastard that raped me over and over! I see my dad, the man that damn near drove me insane! And I see him all the time," I said as my heart pumped hard and my chest heaved up and down.

I was enraged, tired, hurt, sick to my stomach with my fucked up life. And I spewed all of that out in every word I said to Samael. "Every time I try to ignore the fact that you were created from rape, from incest, from abuse, you look at me and I see his face. I see his eyebrows. I see his eyes. And I'm reminded of what the fuck I had to endure. I look at you and see not only my son, *not only my fuckin' brother*, I see *him*!" I was on the verge of hysterics by that point, on the cusp of losing my grip on reality. "It may not be your fault, but it's something I can't get over because even though you're half me, you're still half of him, half of the monster that tormented me! Now, ask me again, Samael," I said as my breathing hitched, as my heart raced as if it wanted out of my chest. "Why would I love you? How could I love you? Why the fuck would I love you?"

Suddenly, I couldn't stand to be there anymore, and without another word, I pushed past him with my bottle in my hand and left the house.

Twenty-Six

I had finished my bottle and threw it in some bushes right before I got to the bar. I wasn't gonna let anything taint my happy place. I walked into my normal spot and a few of the regulars greeted me. "Aye, Zell, we thought you wasn't coming tonight."

"Herb, you know I wasn't gonna miss seeing your ugly mug."

"Aaaahhh, Zell, you're a charmer. Let me buy you your first round."

The drinks were flowing, and my problems floated further and further away with each drink. Over the years, that place had become my family. No one judged me in there and nothing mattered in there. We just drank and laughed, escaped our madness, whatever it may have been. That was my happy place and I liked being there. As usual, I stayed until closing time, then I said my goodbyes as we all piled out of the bar and headed our separate ways.

On my way home, I stopped by the local bootlegger, grabbed me a bottle for bed, and stumbled back home. I didn't stop at all because I didn't want Ms. Jones nosey ass to call Sam even though he probably wouldn't have come this time. When I got to my door, I fumbled with the lock for a minute. Although it took me a while, I finally got in, closed the door, and plopped down on the couch in the dark with my bottle. I cracked it open, took a swig and mumbled inaudibly before I fell into a deep sleep.

The next day, I opened my eyes to the sunlight peeking through the curtain, burning my eyes as I tried to focus. The first thing I reached for

Why Would I Love You?

was my bottle, when I heard paper rustling under my fingertips. I blinked, trying to focus, and saw that it was a note titled *ZELL*. Immediately, I unfolded it and read it.

Zell,
I'm sorry that you went through all those things, but you were right, it wasn't my fault. I didn't deserve to feel the way I did growing up. I know you thought I was just a kid, but I was mature enough to know something was wrong with our mother/son relationship. I remember you never telling me that you loved me and only hugging me when you picked me up from daycare. I honestly pined for your approval since as far back as I can remember.

When Papa Blu died, I tried to be the man of the house. I wanted you to be proud of me. I looked after you even when you didn't want me to. I tried so hard to make life easier for you by being a good kid. I didn't fuss, I was low maintenance, and I cleaned up so you didn't have to worry about anything. I'm sorry it wasn't enough.

Well, for my birthday I want to give you a gift, one last chance to make life easier for you. By the time you read this, I should be in the bathroom. All you will have to do is turn on the water once they take me, and any remnants of me will wash down the drain. You won't have to see the half of him that torments you ever again.

This is why you should love me.
-Samael-

For a moment, I sat on the couch in my spot, holding his letter to my chest, confused. *What is he talking about? Who is going to take him?* I thought as I tried to process what Samael was saying in that letter. Then it hit me like a ton of bricks and I scrambled to my feet. My head was spinning, my muscles were shaking, my breathing was shallow and quick. I steadied myself as I hesitantly walked the walls to the back of the apartment. This wasn't happening, no way in hell was this happening. Finally, I made it to the bathroom and for a moment I just stood there, not believing anything I was experiencing. But that letter was real, the words on it were real.

Terrified, I reached my hand out and touched the door. Then, as slowly as I could, I pushed the bathroom door open. When I did, I saw Sam, he was in the tub, eyes open and unfocused, wrists slit. My son was dead and covered with blood. I stood there in absolute shock. I tried with everything in me to inhale but my throat felt like I was being choked. I couldn't breathe. I gasped for air, fought to take in a single breath as I held onto the frame of the door.

Finally, I found my voice, and when I did, I let out a blood curdling scream that came from the depths of my tormented soul. "NOOOOOOOOO!" I screeched as I dropped to the floor at the side of the tub.

So now, here I am just like I said, on the floor, curled up in a ball, crying. I know I'm not in physical pain, but what the fuck? I hurt everywhere, all over. My mind hurts, my heart hurts, my soul hurts. I'd spent so many years learning to shield myself and living in the hate that had been inflicted on me by others, that I couldn't see my own damage, couldn't see the damage that was alive and well in me, or see that I was damaging others. I had been so blinded by my pain that I couldn't see past it. My own pain had rendered me emotionally mute and as a result, I hadn't loved my own child. Samael had killed himself because of it.

Staring at the side of the tub with tears falling from my eyes, I can feel each one dripping from my nose and cheek. I'm ashamed that it took such a drastic incident for me to shed tears, real tears of love and not tears of pain. I love Sam, I never gave him up because I loved him even back then, I was just too selfish to show it or to know it. But I'm done making excuses. Bottom line, I was a shitty mother.

"I'm sorry, Sam. I'm sorry. I'm sorry!" I practically chant the words as I rock to and fro on that floor

Why Would I Love You?

Bam! Bam! Bam!

"Police, open up!"

Police? How do they know? Maybe a neighbor heard me screaming. I hear them but I don't even bother to move. I hear more voices at the front of the house and then the door unlocks. Men come rushing in with guns drawn.

"Front room clear. Bedroom clear. Put your hands where I can see them. I have one in the bathroom. Holy fuck! We might need a bus, send the medical team!"

I straighten my body so they can see my hands. One guy grabs me up off the floor but I'm kicking and screaming, "Don't you fuckin' touch him! Get your hands off of him!" to the medical team that has now rushed into the bathroom to save Sam.

How ironic is it that I'm trying to defend him now that he's dead? Just that thought is enough to drive me mad and my behavior is making everyone around me think that I am actually insane. After I give them one hell of a struggle, they finally manage to put me in an ambulance and strap me to the gurney. That doesn't help at all because I can't bring myself to stop screaming and kicking. I'm out of control. I know that I'm finally broken because I just keep talking nonsense. I can feel my world collapsing around me and I can't seem to control anything. I watch helplessly as the EMT's put a needle in my arm, the next thing I know, my whole fucked up world goes slowly and completely dark. When I finally wake, I'm completely drained and in an empty room.

Sitting in a white, padded space with nothing but a bed is a mix of scary and peaceful for me. It's scary because that means I can't be trusted with myself. It means they think I'm dangerous and therefore I can't be trusted to even move around the world on my own. It's peaceful because I'm finally free of the pain and the torment that was once my life. There is nothing in this room but me.

After some time I've come to understand that I've been committed to a mental institution where they're keeping me heavily medicated.

There is no one on the outside of these walls that will ever come to check on me or to advocate for me. Everyone that has ever loved me or that I have ever loved is dead. My mom. Jazz. Aunt Lori. Blu. Samael. No one else is checking for me. I'm in this place and that's that.

When I first got here, I was so mentally messed up that when they took me to court, I couldn't even defend myself to say that I didn't kill Sam which is what the cops originally believed. Eventually, the police investigated and found that from the angles of the slashes on Samael's wrists, he had to have sliced himself like that. His death was ruled a suicide, everybody knows that my son killed himself. However, even though they no longer blame me for his death, I blame myself. And there is no court in the land that can drop my own charges against me.

As a result of my nervous breakdown and my deteriorated mental capacity, my stay in this facility has been determined to be indefinite. I can be here for one month, or I can be here for the rest of my life. From what my doctor has said to me in our sessions, the level of trauma I've endured over the years of my life has altered my state of mind so much that I struggle to tell the difference between what's real and what's not. I've created a happy place inside of my head that the years of alcoholism couldn't do for me.

"But you can come out of your head and live in the real world anytime you want to," he tells me.

Except I don't want to come out. I'd rather live in here, in my head, than out there in the real world with the bad monsters that keep torturing me. If there's one thing my life has taught me, it's that sometimes, for some people, real life is not a bed of roses. It's not all smiles and happiness, and dreams fulfilled. Sometimes it's heartache, and torment, and nightmares come to life. That was my experience and I've had enough of that. So, since the final decision is ultimately mine, since my freedom is determined by me, I'll take forever in a nut house for five hundred, Alex. This institution will be my last home.

Why Would I Love You?

THE END!

Resources

If you or anyone you know is being abused, please call one of the numbers listed.

The Childhelp National Child Abuse Hotline
1-800-4-A-CHILD OR 1-800-422-4453

National Domestic Violence Support
1-800-799-SAFE (7233)
CALL OR TEXT "SAFE"

All calls, texts and chats are confidential. Staffed 24/7

National Suicide Prevention Lifeline
1-800-273-8255

Text "Go" to 741741 to reach a trained Crisis Counselor. Staffed 24/7

About the Author

S. Shine was born in Maryland and raised in Rochester, NY. She has been writing short stories and poetry from a young age. S. Shine was published in a poetry compilation book in 1997. In 2017, she picked up her pen and paper and began the journey of writing a book. Since then she has written the trilogy of Against Every Odd and the novel, Why Would I Love You under her publishing company name, Messy Mind Publishing. She continues to create messy mind masterpieces for all to enjoy. Her writing is a mirror image of her free and creative thinking.

Connect with author S. Shine:
Instagram: @s.shine_the_author
Email: sshinetheauthor@gmail.com
Website: sshinetheauthor.com
Snapchat: shayshine82
Facebook: sshinetheauthor

Made in the USA
Monee, IL
04 October 2021